Readers Love
RHYS FORD

Savior

"I can always count on Rhys to give me well thought out characters and beautiful stories, and this one didn't disappoint."
—Jessie G Books

"…I absolutely adored this book. I couldn't stop reading it once I started."
—The Blogger Girls

Sin and Tonic

"As a longtime fan of this series and of Rhys in general, I want to say thank you for giving us such wonderful characters to know and love and feel as if they've been a part of our family for the past five years."
—Diverse Reader

"Rhys Ford has with mere words created a magical, at times rambunctious, blue bleeding family that loves deeply and fully."
—Love Bytes

Once Upon a Wolf

"As always, Ford's writing is descriptive and evocative and these characters and their surroundings just leap off the page."
—Joyfully Jay

"*Once Upon a Wolf* is a perfectly crafted novella that will have you riveted from the first page to its highly satisfying HEA."
—*Divine Magazine*

By RHYS FORD

RAMEN ASSASSIN
Ramen Assassin

415 INK
Rebel
Savior
Hellion (Coming Fall 2019)

HALF MOON BAY
Fish Stick Fridays
Hanging the Stars
Tutus and Tinsel

MURDER AND MAYHEM
Murder and Mayhem
Tramps and Thieves
Cops and Comix

HELLSINGER
Fish and Ghosts
Duck Duck Ghost

SINNERS SERIES
Sinner's Gin
Whiskey and Wry
The Devil's Brew
Tequila Mockingbird
Sloe Ride
Absinthe of Malice
Sin and Tonic

WAYWARD WOLVES
Once Upon a Wolf

KAI GRACEN
Black Dog Blues
Mad Lizard Mambo
Jacked Cat Jive

COLE MCGINNIS
MYSTERIES
Dirty Kiss
Dirty Secret
Dirty Laundry
Dirty Deeds
Down and Dirty
Dirty Heart
Dirty Bites

There's This Guy
Dim Sum Asylum
Ink and Shadows
Clockwork Tangerine
Creature Feature 2 *with Poppy Dennison*

Published by DREAMSPINNER PRESS
www.dreamspinnerpress.com

RHYS FORD

RAMEN ASSASSIN

Published by

DREAMSPINNER PRESS

5032 Capital Circle SW, Suite 2, PMB# 279, Tallahassee, FL 32305-7886 USA
www.dreamspinnerpress.com

Trade Paperback ISBN: 978-1-64405-474-1
Digital ISBN: 978-1-64405-473-4
Library of Congress Control Number: 2019932250
Trade Paperback published June 2019
v. 1.0

Printed in the United States of America

This paper meets the requirements of
ANSI/NISO Z39.48-1992 (Permanence of Paper).

One

KURO KNEW they weren't going to make it.

He just couldn't tell that to the kids he'd pulled out of a squalid shack not more than an hour before.

In his line of business, an hour was a lifetime. Stuck in a bullet-ridden van with eight screaming kids, an hour became being stuck on the edge of a black hole waiting an eternity to be sucked into nothingness.

Dawn was a ghost on the horizon when he'd started the van up. Now it was slipping over the edge, swirls of pink and gold light chasing away the night sky. Only a few hours ago he'd crawled on his belly under what felt like a mile of barbed wire, intent on reaching the ramshackle shed his handler was certain held the ambassador's young daughter. Holly was wrong. It was a rare moment in life when Holly was wrong, but when she was, it was usually bad news for Kuro.

He'd been expecting to find a frightened ten-year-old girl and her kidnapper. Instead he'd punched through the front door to discover eight children shackled to cots and iron rings set into the floor, their dirty young faces streaked with tears and worn out from dehydration. It was clear they were all well-off. Their clothes were filthy but finely made, designer labels paired with expensive shoes. Or at least those who still had shoes. Some of the kids sported welts and dark mottles from being hit. The youngest of them was three or four—having little experience with kids, Kuro had to guess—but his round, pink-cheeked face was bruised, and one dark brown eye was nearly swollen shut.

It'd taken him nearly fifteen minutes to calm them down and another half an hour to free them all. Weak with hunger and frightened half to death, they followed him in a shambling mass of filthy flesh and mewling, unable to keep silent through their mad dash to the nearby barn where he'd stashed the van he'd stolen from a bakery down the road. A delivery transport wouldn't have been out of place in either the bucolic countryside where the children had been stashed or the bustling streets of London where Kuro needed to drop off his original target. A bakery would have very early-morning deliveries, rambling through the motorways toward the shops it serviced. The van *would* have been the perfect cover if only one of the children hadn't started screaming.

But then, Kuro supposed he would have started screaming his head off when he was six if he'd spotted the man who thrashed him within an inch of his life scrambling across the dew-wet fields and spraying the ground with machine-gun fire in an attempt to stop their escape.

That was over an hour ago, and since then, they'd rammed a jeep, had their windows shot out, nearly rolled over, and dislodged a man who'd jumped from a Rover to cling to the van's driver-side door and put several bullets into Kuro's right side.

He hit the city streets with a vengeance, hoping he could lose the remaining Rover, but his gamble on the early hour traffic being thickened by people commuting in hit a serious snag once Kuro found the roads mostly empty. It was too close to dawn, and London hadn't quite shaken off its weekend.

A heavy lorry turned out to be his undoing. Well, that and the little boy screaming in his ear. The kid spoke Farsi, one of the languages Kuro was spotty in at best, and nothing he said or did seemed to calm the boy down. The other kids alternated, some yelling, then babbling for their parents or crying while the eldest girl sat stiffly behind him, holding the barely-not-toddler in her lap, her arms clenched tight enough around his tiny body to cause more bruises. The screaming boy didn't seem to even take a breath, his wailing reverberating in the small, confined space of the van's front compartment.

Either way, the kid couldn't or wouldn't listen to Kuro telling him to sit down, and the lorry punching out of a back alley nearly killed them all.

They were so close. Only a half a mile away from the embassy and the van went up on two wheels, its tires smoking when they hit the curb. They hit something sharp, maybe even bending the rim, because a tire blew, rocking the van askew and then drawing up sparks when it landed back onto the street. The jolt rattled Kuro's teeth, and for one blessed instant, all the children were silent, either from shock or fear, but whatever the reason, Kuro relished the quiet. Spotting the truck in the van's remaining sideview mirror, he braced himself for a long, drawn-out fight where he'd not only fail to deliver the young girl back to her parents but also get seven other children killed in the process.

And probably himself too.

His shoulder was soaked with blood, and a dizziness tugged at the back of his brain. The road wavered in front of him, and no matter how much he coaxed and cursed the van forward, it lagged, its chewed-up rim and shredded tire barely able to push the heavy vehicle forward. For all he knew, there was nothing left of the rim and he was dragging the van along on its rotor, digging grooves into one of London's oldest streets.

Sirens were going off, the distinctive wah-wah of a British copper's car, but Kuro knew he couldn't stop. Not now. Not when the truck loomed up behind them and he could see the wild-eyed stare of its driver caught in the van's side mirror. There wasn't enough sun to glint poetically off of the mean-looking muzzle poking out of the truck's passenger-side window, but Kuro recognized a promise of hot-leaded death when he saw it. They weren't going to make it to the front entrance. Not at the speed they were limping along and certainly not if the men chasing them had anything to say about it.

A block away from the embassy, Kuro hit the emergency beacon on his watch. The speaker set into its band flared green, alerting him he had less than ten seconds to transmit before the line was locked down to prevent any security breach. The wailing had begun again, then a brief burst of gunfire broke through over that, the van's windshield blowing out from a heavy blast coming from behind them. Something hot creased his left shoulder and he sucked in a breath, mentally steeling himself for even more pain.

"Coming in hot with the package," he screamed into the band, hoping someone could hear him over the caterwauling and chaos surrounding him. "US embassy. London. Again, coming in hot. White van."

He didn't know if anyone heard him. There'd never been a time when he'd activated the channel in the past, and for all he knew, he was yelling at an unmanned station where some low-level clerk wandered off for a cup of tea not moments before. It didn't matter. He was going to break through one of the gates and hope for the best. Either they'd all die on the road being shot to hell and gone by the men who'd kidnapped the kids or the embassy's security would blow them out of the water for breaching its walls. Either way, it was his only chance of getting the kids someplace safe.

"Get down on the floor!" Kuro screamed over his shoulder. "Flat. Now!"

There wasn't time to spare. And he sure as hell couldn't look over his shoulder to see if anyone was listening to his orders. There was some rustling and more screaming, but this time it sounded like the older girl was pulling the others down, yelling at them to be quiet. The yelling boy was out of Kuro's ear, but the high-pitched mewling hadn't stopped. It was coming from the van's floor this time, muffled by the bench seats, and Kuro sent a silent prayer to whichever god was listening that the van's heavy floor and sides would protect the kids from the embassy's massive firepower.

Another turn and Kuro could see the embassy's gates. The van was barely lurching forward, but he gunned it, the engine giving everything it had. A big boom hit them from behind and the van rocked forward, nearly pushing them onto the curb. Fighting the wheel strained Kuro's right shoulder and it began bleeding again, something he'd not thought possible. Blood dripped down his arm, running off his elbow and dribbling down the inside of the van's door. A splatter of red painted the windshield, and his fingers shook despite his firm grip on the steering wheel. He was losing too much blood way too fast, but with the embassy in sight, there would be no giving in to the pain.

Especially since the gates were slowly opening and a pair of heavily armored men were stepping out onto the street.

"Hold on," he yelled at the children behind him. "We're going to go in."

The gates weren't fully open, but Kuro wasn't willing to put on the brakes. The truck slammed into them again, fishtailing the van to the right, and it took everything he had left in him to straighten it back up. The men in front of him lowered their weapons and shouted at him, their faces going red in the sticky London morning heat. Cars were flying past them on the other side of the road, long sleek black sedans pouring out of some other driveway, but Kuro kept his focus on the partially open gates ahead of him.

A moment later, they were through the cramped opening, the reinforced gate ripped into the van's bullet-weakened sides. The sound of metal tearing was nearly as torturous as the boy's screaming, but it was a keening pitch Kuro welcomed. Someone close by was shooting, but he didn't think the gunfire was aimed at them. Or at least he hoped not. The van lurched to a stop, caught on something, or perhaps someone closed the gate on it, but either way it wasn't moving another inch.

Forcing the door open with his blown-through shoulder, Kuro shoved his way out of the van, then threw open the sliding door. Its hinges refused to cooperate, and he wrestled with it as bullets whizzed around in the air. One mighty heave and it finally cracked apart, leaving a space open for the children to escape.

This time, they didn't need to be told what to do. Ducking down, they scrambled out, and Kuro grabbed the little boy in the ten-year-old's arms, hefting the three-year-old up and cradling him against his chest. Turning, he followed his band of weary rescues, ducking his head down to protect the crying child in his arms as he ran straight into a herd of hungry photographers, their cameras flashing a barrage of blinding lights from the relative safety of a reinforced barricade.

Someone grabbed at his arm and Kuro elbowed them, savagely fighting whoever it was trying to tear the little boy from his grip. Then reason took over what was left of his mind. The weight of the boy left him, and Kuro stumbled one final time, going down on his left knee, unable to take another step. His right shoulder hit the ground, and he fought to free the Glock he'd tucked against his left hip, wondering if there was another bullet in it, laughing at the irony of making it through the gates only to kill himself with his own gun by falling on it.

The ground was cold, too cold for Kuro's liking, but that no longer mattered either. It was warmer than his flesh, which seemed to be quaking and seizing up around his bones. A pair of alligator-skin red heels floated into his line of sight and Kuro blinked, a swirl of sidewalk grit peppering his face. A long shadow stretched over him, and the delicate flutter of fingers across his cheek made him flinch, but nothing was as cold and chilling as Holly's familiar cut-glass accented words digging into his brain.

"Well then, Jenkins, it appears as if you've just burned your own identity. There won't be a newspaper left in this world that won't have your beautiful face plastered all over it. Quite a feat. Saving a van full of stolen children held hostage by a terrorist organization. Pity about the photogs covering the garden opening, but that's how our lives go," she murmured, stroking his temples while someone he couldn't see shouted for help. "Welcome to civilian life, dear. Hope you have a backup plan ready for your retirement or else you're going to be bored out of your mind."

TWO IN the morning was a horrible time to be awake and on the streets in Los Angeles, especially when winter had a firm grip on the city's balls, squeezing hard enough to make its jutting skyscrapers whimper from the cold. The damp in the air scraped any warmth from Trey's face, arms, and legs, peeling away the layers of heat he'd worked up in his moving limbs, but he kept pushing on, losing himself in the shadows edging into the watery pools of light coming from the avenue's gauntlet of streetlamps.

His lungs were screaming from the razor-bite chill filling them with each heaving breath. A tickle of pain was beginning to form in the center of his knees and a stabbing ache crept along his ribs, ratcheting spurts of agony across his right side. His feet hurt, and a twinge sparked up from his left ankle, coursing a bright sharp line of tingling nerves up his calf.

A sane man would have stopped running miles ago, succumbing to the fatigue in his bones, but Trey couldn't. If he stopped running, his demons would catch up with him and he'd have to deal with all the poor choices and disastrous mistakes he'd made since he let loose his first scream after the doctor slapped the afterbirth off of his pallid, blood-caked body.

He was also a little more than a mile and a half away from home, and even if his sneakers were beginning to rub against the sides of his feet, Trey couldn't stop. Not now while he was in the worst tangle of streets in Koreatown's sometimes dark underbelly.

Most of the businesses along Sixth Street were closed, and MacArthur Park was empty of anyone with any good in their hearts. Trey could make out shadowy silhouettes moving about near a picnic bench, their bodies taut with tension as he jogged by. The slap of his sneakers on the sidewalk missed a beat when Trey took a long stride to avoid a crack in the cement, and the break in the snapping rhythm seemed to agitate the lurkers, and they moved together, closing in around one end of the table.

Trey left them behind in a rush of sprinting legs, thankful for the tall chain-link fence surrounding that end of the park.

It was probably nothing. A group of teenagers bored out of their minds and gathering in the park to catch a smoke. Perhaps even a bunch of kitchen workers from one of the nearby restaurants having a quick beer under the stars before heading home after a long shift. Just the ordinary gathering of some people hugging the shadows in the wee morning hours of a dimly lit park.

Trey ran faster.

Outrunning trouble was something he'd thought he was good at. It took a headlong crash into the darkest points of his life to realize no one could really outrun their own demons. Demons just piggybacked onto their victims, sucking out their dreams and hopes until they became bloated ticks made fat from a daily diet of ego and hubris. Their burgeoning weight slowed Trey down, making him stumble on the sharp remains of the shining yellow brick road he'd once laid down to follow. He'd taken a hammer to the glass house he'd constructed, scattering its corpse in his path. He'd bled out every last bit of his life on those sparkling, arrogant-whetted shards, wondering how he'd sliced up his feet and why he was hunched over, unable to take another step forward because of the pressing burden on his back.

The thirst at the back of his throat ached less. His knuckles hurt from clenching his hands into fists, but it was the only way Trey knew to keep them from shaking. As stupid as it was to be running through the rank, shadow-clotted sidewalks of Los Angeles's tangled streets, it would have been nearly suicide if he hadn't tugged on his sneakers and pounded his knees into throbbing knots.

So long as he didn't put a whiskey bottle to his mouth, Trey was willing to put up with any kind of pain his body dished out.

Best thing about running before the sun was even a whisper on the horizon was that no one recognized him. Being honest with himself meant Trey admitting very few people connected him with the cherubic-faced, smart-mouthed little kid he'd been on *Down the Tracks*. No, it was the insane drug-fueled rages and widely photographed tantrums most remembered him for. There were too many to count. His downward spiral from prepubescent Emmy-award-winning actor to has-been took years, but Trey'd been too wasted to notice the time and his sanity slipping away. Until the morning he woke up strapped down to a hospital bed with his stomach feeling like it'd been turned inside out, Trey thought his life was going great. Everything was at his fingertips. Hot, willing men, any drug he could think of asking for, and a never-ending supply of parties to get drunk at.

The crash had been hard. He was still recovering from it. Probably always would be recovering from having to pick up the pieces of himself off the ground and put a new Trey Bishop back together.

Even if it meant running himself to death in the wee hours of a Los Angeles morning.

The end of his nighttime jog was near. Trey could taste it along the slimy stickiness on his gums. He was three blocks away from the 1920s house his father turned into vacation apartments, a rambling old place with a separate guest quarters Trey moved into after his collapse. He'd make it home in time to get a hot shower out of the water heater before the main house sucked it all down, and maybe even fall into bed for a few hours.

"Okay, ramen shop. Almost there," Trey panted out through his teeth. "Still, what the fuck is a ramen shop doing in K-Town?"

His stomach growled, probably recalling his dinner consisted of a granola bar and a Diet Coke at five in the afternoon. The ramen place didn't have a name, or at least not one Trey remembered. It sat twelve people, although there was a table at the back of the long, tight space for employees. More than a few times, he'd wandered in and the shop's smoking-hot owner nodded his head to the back table, silently giving Trey permission to sit there and have lunch. He'd never spoken to the man, but his arresting Asian European features, silky black hair, and stormy blue eyes were the reason Trey stopped by in the first place. The food put in front of him was delicious enough to bring him back, but mostly it was the sight of the silent, trim-hipped, tall man behind the counter as he pulled together ramen bowls that had Trey eating there more than twice a week.

He ducked into the sliver of a break between the buildings, intending to cut across the small parking lot behind the alleyway beyond. It would shorten his run by ten minutes, ten long minutes of torture and darkness he wanted to leave behind him in a cloud of dust. Problem was, there weren't many clouds of dust to be had in Koreatown at three-something in the morning.

Trey had to be satisfied with sprinting past a sour-smelling dumpster, startling something with scrabbling claws as it fed on the trash in the deep rectangular receptacle. Halfway across the parking lot, he plunged into a well of shadows, then headed to the street on the other side, cutting through a narrow pass between another set of buildings. Avoiding a pile of smelly cabbage leaves dumped on the walk, he sidestepped quickly, dodging a puddle before unceremoniously slamming into the open back door of an old van parked on the street.

And apparently startled a pair of scowling brawny men loading something heavy into the back of it. Trey couldn't figure out what they were holding, but his eyes were watering, and somehow he'd smacked his nose hard enough to make it bleed. Too thick around the middle to be a carpet but long enough to need two men to carry it, whatever it was bundled up in the thick sheets of frosted white plastic curved down in the middle when the men stopped moving. The van's door swung in, striking a thickly muscled giant across the side, and he turned, scowling at Trey from under an impressive pair of bristly black eyebrows. At first Trey thought both were bald, but the one at the other end shuffled his feet and the streetlights teased out the burr of his closely cropped crew cut, its short strands nearly translucent against his pale skin.

"Hey, watch where the fuck you're going!" Black Eyebrows barked, his shoulders bulging around the thin straps of his grimy white tank top. He struggled to maintain his grip on what he was hefting, trying to push the van's swinging door back with a nudge of his shoulder.

"You're going to—" The blond wavered, unable to catch the slithering mass shifting between them. Unlike his partner, he wore a heavy windbreaker, and it flared open when he moved, giving Trey a very good look at the gun holster strapped under his arm. "Fuck."

Everything happened too quickly for Trey to follow, or at least that's what it seemed like. One moment he was backing away quickly from the van and its two menacing companions. Then in his next breath, the long package they were carrying dropped, the sheets unfurling as they grabbed at its ends, battling gravity and bad luck along the way.

The men lost, and they stood there, mouths gaped open and hands full of plastic sheet ends, while a paunchy gray-skinned man plopped out onto the street and rolled across the asphalt to rest against the curb at Trey's feet.

It was amazing how much energy Trey found in his legs at that moment. Apparently, nothing motivated a man quite like having a corpse run over his toes, then discovering two guns being pulled on him by the two thugs trying to move said dead man's body.

He knew the man was dead. No one could have survived a hole that big in the middle of his chest, and what was worse, Trey knew he'd seen that man before. Many times before. But none of that would matter if the two men trying to dispose of the body caught up with him. He'd be nothing more than another bundle wrapped up in plastic, yet another failed child star who'd gone missing in the middle of the night.

The alley behind him was his only avenue of escape, but it led to the small parking lot he'd crossed just minutes before. If he could make it across the lot and between the other buildings, he had a good chance of losing them along the main road. There were enough alcoves and oddly shaped buildings to hide a man, or push came to shove, he'd be hit by a passing bus and the driver would be forced to stop. Either way, he wouldn't be dead of a gunshot wound to the back of his head.

Providing he could make it across the lot in time.

The first shot he heard nearly broke his stride. It was louder than he'd ever imagined a gun would sound. Even on the set of *Down the Tracks*, the sound effects were added in later, more to ensure no one on the set handled a weapon with anything loaded into it. Even blanks were dangerous, or so he'd been told. Either way, the boom caught him unawares and he stumbled, catching his balance before he tumbled onto the broken-apart asphalt.

The next shot was closer. Mind-numbingly closer. It hit the ground near his feet, kicking up sharp black nodules into his shin. Suddenly the shadows didn't seem dark enough, cloudy enough to hide him, and Trey could have sworn he felt the heat of a gun being aimed at the spot between his shoulder blades.

He got into the alleyway just as a dark form emerged from one of the doors.

"Get down," a deep, melodic voice ordered. "Behind the bin."

The voice tickled at parts of Trey's psyche, parts he'd long thought were dead. It tickled other parts too. It was wrong to drop to the stinking, filthy ground with a hard-on but not impossible. But then any arousal that sensual flow of voice invoked fled the scene as soon as Trey got a good look at the menacing piece of steel in the man's hand. Long legs stepped over him, straddling Trey's hips. The darkness in the tight alley grew, enveloping Trey, and he pressed his cheek to the ground, ignoring the rank stench of a puddle near his face and the stickiness of something under his chin.

There was a silence in the man's stance Trey could feel down to his bones. Sneaking a glance upward didn't do him any good. All he saw were a pair of powerful shins in blue jeans on either side of his body and long stretches of muscular arms lifting up to aim the small cannon the man held in his hands.

This time, the boom was massive, shattering any sense left in Trey's mind. His ears were ringing when another blast went off and the smell of gunpowder filled his nostrils, the heat of the weapon's fire smoking the air. Trey closed his eyes, flinching in the tinny quiet left behind after the man's second shot. He hurt, more from flattening himself against the ground than anything else, but as he lay there, Trey took inventory of his body, noting the throbs and pains along his joints and exposed skin.

It seemed like forever before those long gorgeous legs stepped away and one sneakered foot nudged Trey's shoulder.

"They're gone." The man purred when he spoke, a delightfully rolling undertone to his words. Trey couldn't place it as an accent. He'd gone to more voice coaches than he could count when he was younger, anything to hone his craft, or so his mother said then. He'd known better. She'd slept with every coach and tutor he had, and none of them sounded like the man crouching down next to him. "You hurt?"

"No," he admitted, slowly sitting up. "Just my pride."

"They would have hurt much more than that if they'd gotten ahold of you." The man's voice was stronger, layered with a bemusement bordering on mocking. He tilted his head, and Trey got his first good look at the man who'd saved his life.

It wasn't fair to be saved by the object of one's wet dreams. It was even more unfair to be helped up off the ground while wearing a pair of shorts that had seen better days and a T-shirt torn in places from being snagged on uneven surfaces.

Up close the damned man was even sexier, more dangerous, but Trey imagined that the gun he easily held in his hand probably had something to do with that impression. He was beautiful, sleek and sinewy with long legs and a trim waist, jeans slung low across his hips, his shirt riding up a bit, showing Trey a peek of his golden-brown skin. His lashes were long enough to throw shadows across his face, even in the sparse light, but there was enough of a glow from the street to flicker across the amber speckles in the man's tilted-up green eyes.

Still, the gun made Trey pause, and he sat up, more confused than ever.

"You're the ramen shop guy," he gulped out, swallowing hard when the man's sexy mouth curved into a sardonic smile. "What the hell are you doing with a gun? At three in the morning?"

"Really?" He gestured toward the parking lot Trey sprinted across, chased by a hail of bullets and deadly thugs. "I think the question you should be asking right now is why the hell don't *you* have one? Get up off the ground. I'm going to go inside and call the cops."

Two

FIRST THING the cops did was take his gun. Kuro didn't mind. It was procedure. Just like someone scrubbing at his hands to gather evidence and having to retell the same story to ten different people and three more times to the same detective. He had other guns but only one story. He'd been restless, unable to sleep, and figured he'd start the day's prep early, intending to go home after a couple of hours and catch some sleep. The sound of gunshots drew him out of his kitchen, and he'd returned fire after telling the blond jogger to drop to the ground.

He'd forgotten how tedious police were, especially baby detectives so new to the job the gold paint was still wet on their badges.

The back of the detective's hands were freckled, but the spread was not nearly as thick as the splatter of brown across his nose. He might have been in his later twenties or even early thirties, but with his shock of red hair and buck-toothed smile, Detective Max O'Connor looked more like a human reincarnation of an old children's puppet than a sworn-in officer of the stalwart Los Angeles Police Department.

Kuro wondered if the kid was even old enough to cross the street without someone else holding his hand.

"So you didn't recognize Trey Bishop?" the kid asked, barely looking up from his note scribbling. "Hard to imagine missing the train wreck he's been on these past few years. Don't watch a lot of television, huh?"

"Enough. Mostly the classics like Bugs Bunny, but the Warner Brothers and Sister are pretty decent," Kuro drawled.

"Don't watch as much as I used to, but it's a good way to wind down," O'Connor replied. "But you'd have to be living under a rock to miss Trey Bishop crashing and burning."

There was a lot of television about the cop, mostly in the way he held himself. He wore his gun in a shoulder holster, very old-school, small-screen cop, and his badge dangled from a loop on his belt. O'Connor came off as nervous, his eyes shifting and sliding off of Kuro's face while he spoke, but there was an intelligence behind his guileless blue gaze, a sharpness he'd have to hone in order to climb the ranks. He'd do well, Kuro decided, if he stiffened up his backbone before the system chewed him up and spat him back out.

"I recognized him as a customer who comes in a couple of times a week," Kuro said. "Never knew his name. I can tell you he usually orders the miso with extra soft *shoyu* eggs and seared *kakuni*. Every once in a while, he livens things up by asking for extra *kamaboko*."

"I'll have to try that sometime. It sounds good," the detective murmured. "So you really had *no* idea who your customer is? Or was?"

"Before or after I returned fire?"

"Either," O'Connor replied, glancing up at Kuro momentarily before flicking back to his notebook. "Most people would think twice about stepping into the line of fire for a stranger."

"Never done it before, but the guy brought nothing to the fight," he lied. "He came running across the parking lot being chased by two men with guns. Seemed like he was in fear for his life. I aimed to scare them off. Not to kill."

Kuro was very curious about why the cop kept bringing up Bishop's name and alluding to something. What, he didn't know, but it was there. An overt probing at Kuro's thoughts about the man he'd watched coming into his shop over the past few months, a man he'd silently lusted for even after he'd put away those kinds of thoughts and feelings. The last thing Kuro needed was a complication, and the sexy, lanky dirty blond was certainly that. He wore trouble on him like a cologne, a subtle but evocative scent promising all sorts of nasty things and heartbreak.

Then the cop threw a curveball, one Kuro didn't see coming, and he pulled his curiosity back, shoving it behind a firm brick wall next to the lust he'd banked there. "So you didn't see the dead body Bishop claimed was lying in the street?"

"I didn't see any dead body." Kuro frowned. "I didn't go further than the alley. Didn't have to. I could see across the lot, and once the two men pursuing him went around the building, I didn't give chase. Was more interested in calling the cops, but you all showed up before I even hung up."

"Bishop says the men were carrying a man wrapped up in plastic sheets and were loading him into the back of a van when he came across them." The detective peered down the parking lot, shuffling a few feet to the right until he was lined up with the alleyway leading to the ramen shop. "If you were standing about here—well, further back—so you should have been able to see a van pulling away. Did you see something? Hear anything?"

He was getting old. Or the sight of Trey Bishop lying facedown on the ground distracted Kuro more than he'd like to admit. The shorts he'd worn running bordered on indecent, or at least that's what Kuro thought when he'd glanced down and caught sight of Trey's butt under the silken fabric. He seemed to be mostly leg, firm calves and lean thighs, but there was a hint of nice shoulders beneath the ratty T-shirt stretched across his back. There hadn't been enough time to get a good look. It was hard to ogle a man sprawled out between your feet when bullets were flying around in the air.

But he'd given it his best shot.

Literally.

"I didn't hear or see a van, but to be honest, I wasn't listening for one. There wasn't exactly time to talk about what was going on," Kuro said, glancing over his shoulder toward the edge of the parking lot where Trey stood speaking to the other detective, a handsome blonde with a sour look on her face. "I was more concerned with Bishop's safety and then getting LAPD on the scene. And of course, handing over my gun."

"Handy for Bishop you were armed, but that's kind of a funny thing, right? I mean, you make ramen. What's a guy who cooks noodles up for people doing with a concealed carry permit and a small cannon?" O'Connor shifted the conversation in a quick dodge of words, obviously meant to throw Kuro off stride. There was no way the young cop could have known Kuro cut his teeth on that kind of slice-and-cut interviewing, and the detective's narrowed glance up at Kuro simmered with a barely held back curiosity.

"Rats. Ever since they laid down the new waterlines, they're getting into everything," he replied, keeping his face schooled into a flat, serious expression.

"You got off five bullets from that gun. An Eagle, right? Kind of overpowered for rats, don't you think?"

"K-Town grows them big. Baby rhinos, really."

O'Connor's expression soured a bit, and Kuro knew he was reaching the end of the cop's patience. Clearing his throat, the detective took a breath and once again shuffled up the dumb kid expression he'd used a moment before.

"Did some checking up on you. Quickly, you know, because here we are at a shooting and you've got that conceal license." O'Connor was fishing, fishing hard enough for Kuro to see the massive, glittering hook badly hidden behind his opening gambit. "Thing is, usually if someone's got that kind of paper, I get more than name, address, and serial number on them. But not you. There's nothing there, Mr. Jenkins. No parking tickets. Not even a citation for jaywalking. Or even a health violation for your restaurant."

"Considering it's been three hours since I called the shooting in, I'm surprised you dug down that deep." He shrugged, his attention drifting back to Trey and the detective interrogating him. "And I'm pretty sure we were cited once for not having enough ice on one of the prep stations. Or at least warned."

"Thing is, my partner and I get a bit leery when a guy who makes noodle soup for a living has a weapon big enough to stop an elephant, and when we call it in to check on his license, we find out he's licensed for an armored tank if he wants one, and oh by the way, if he wants to tuck it into his jacket, the state of California's okay with it." O'Connor nodded toward the far wall where a forensic tech was standing on a step stool and extracting bullet fragments from the building's exterior bricks. "It also makes us pretty itchy when a noodle shop guy lays down five shots in a perfect line exactly a few inches higher than the heads of the guys he says he was shooting at."

"I figured it would be easier to identify them if I had an exact measure of the tall one's height," Kuro rumbled, his voice deepening. The female detective was poking Trey's chest with a stiff finger, right below his collarbone, and Trey was taking it, mostly. His face was turned away from her, even though his shoulders were squared off to face her, but his spine was rigid, tightening his body into a hard, firm line. "So two things; when can I get my gun back and are we done here?"

"You planning on answering any of my questions?"

"They're not relevant to what's going on, are they?" He cocked his head slightly, taking advantage of the few inches he had on O'Connor.

O'Connor's lips peeled back into a mockery of an aw-shucks grin, but the newbie sheen wasn't holding up. The man probably played this game often enough, skilled enough to maneuver an unsuspecting person into coughing up tidbits of information he could use to piece together something solid.

Kuro had no intention of giving the man anything to hang even the tiniest hat on.

He didn't smile back but held O'Connor's steady gaze.

"No harm in asking. You got my curiosity up." The detective shrugged. "I'd really like a couple of answers."

"I'd really like some coffee, but something tells me I'm going to be sadly disappointed for hours to come."

"Well then, I think you and I are done, but I'm sure the lieutenant's probably going to have some questions for you. You can ask her about your gun." His smile did little to lighten the bitterness in his words, and O'Connor gave a slow performance of putting his notebook away into his jacket pocket, tucking his pen in beside it. "So just stand around here, kicking up your heels like you've had me doing right now. Maybe you'll be cut loose in time to serve up lunch tomorrow."

Kuro returned O'Connor's smile, baring enough teeth to make the cop uncomfortable. "Any idea on when she's going to get around to me? Because if you all like it or not, I'm serving lunch today."

"She'll get to you in a bit," O'Connor ground out, nodding curtly. "Probably right after she's done chewing her baby brother over there a new asshole."

"I'M TELLING you, they were shoving a dead man into the back of a van," Trey ground out again through his clenched teeth. "I'm not making this up, Kimber. The worst thing is, I recognized him, but I don't know where I'd seen him before."

"Trey, I'm going to ask you this one more time and then we're done here." His older sister tilted her chin up, a gesture he'd seen his father make more times than he could count. "Tell me the truth and I will make sure you don't get into trouble. The guys shooting at you? You stiffed them on drugs, didn't you? You're using again, and you just don't want anybody to know it."

It was bad enough having his life played out in front of millions of people, every misstep and stumble reported on in intimate detail. The *Inquirer* probably paid its admin staff's yearly salary on his volatile breakup with the very closeted Lance Markham, one of America's muscle-heavy leading men. He'd trashed the restaurant they'd been having dinner in, his uncontrollable rage fueled by frustration and a drug cocktail he'd gotten from the studio doctor. Lance went on to deny any romantic relationship, turning the incident into a long-suffering friend making one last-ditch effort to attempt to help Trey get onto the road to sobriety.

That was a joke. Lance was often higher than a kite and had simply wanted to play the field. It made good press and was one of the many nails in Trey's coffin.

There were other blowups, other overdoses, until the day Trey found himself waking up from a weekend-long binge in Vegas, only to discover himself strapped down to a hospital bed in a Santa Monica rehab following a two-week coma.

And at every step, there'd been cameras, capturing his disastrous life a frame at a time.

Rehab was a revolving door of therapists and more drugs, lesser strains meant to wean his blood system. Nothing took. Not until he ended up in what was basically his last-chance stop. Locked in by a judge who'd seen him at least ten times before, the program preached a cold-turkey approach, and its staff was incorruptible. He shared the compound with everything from a fallen rock star to a grand dame of theater. They all had something in common, an addiction they couldn't control and a support system that had reached the end of its rope.

The rock star made it out before he did, but as far as Trey knew, the mistress of the stage remained behind its closed doors, barricaded from the outside world by a wrought iron fence and a locked-down trust.

He'd come out of the experience flat broke and desperate to regain his dignity.

It was just a pity that he'd been captured on video having very violent hallucinations about dog-headed aliens landing at Venice Beach. A few bad trips alongside a well-publicized breakdown or five and no one was willing to give him the benefit of the doubt. Especially his family.

Not that Kimber had ever given him the benefit of the doubt.

"I'm not using. I've been sober since I got out. Shit, I'll take a drug test if you want me to." Trey rubbed at his shoulder, the spot still aching where she'd stabbed at it with her finger. "Dad will tell you—"

"Dad's blind spot where you're concerned is huge, so you're going to have to forgive me if I don't believe anything he says about you.

You're the son he finally got, and there's nothing he won't do to bail you out," she replied sarcastically. "If I found you in the middle of Malibu trying to snort up the sand through a red licorice straw, he would say you were vacuuming the beach to keep it neat. That's your biggest problem, Harry. No one's ever held you accountable for anything, and the only reason Dad put you into rehab was because if he didn't stop you, you were going to kill yourself and he would have to make another son. And the man's getting too old to do that with any of his bimbos."

"First, don't call me Harry." Trey struggled to keep his temper. "And if that crack about bimbos is about my mom, then you can just fuck off. If I were anyone else, you would be looking for that van and those guys, but since it's me, you're saying it's a lie just to cover up some drug deal gone bad."

"All I've ever heard of you has been lies. What makes this time so different?"

He didn't know what else to tell her. She was his oldest sister, his father's firstborn and fifteen years older than Trey. She looked like her mother, a blonde-haired, blue-eyed former Russian high fashion model turned actress, but Kimber was 100 percent their father's daughter. Turning her back on the family's vast empire, she instead decided to be a cop. It was a turning point in her relationship with their dad. Harrington James Bishop the Second hadn't greased palms and worked his connections for his daughter to get an Ivy League education only for her to spit in his face, head to UCLA to get her degree, and promptly join the Los Angeles Police Department. Now a lieutenant, she still worked the occasional case, usually high profile or politically sensitive incidents or whenever her baby brother fell down into the gutter.

It was just a shame that's the only place she thought he belonged.

"What do I have to gain by lying about seeing a dead man?" Trey asked. "It wasn't like I imagined those two guys. The ramen shop owner literally saved my ass. They were shooting at me, Kimber. I wasn't making that up. I don't even have any money on me. I told you, I went running because I needed to work out some energy. It keeps me sober. I don't know what to tell you to make you believe me."

She was a beautiful woman, the kind of woman who turned people's heads when she walked by. Her beauty only intensified as she got older, and in her early forties, she was now stunning, infused with a powerful confidence and keen intelligence. When he was younger, there was nothing Trey wanted more than his older sisters' attention, but the years between them and the acrid animosity among their different mothers made building relationships nearly impossible. He'd envied her poise and confidence, as well as the affectionate relationship she had with her mother, a far cry from the emotional upheaval of his own mother's neediness and violent behavior. Kimber represented a stability he'd always wanted, yet it appeared nothing he did would ever bring them closer.

But then he had no one to blame but himself for that. They were no longer young. No longer living under their father's roof and forced to have holidays together. He'd destroyed any fragile thread connecting them, and now when he needed her to believe him, Trey mourned what he'd destroyed.

"I'm going to have one of the uniforms drive you home," she said, glancing back over toward where the handsome black-haired ramen shop owner stood with one of the detectives. "I've got a few questions for him, and then I'm going to thank him for saving your life. Because if he hadn't been here, I'd probably be making a condolence visit to Dad. As it is, I'm not sure what to do with you. I'll ask around to see if there are any security cameras, to see if any place down the street caught video of a van, but beyond that, I only have your word about the dead man. And that's less than shit to go on."

"I swear to you, Kimber, I am telling the truth," Trey murmured, wishing he'd brought a jacket or something because the morning air was cold against his skin, or maybe the glacial crawl through his bones was the realization his sister not only didn't trust him but didn't love him. It'd been too long since he'd seen anything but disappointment in her luminous eyes, and he couldn't remember the last time he'd seen her smile. "I'll do anything to prove it to you. Hell, if I could find them myself I would."

"See, Harry, that's where I think the problem is. I think you know who they are. I believe you know where to find them, but if you rat them out, you'll be burning bridges you don't want to. Just don't sell everything off in the bungalow to pay for whatever mess you've fallen into," she said, then sighed. "You are going to break Dad's heart, and as much as I sometimes hate the old man, he doesn't deserve to have you as a son. He's given you so fucking much, and you just throw it all away. Just stay out of trouble, because the last thing I want to do is knock on his front door at two o'clock in the morning to tell him someone found your body. Go home, get some sleep, then get some help. Because the next time I get called into one of your little episodes, I'm tossing you into jail, and there's not going to be a damned thing Dad can do to get you out."

Three

"I'M TELLING you, babe, your sister's a bitch," Sera declared from the bungalow's kitchen. The smell of grilled cheese sandwiches woke Trey up a little bit, but not enough for him to crawl off the gray sectional set at the far end of the great room. "Never did like her. Actually, all of your sisters are raging bitches. You're the best one out of the bunch."

"That's a scary thought," he mumbled into the decorative pillows, willing his head to stop pounding. "Icarus looks at me and says, 'Damn, that boy's gone and fucked up his life.'"

"Can't fall up from Hell, kiddo." Sera chuckled under her breath. "Listen to me. I sound like one of my hat-wearing aunties at church. You planning on sitting up so you can eat these things, or am I going to have to feed you like some little bird I've found on the sidewalk?"

Sitting up was going to be a challenge. He was worn down past the ache in his bones, and after stumbling out of the police car, the bedroom had been too far away. Or at least that's what it felt like, despite the fact the guest house was a 1920s one-story square bungalow split down the middle by a single wall, and all he'd needed to do was walk through the long great room with its kitchenette and living area through a door to get to his king-sized bed.

It'd been too much. Too far. Much like everything in his life. The crash after the rush of overwhelming adrenaline knocked Trey down to his knees, and after a mind-numbing ride through Koreatown while sitting in the back of a black-and-white driven by a stone-faced cop, he'd been ready to crawl into whatever hole could swallow him up. The cop insisted he sit in the back, droning on something about procedure, but Trey gave it his best shot to squat in the passenger seat. He'd lost that fight, much like he'd lost all other battles to avoid being transported in the back of a police car, but at least this time he wasn't cuffed behind his back.

Thank God for that small little favor, even if the little old lady who lived next door sneered malevolently at him when the squad car pulled up to the main house's curb. She didn't even try to hide her phone as she filmed him doing what she believed was a walk of shame to the back of the property. Blowing a kiss to the cop and waving goodbye probably hadn't helped things, but at least it made Trey feel better, and gave the illusion he'd been taken for a good ride.

Mrs. Hornswaggle hadn't bought it. Not one damned bit. He could hear her tsking, and the sound of her pressure-hosing her front walk haunted him until he closed the bungalow's front door.

"I'm burning these like you like them, so you've got about two minutes to get up off that couch," Sera warned him again, the kitchen's transom windows above the Shaker-style cabinets playing flicks of light over her lush sienna skin and teasing the gold flecks out of her honey-brown eyes. "Don't think for one moment I'm babying you like I did your daddy. You don't get up and you're not going to like what I'll do to you."

Trey knew she meant it.

Of all of his father's ex-mistresses, Sera was the one he was closest to. Probably because she wasn't much older than he was. A leggy, strong-featured black woman originally from Georgia, she'd come out to Los Angeles to make a splash in the art world with her edgy paintings of urban landscapes, scoring a big show only a few months after touching down in Southern California. Meeting Harrington Bishop the Second was probably the best and worst thing ever to happen to Sera, but in the long run, Trey got a best friend out of the deal.

She was also the first one his father didn't insist he call Auntie, which was a damn relief by then, because as he got older, his father's mistresses got significantly younger. The current one was barely out of braces and couldn't buy alcohol by herself. His mother ignored them all, drowning herself in shopping, country club activities, and long trips to Europe accompanied by a variety of buff, handsome men with umlauts in their names.

The grilled cheese sandwich came with a huge mug of creamy tomato soup, bits of parmesan cheese floating across its steaming surface. He'd been right about sitting up being painful. His thighs hurt in places Trey didn't think possible, and for some reason, his hip bones creaked when he moved, belatedly remembering he'd dropped facedown to the alley's cracked concrete walk when the ramen shop guy ordered him to get out of the way.

"I'd offer you painkillers but that's a hill I don't want you tumbling down," Sera pronounced, looming over him with her hands on her hips. "Get some of that into you and I'll go get you some ibuprofen. Then I want the scoop on the guy who saved your scrawny ass from being used to wipe up bum puke."

His first sip of soup was manna pouring down his throat. The weather snapped cold while he'd been passed out on the couch, and a chill settled into him, leaving Trey shaky and unsteady. He was reluctant to contemplate why his hands were trembling, but the shaking and his iced-over backbone were the result of almost being gunned down in the street like some bad TV show victim. There were better ways to die. Or at least more flashy ways. It would have been irony at its highest snark for him to be killed in a random shooting, especially since Death came for him so many times before and he'd dodged its bony finger.

Sera came back with a handful of orange tablets and a glass of sparkling water, sticking both under his nose with an imperious sniff. "Take these. You'll feel better."

If there was one thing Trey appreciated more about Serafina Tate than her friendship, it was that she believed him when he told her he hadn't been drinking. He'd grown used to the suspicious glances and disapproving looks from nearly everyone around him, including his mother, who'd spent most of Trey's life ignoring him. Sera stood firmly by him, welcoming him with open arms when he'd arrived at the converted mansion, licking his psychological wounds after his stint in rehab and looking for a place to hide. She'd taken over the running of the old house, a deal she'd worked out with his father in exchange for a hefty salary, one well above what an estate manager normally was paid, and possession of the top-floor apartment, where she lived and worked. The guest bungalow on the back had been set up for sporadic rentals, but Trey's father offered it up to him as a place to live.

He took it, swallowing his pride. He'd learned to choke down the taste of crow being served up hot and heavy on his plate, drowning in a gravy made up of his own remorse. His descent into a breakdown included losing everything he'd gained over the years, including the glass-walled mansion he'd purchased in Malibu.

Trey was broke and alone, living off the scraps his father threw his way and desperate for a way to fix the life he'd fucked up. Sera was a huge part of that fix, a steady rock he'd clung to more than a few times since he'd earned his release.

Much like taking the bungalow's keys from his father's hand, Trey took the ibuprofen.

"Tell me about the ramen shop guy." She sat down next to him, folding her legs under her. Leaning over, Sera pinched off a corner of Trey's sandwich, taking a bit of cheese with her. "I've been by that place. Boy's hot."

"Boy's not a boy," Trey grumbled back. "But yeah, he's hot as fuck. And scary. Turned the corner and there he was, big-ass gun in his hand and a face made out of granite. Like, no expression. No shaking. No nothing. Told me to drop to the ground and stay out of the way."

"Whatcha do?"

"I dropped to the ground and stayed out of the way," he said around a mouthful of grilled cheese and nearly blackened bread. "I dropped, then he stood over me. Like some kind of half-Asian Colossus of Rhodes. Scared the shit out of me. I thought I was going to die. Couldn't run anymore. Hell, couldn't even breathe anymore, then boom-boom-boom, his gun went off. Damned thing was so loud because the alley's tight, you know? But he was as cool as a cucumber. Didn't even flinch."

"And you could tell that facedown and sucking up gutter juice?" Sera lifted one sculpted eyebrow, rubbing at her nearly shorn hair with one hand. "Nice legs?"

"Great legs. Even better ass," Trey admitted. "I looked up a couple of times, because shit, if I'm going to die, I should at least take a good look at the guy trying to save me."

"Kind of funny he was there. At three in the morning? Shop doesn't open until eleven, right? But there's this guy, and with a gun." Leaning back, Sera rolled her shoulders, getting comfortable against the couch. "Not exactly a rough neighborhood."

"Lots of people there remember the riots," he reminded her. "Sure, it was a long time ago, but that kind of thing stains the area. People are always looking over their shoulder late at night, and back then, it wasn't like the cops were around to help. Hell, there's pictures of guys with bulldozers parked in front of their stores to protect their place. Maybe he's just prepared."

"Or maybe he's an ex-cop," she shot back. "You said the gun was big—"

"Huge. Like a cannon. Sounded like one too."

"And the cops didn't even blink at him, right?"

"Kimber didn't say anything. Hell, she talked to him for a few seconds after she was done with me and then walked away." He sipped again, grateful for the soup cooling down, because his tongue tingled from the last time he'd put his lips to the rim and drank. "I didn't even get to thank him for saving me. She had me shoved into a police car and off the property before I could even cross the parking lot."

"You shall have to go back to the shop and see him." Sera grinned slyly, a deep dimple forming in her left cheek. It wasn't hard to see why his father had become enamored with her. There was an earthy sassiness to her personality, and combined with her gut-punching sensuality, she was a potent mix of vixen and power. "I'd say you could cook him dinner as a way of saying thank you, but let's face it, you'd burn air if it was possible. Maybe you can do takeout. Dish it up here. Pop a bottle of sparkling cider and take your time expressing your gratitude."

"One, I don't think he's gay. Two, he is way out of my league." Trey shook his head, moving his grilled cheese out of Sera's reach after she helped herself to another pinch. "Go make your own. This is supposed to be my convalescence meal. What kind of nurse eats her patient's food?"

"A hungry one," she shot back. "And how can he be out of your league? You were in teen magazines! The kind of shit where they tell infatuated little boys and girls what your blood type is and what kind of toothpaste you prefer."

"Those days are long gone, honey." Trey nearly choked on his sandwich. "Besides, no one ever really asked us those questions. They just made shit up and printed it after we spent a couple of days getting our photos taken in different outfits. And it's not just looks. He's got his shit together and I haven't even picked all of mine up from the backyard. So, *way* out of my league."

Sera was about to respond when Trey's phone chirruped and vibrated across the coffee table. He began to chew quickly, regretting taking as big of a bite as he had when she picked up the device. Easily avoiding Trey's flailing, grasping hand, Sera frowned as she read the incoming text.

"Don't you know better than to open up a gay man's phone?" Trey made another attempt to grab it from her, nearly falling off the couch when he leaned over.

"Please! You've got Miki St. John wearing a My Little Pony T-shirt as your wallpaper. The biggest question I have about you is did you photoshop this or is he secretly a brony?" She gave another frown when the second half of a text scrolled up across the screen. It was too far away for him to read, mostly because he was tired and his astigmatism blurred anything past six feet away. "Well, shit."

"His guitarist dared him to wear the shirt. I thought he looked sexy. And give me my phone so I can see what you're pissed off about." He resigned himself to sitting back on the couch. Fighting with Sera would do no good, and honestly, his joints hurt too much. "Tell me it's Kimber and they found the dead guy."

"No such luck. My guess is, Kimber squealed like a greased piglet being chased by a bobcat," she sighed at him. "Better go take a shower and get dressed because the car's going to be here in half an hour. It's your dad's secretary. It looks like you're being called on the carpet."

THERE WAS never any question about Harrington James Bishop the Second's immense clout and long-reaching power. His father's unshakable grip on other people's lives was evident in every inch of his environment, including his children.

One of the benefits of being Harrington Bishop's son was never having to wait for an elevator. Still, getting from the parking garage to the top floor of Bishop International's glass shard of a skyscraper in downtown Los Angeles meant crossing over an ocean of gray-veined white marble on the lobby level. It was a gauntlet of disapproving looks and barely concealed sour expressions. If there was one thing his father commanded besides others' attention, it was their loyalty. He inspired a nearly slavish devotion from his employees.

Trey couldn't make heads or tails of it, but that could have been because he was too close to the man himself. He didn't know the Harrington Bishop who was an industrial giant with an alleged heart of gold. He was only acquainted with the cold, brutal truth of a man who demanded his children be excellent in every way possible, something Trey never could achieve. There was no grade high enough or award esteemed enough to satisfy Harrington Bishop's hunger for perfection in his offspring. Kimber's defection to the police force dealt the man's ego a nearly fatal blow, and he'd tightened his grip around his other children. Trey's sisters, Margaret and the unfortunately named Scooter, were powerhouses of industry at BI, cutting their teeth on deals and acquisitions before Trey could even walk.

And if Kimber wearing a badge was a nearly fatal disappointment, Trey didn't even want to imagine what his father thought of him.

Harrington never told him. Never exploded in a rant or diatribe like he did about Trey's sisters. With his son, Harrington Bishop remained silent but steady, refusing to entertain any suggestion he turn his back on Trey, but at the same time, never dropping a word of encouragement. It made Trey feel like some kind of experiment, some kind of social engineering data point his father leveraged in his business dealings with self-destructive former child stars.

His father's bulldog waited for him at the top floor's elevator, a cold-faced sentinel with flame-red hair and wearing a black leather skirt. There was nothing sexy about Tatiana. Or at least nothing Trey could see. She looked like she was carved out of the same marble they used in the lobby, her translucent pale skin with faint indigo lines running under it where Trey assumed her blood had frozen. Her eyes were a pale blue, frosted over with gray, and her lush mouth sported a dark red lipstick, a slash of vibrance against her nearly bloodless white face. He didn't know how old she was, but then stones rarely showed their age. She'd come into his father's life when Trey was a kid, replacing the grandmotherly Marion, who'd gone to Florida to be with her family.

If ever there was an apocalypse, Harrington Bishop would survive solely because his right-hand woman probably could kill the grizzly bear with the power of her glare, then skin it with her sharp fingernails.

God knew the tight smile she gave him probably hid her rows of bristling pointed teeth.

"This way please," she said in her lightly Russian-accented voice. "He is waiting for you."

"I know the way, Tatiana." Trey slipped past her, nodding at the receptionist behind the swoop of wood and metal the company's designer decided was forbidding enough to use to welcome guests to Harrington Bishop's inner sanctum. "Good to see you, Gloria."

He didn't need to look behind him to know Tatiana was hot on his ass. He could practically feel her ice-cold breath on the back of his neck and imagined he could hear her high heels clicking a fast tempo despite the thick gray carpet, much like a rattler signaling its intent to strike. No one went anywhere near Harrington Bishop without Tatiana hovering nearby. Oddly enough, she was the one woman in his father's life who he'd never slept with, or at least he'd never heard about his dad's dick falling off in some tragic sexually induced Arctic accident.

The top floor wasn't a cubicle farm. No, his father had the outer perimeter chopped up into offices styled after a gentlemen's club with one wall of floor-to-ceiling glass, giving the lucky occupant a stunning view of Los Angeles. Each office came with an assistant, their doorless space enclosed by more glossy wood paneling and glass panels. It was meant to look lush and rich, but Trey was a little unnerved by the lack of windows. It felt like a cloistered, stuffy cage, and not one he ever wanted to be trapped in. His father's office was directly across of the reception desk, taking up nearly half of that part of the space, with two enormous corner offices on either side. Those belonged to his half sisters, two women from different mothers who shared their father's ambition and need for power. Chances were, he wouldn't see them during his visit, but then he hadn't seen them in years.

His father's current assistant, a spindly balding man named Bruce, was manning the phones at his own desk, rattling off something in German, then placing his call on hold to stand up and greet Trey. "You can go right in. He's expecting you."

Trey didn't know where Tatiana sat. He imagined his father probably had a falcon perch she squatted on in between meetings, or perhaps a restaurant-grade freezer hidden among the cabinets where she folded up into her space, waiting for Harrington Bishop to summon her to fight battles. What he did know was he felt immense satisfaction in closing the inner sanctum's door in her face.

His father didn't even look up from his desk. Whatever was on his computer screen was much more entertaining or compelling than saying hello to his only son, and Trey fought the nearly overwhelming instinct to help himself to a tall glass of whatever potent amber liquor his father had on the wet bar. He'd taken his first drink in that office, stealing a sip of something expensive from an unmarked crystal decanter. It burned going down. Much like it burned coming back up. But the numbness it left on Trey's tongue and eventually his brain was glorious.

Also destructively seductive. Or seductively destructive. He still hadn't determined which.

Despite being in his early seventies, Harrington Bishop was a giant of a man. Sporting a full head of silver-white hair and a firm lantern jaw, he looked more like a vintage movie star ready to storm beaches and have a shootout in an old corral. Lightly tanned from spending a few hours on the golf course or the yacht he'd purchased years ago, the man was still fighting trim, with broad shoulders bulging with muscles beneath his expensive fitted gray suit. His teeth were white, sparkling, and still his own, or at least he liked to brag. His mother, Joy, liked to point out she could claim her boobs were her own as well, having paid for someone to install them.

The only thing he'd gotten from his father was his nose and hair color. Everything else passed down the genetic stream came from his allegedly Scandinavian mother with her five-hundred-yard legs, high cheekbones, and an addiction to anything and everything bad for a sane human being.

"Sit down, Harry… er, Trey." His father glanced up from his screen, motioning toward one of the high-backed armchairs set in front of the massive oak desk he'd inherited from his own father. "Let me finish this up and I'll deal with you."

"Deal with me? There's nothing to deal *with*," Trey scoffed, willfully ignoring his father's order for him to take a seat. Ambling over to the wet bar was a habit, but this time, like the last few times he'd been called in to the old man's throne room, he reached for a bottle of sparkling water from the fridge. "Want one?"

His father spared another glance, eagle-eyed and wary. Nodding when he spotted the bottle, he returned to what he was working on, only paying attention to the scrolling numbers on the screen. Behind him, Los Angeles was having a glorious day, clear skies with the barest of clouds laced over its crystal-blue canopy, and the city stretched out beneath the sun's warming rays. If he squinted, he could make out the edge of the ocean peeking up over the horizon or imagine it was there. The cloud cover was thicker on the coast, layering a brushed aluminum filter over the edges of the sky, but everything else was in crisp, hard contrast, clean-lined buildings bristling into the crowded downtown grid.

Turning back to grab another bottle of water for his father, he caught sight of a very familiar face in the photos hanging on the long pale stretch above the wet bar. Amid the sea of framed images arranged on the watered damask silk–covered wall, one stood out, a cherubic red-cheeked older man with a white streak across one eyebrow and thinning hair he trimmed close down to his scalp.

Trey'd seen the man only hours before, bled out white and slack-fleshed, his flaccid body wrapped in sheets of opaque plastic. The dead man was grinning widely, nearly a foot shorter than Trey's father, but he'd somehow forced his arm up over Harrington's shoulder, dangling his plump hand down across his collarbone. Another man Trey didn't know stood on the other side of his father, his hatchet face sporting a forced smile, and his arms were firmly against his sides, locked into place while the other men were clearly having a good time. They were all dressed for some event, a black-tie affair with a crowd of diamond-wearing, smug-faced people milling about, but the photographer captured the discomfort of the one man compared to the friends on the other side, a genuine grin on Harrington's face instead of the practiced, politically correct half smile he normally wore in photos.

Trey *knew* that other smile well. He'd seen it often enough in family photos, especially the ones where Harrington annually gathered up all his offspring, forcing them to sit in one another's company long enough to capture the moment. Not being asked to sit in on the family shoot was a dire indication of how displeased Harrington Bishop was with a particular child, and since Trey hadn't sat down for one in years, he figured he was the current record holder at being the subject of the old man's ire.

After shoving one water bottle under his arm to hold it and taking another one out, Trey lifted the photo from the wall, turning it over to see if there was a name or something scribbled on the back. Most photos on the wall were transients, cycling in and out depending on Harrington's moods, but there were a few core shots Trey no longer saw when he was in the room. They'd been up *that* long. This was one of them, and its back was sealed brown paper, wetted down to tighten up against the frame, and no note on the back to indicate who was in the image. Frowning, he padded back over to his father's desk, placing the bottles on the desk.

"Dad, who's this?" He held the photo up.

"Can't this wait until I talk to you about what you did last night? Kimber said you're using again. Hallucinating dead men and such, so you and I are going to have a little discussion, mister, then I'm going to figure out what to do with you. I can't carry you anymore, Trey. You've got to man up." Harrington scowled at the screen, clearly displeased at what was there. "I need ten minutes. Play with something on your phone."

"I'm not five anymore. Video games aren't going to keep me quiet for half an hour. And I was stone cold sober this morning. I went running so I wouldn't take a drink. I wasn't hallucinating. Not the dead guy. Not the guys shooting at me. I get Kimber not trusting me, but shit, you've got to believe me on this." Trey leaned across the desk, putting the photo right under his father's nose. "Who's the guy on the right?"

"Son, that's Robert Mathers. Known the guy for years. You've met him before. You just probably don't remember." Harrington stared at the photo, his steely eyes fixed on the man's face for a moment before looking up at Trey. His frown intensified, growing stormy, then disappeared, wiped away as if it never existed. His father didn't like to lose control of his emotions, keeping a steady, calm expression even in the worst of storms. Only Trey seemed to be able to break it, cracking the man's authoritative serenity. "I played golf with him this morning, Trey. His game was off, but everyone has a bad day. Why?"

"Because this is the guy I saw this morning. The one I saw dropped into the street." Trey hated how his hand shook, but the cold was back in his bones, doubts beginning to form icy shards along the edges of his thoughts. He'd blacked out before, waking up without a single memory of what he'd done or drank, but this time it was different. He recalled every single second of his early-morning run, and despite the weight of confusion pressing in on him, he refused to believe he'd slid back into his old ways. Not without a hell of a fight. "This is the dead man, Dad. I saw him as clear as day. Like I'm seeing you now. So I don't know who you played golf with this morning, but it sure as fuck couldn't have been Robert Mathers."

Four

MAKING NOODLES for a restaurant took a lot of time, but it was one of the things Kuro enjoyed the most. While the Tako Shop storefront sat only twelve customers, not counting the employees' table, its back kitchen was huge, a master chef's workshop hidden behind a wardrobe—in reality a steel door—where Kuro and his crew could prep the day's offerings in a luxury of space.

It was a delight to work in the kitchen, its long walls filled with bins of fresh vegetables dropped off early that morning, and a bank of walk-ins and freezers bulged with rendered soup broths and prepped toppings for a couple of days' seatings. A delivery of fresh eggs arriving two hours too early forced Kuro out of his bed that morning, a stumbling run down the stairs from his apartment upstairs to let the man in. There'd been apologies and a smatter of catching up, a gush of formal Japanese Kuro struggled with until his brain kicked in. The night before had gone late, stretching into the early hours of the morning, and for nothing other than sleeplessness and the image of Trey Bishop's crestfallen face burned into his memory.

So instead of going back to sleep, Kuro stayed in the kitchen and began to make noodles.

They made everything on-site. It was one of the things he'd insisted on, paying hefty wages to bring in people who knew what they were doing to work the kitchen and the bar. More than a few of his servers "graduated" to the kitchen or ramen assembly, earning their way up the ladder through hard work and drinking in everything the shop did. But there was something peaceful about noodle making, or at least the kneading of the dough and the delicate wrapping of the sectioned-off pale balls so they could be set aside to rest. Cutting would come later, something the morning crew would do for the rushes, but for now, the kitchen was empty, the silence before the storm of chatter his employees would bring with them in a few hours.

But then again, silence was only possible if Eugene Aoki wasn't there, because no matter how still Kuro's second-in-command sat, he was surrounded by a sea of white noise.

It wasn't that he didn't love Aoki. He did. Mostly. He owed the man a lot. Aoki had pulled his ass out of many a tight mission, cutting in with information and escape holes Kuro couldn't have found on the fly. More than a few times, other operatives tried to lure Aoki away, promising him a higher profile or greater pay. Kuro's department head always countered the pay offers, then surreptitiously shared recordings of Aoki working an extraction. Normally that was enough for the headhunters to quietly wither up and drop off.

Because the man *never* shut up.

The leg bouncing was usually a sign Aoki was about to burst into a rattle of noise, and right now if Kuro attached a tub of heavy cream to Aoki's knee, he'd have butter in about ten minutes. Then came the shifting on the barstool, an ominous creaking and swaying broad enough to stress the screws holding its metal legs to its stabilizing base. They'd already had to replace two of the wooden stools, and Kuro'd hoped the metal-and-vinyl one would be able to hold up under Aoki's fidgeting, but from the sounds of it, the poor seat wouldn't make it another day.

A slightly plump man with a moon face, Aoki was the picture of a happy soul, with a broad smile and cold-reddened cheeks. Wearing khaki cargo shorts and one of the shop's T-shirts stretched across his thick torso, he shimmied in place for another minute, shattering Kuro's concentration, and not for the first time since he'd opened the shop, Kuro wondered if he'd added enough eggs to his dough, having lost count after a particularly loud throat-clearing behind him.

"Just say it," Kuro finally muttered, folding a piece of wrap around a ball of dough.

"I'm fine! Don't need to say anything!" Aoki burbled, his tongue tripping over his words. The rocking began anew and the stool groaned, tired of the abuse. "You work. I'm just watching!"

"You're holding something in, and if you don't get it out soon, your head's going to explode." He glanced over his shoulder, shooting his former communications liaison a skeptical look. "I don't want to have to wipe your brains off the walls or equipment. You know how Tanaka gets if you spoil his vegetable prep time."

"Tanaka can go—" Aoki gulped when Kuro narrowed his eyes. "Sorry. Look, that guy you saved yesterday—"

"Trey Bishop," Kuro cut in. "His name is Trey Bishop."

"Yeah, I know. I've read up on him." Once Aoki got started, there was no stopping him, and from the fiery light in his beady black eyes, he was about to roll out every bit of information he'd scraped together. "Honestly, I know you live under a rock, but I can't believe you didn't know who he was. Trey Freaking Bishop. He's like the poster child of how not to be a human being."

This time, the look Kuro shot Aoki was as cold as the stone in the pit of his stomach. The man he'd observed in the parking lot was shaken but resolved. Even from a distance, Kuro understood Bishop was struggling to be heard, to be believed, and the few probing asides he'd been able to slip into his conversation with Bishop's detective sister hadn't reaped much. The woman was more close-lipped about her brother than she'd been about the case, willing to share information about the alleged van he'd missed seeing and the possibility the men shooting at Trey Bishop were drug dealers he'd crossed.

"His sister thought he'd fallen off the wagon. Said he was using again." Kuro wrapped the last of the dough, tucking it in tight.

"Makes sense. Bookies in Vegas have pretty good odds on him crashing again. He's been on the Dead Pool for at least two years. I've got fifty bucks on him and a couple of others not making it to Christmas."

"You bet on people dying?" He cocked an eyebrow at his friend.

"Hey, I also bet on what kind of dog wins Westminster," Aoki protested. "Not like I'm paying someone to go out and kill them. Hell, you know that kind of thing costs more than I'd make playing penny bets."

"I worry about you, Aoki," Kuro sighed. "Do me and Tanaka a favor, if you're going to sit here and talk, go clean the green onions. I'm going to make up a batch of *char siu*. We're running low."

The drug dealer thing lined up with what Aoki was spooling out. It was a classic tale of a spoiled young man with too much money and too little to do. Burdened with no personal responsibilities, Trey Bishop crashed and burned before he'd even truly taken off. Or at least that's what it sounded like.

Kuro wasn't so sure.

He'd seen a lot of failures in his life. Hell, he'd stood over many of them much like he'd done for Trey Bishop, straddling their prone bodies while firing off shots at people intent on getting blood on their hands. Most of the time, those people cowered, shaking in their shallow trenches, but not Bishop. Not *Trey*. He'd dropped without questioning Kuro's order, but he'd been firm, keeping an eye on the situation, and his head was down.

Except when he looked up and caught Kuro glancing down at him.

Kuro couldn't recall the last time he'd seen such *hopelessness* in a man's eyes. He'd stared down the barrel of a gun with a dying man holding firm, ready to take Kuro with him, but nothing compared to Trey Bishop's resignation. He'd accepted a fate being handed to him with a clear awareness of the danger they'd been in, but put enough faith in Kuro to drop to the ground. Death was simply another obstacle put in Trey's way, something else for him to climb over to get to the other side.

In hindsight—and with unwilling assuredness—Kuro knew he should have killed the men chasing after Trey. If only to bring a sense of peace to the handsome man who'd placed his life and trust in Kuro's hands without so much as a whimper.

"So, the latest is that he's broke and living on his dad's handouts, but a lot of people think he's turning tricks," Aoki rattled on. "Or at least keeping company with some high-powered Hollywood people in exchange for goodies, you know?"

"Where are you getting all of this?" They were running low on hoisin, so Kuro marked off the resupply sheet plastered to the whiteboard listing the specials for the week. "And why are you pulling intel on Trey Bishop?"

"Not intel. You can read all of this stuff online. Just hit up any gossip site. A few clicks and you can find out everything you want to know about the guy," Aoki remarked, shaking his head. Holding up a withered bunch of green stalks, he shook them at Kuro. "This one isn't good. Whoever did intake should have rejected them."

"Put them aside. I'll take them up and use them in a pancake." He nodded toward a brown paper bag he'd left open on the counter. "Toss them in there, but be careful. I've got some eggs and stuff in there."

"They're green onions. Not grenades. Sheesh, blow up *one* duffel bag and no one lets you forget it." His friend shuffled over to the counter, grumbling under his breath. "Anyway, you're better off seeing the last of him. *That* kind of trouble you *don't* need. It's why you retired. So you wouldn't have to babysit idiots anymore."

"I retired because my cover was burned by an international corps of photographers and I was shot up with more holes than swiss cheese." He rolled his left shoulder, feeling the bones ache and rub. The cold got to him now, and there was a suspicious hitch in his side when he worked out too long. The breaks and fractures he'd logged over the years were catching up to him, the scar tissue running down into his healed-over muscles pulling and contracting when he least needed it. "That and I was sick of babysitting idiots. Don't think Trey Bishop's one. His sister was damned insistent the dead man he'd seen was made up to throw the cops off of him, but I don't know. He didn't smell like a liar. Seems to me, he was used to being shoved aside, and no matter what he did, he couldn't make her listen."

"And you got all that from a couple of minutes of listening to him talk to his sister?" Aoki frowned.

"No, I got that just by watching him talk to his sister. She wouldn't let him near me long enough to talk to him. Shuttled him right off into a cop car and took him away from scene." Kuro measured out a few cups of brown sugar, mentally calculating how much he needed to marinate the pork shoulders in the fridge. "My gut tells me something's going on and I don't have the full picture yet."

"Just remember one thing, Kuro," his friend tsked from across the kitchen, elbow-deep in water as he rinsed out a bunch of green onions. "The last time your gut told you something, you ended up with a handful of kids, a bullet-ridden van, and a retirement package. Just make sure this time, your gut doesn't get you killed."

THE CHALLENGER hugged the curve in the road, eating up the asphalt strip winding through Laurel Canyon. Its V-8 engine growled through the pass, a deep-throated purr aching for more power. Having the car shop in Vegas restore its original 440 had been one of the best and worst decisions in Kuro's life. He loved the power it gave the 1970 muscle car, pushing its heavy frame easily through tight turns and steep-angled streets, but it drank gas like it was cheap whiskey and suffering from a deep heartache.

He'd grabbed the keys to the candy-apple-black Mopar and told Aoki he was done for the day, leaving Tanaka in charge. His mind wasn't on the restaurant or its patrons, his thoughts wandering off toward where he'd put the memory of a long-legged dirty blond lying on his belly beneath him. Not exactly the best thing to be happening when ladling steaming-hot broths into shallow bowls and dredging noodles into boiling water baths to flash-cook.

The last thing he needed to do was wield a knife. And since working in the back meant prepping for later in the day, Kuro opted for a drive.

One of the greatest things about Los Angeles was it was built with cars in mind. Maybe not in the beginning. But a few hundred years afterward, its tangled ribbons of concrete and asphalt brought a sense of peace. There was something comforting about driving. Even in Los Angeles's rush-hour traffic, Kuro could let his mind drift away from everything bothering him. He wasn't sure if it was because he had to pay attention to the shifting patterns around him or that the monotony of driving kept his brain at a dull roar, but it was the closest thing to meditation he had.

Or least it had been until the moment he'd laid eyes on Trey Bishop. He'd seen the man come into the shop a couple of times a month, forcing himself not to follow Trey's progress through the narrow dining area. Traditionally, the table shoved up against the back corner was only for staff, a place for one or two people to eat in between shifts, bolting down their food. It was a sacrosanct place of sorts, a normally beat-up perch next to the kitchen door where a chef would sometimes sit a favored customer. Every restaurant had one. Either in the dining room or sometimes in the kitchen if the restaurant ran to that sort of pretension. The Tako Shop did not have a table in the kitchen. It was that corner table some people used only after a nod from Kuro or one of the staff.

Trey had taken to walking to the table, glancing back at Kuro and giving a shy smile when he was given the nod. Tanaka teased him about it, the gruff Tokyo-born cook sniffing out Kuro's sublimated attraction. Aoki hadn't noticed. Or at least not before today. Now he would be looking for any scrap of attention Kuro threw Trey's way.

"I am never going to hear the end of it," he muttered. "Might as well put a bullet in my brain right now."

Certain days felt like he needed the ocean, a silvery-blue embellishment to the black road he drove on. There was something about the salt in the air and the cries of gulls weaving through the wind, screaming their defiance at society's insistence on locking down dumpsters to prevent their scavenging. And then there were days when he needed the smoky bite of overgrown sage in the dryness of the pale brown dust clinging to the hillsides above the city. He drove with no place in mind—no *where* in mind—letting his mind wander while searching out familiar landscapes.

It was always in his confusion and uncertainty, Kuro ran for the hills, climbing its peaks to look out at the world around him, following the lines and noise of the city he'd claimed as his hometown. He *liked* Los Angeles. Sure, there were more beautiful places to visit and more stunning vistas with white, sparkling beaches or ancient buildings built by long-dead artists, but Los Angeles spoke to him. With its hammered metallic blue skies and gritty air, it had enough of an edge to keep him sharp but was mellow enough to let him relax.

There weren't too many places in the world Kuro could relax, and he treasured every second he could spend in the City of Angels.

His problem was Trey Bishop. A man who now haunted Kuro's shadows and thoughts.

"It would be stupid to get involved. Everything Aoki says about the guy is trouble. Hell, even his own sister doesn't believe a damn word that comes out of his mouth," Kuro muttered to himself, listening to the automatic transmission downshift as he slowed. "Just… something's not right."

It'd been forever and a year since he'd been to bed with somebody, and that had been mostly working off steam on the job. He didn't even remember the guy's name or most of his face. It was a Spanish operative he'd been stuck with in a villa while they waited for their target to surface. He'd gone in to grab the two hostages, only to find out the operative he'd slept with double-crossing all of them, standing with their target and shooting down the corridor while Kuro and his charges attempted to escape.

He'd shot the target first, then the man he'd been in bed with only a few hours before. It'd taken eight showers before he was clean, and no matter what his handler said, Kuro felt like he should've known something was off. It was a turning point. His head hadn't been in the game, although he'd reacted well enough. He'd *trusted* that lover, considered him a friend. Counted on him to do the job and instead ended up betrayed and covered in an ex-lover's blood. Although Kuro wasn't sure how long of a time it took for a man to become an ex-lover or if being shot at took care of that situation by itself.

"It's just not right. He's not lying. He *saw* a dead man. At least he thought he did," Kuro grumbled at himself, rolling the window down all the way to let the soft afternoon breeze carry the scent of sagebrush through the car. "And even if it wasn't a dead man he saw, why were they shooting at him? Not drugs. Don't get drugs off of him. It's got to be something else."

Ten minutes into his drive through the hills, Kuro felt a tickle at the back of his neck. A glance in his rearview mirror showed the road was empty, except for a white utility vehicle following behind him about twenty yards back. In the winding roads, it was easy to get lost, and the driveways off the main street were angled oddly, nearly hiding the mansions behind yards of hedges or canyon brush. Making the turn into Laurel Canyon, Kuro slowed the Challenger down, waiting to see if the truck followed.

It did.

"Doesn't mean anything. A lot of people live up this way." Another glance in his mirrors showed the truck's distance was shortening rapidly. "Or I've picked up a tail."

Canyon roads were wide enough for two cars, but the drop-offs in places were steep. There were a few guardrails, usually by turnoff areas people used when they found themselves lost in the labyrinth of Los Angeles's mesas and ridged hills. It'd been too long since someone followed him, but the sticky cloying feeling at the roof of his mouth was the same.

Whoever it was didn't know what they were doing. They kept behind him the entire way through Laurel Canyon, only dropping back when Kuro accelerated around curves, then slowed down to see if they followed. They matched him turn for turn, drifting into the other lane periodically, probably trying to keep him in sight when he disappeared around a bend.

The driveways were now few and far between, larger estates eating up vast expanses of land, their far-reaching buildings buried in the crenulated hills and thoroughly hidden from view. He caught sight of the few house peaks and the occasional juniper stand poking up past a barricade of thick bushes. The people living in the hills valued their privacy, ringing their properties with high walls, barbed-wire tops, and private security. So far from the center of the city meant police support was farther away, and that was too-little protection for the paranoid and rich.

But lack of police coverage meant hitting Kuro along the canyon roads was the truck driver's best chance to either run him off the road or worse, kill him.

The truck sped up, and Kuro punched down the gas pedal. The '70 Challenger was ecstatic to be let off its leash. It bolted forward, grabbing at the road and chewing up the distance toward the top of the peak. Kuro knew these roads like the back of his hand, and while he couldn't depend upon the other driver's unfamiliarity with the twists and turns rolling through the hills, he knew the utility truck wouldn't be able to handle negotiating the hairpins at any top speed. Still, the driver gave it his best shot.

With the window down, Kuro could hear the truck rattling and groaning. It strained with the ascent, falling behind the Challenger on the brief straightaways, catching up only when Kuro slowed to take a turn. The Challenger's windows were too tinted to see much of anything other than the outline of the driver behind the truck's wheel, but Kuro didn't need to know what a man looked like when that man was trying to kill him. Revving the engine, he shot up the hill, watching the landscape for the breaks in the trees he used as markers for the upcoming turns.

He'd raced up and down the canyons' winding streets in everything from a powerful muscle car to a limping SUV. It was like running a pinball through a familiar machine, knowing where the bumpers were by feel and instinctively leaning the board to one side or the other when his silver sphere careened out of control. Taking a curve, he smiled with satisfaction when the truck's right-side tires lifted momentarily off the pavement, slamming the vehicle back down in a hard thump when it straightened out.

A few seconds later and after passing one particular red-berry-laden hedge, Kuro took the Challenger through a hard left.

His tires smoked, the rubber catching on the grooves dug into the cement break in the asphalt. The shallow lines were meant to channel water down the hill, diverting any rushing rainfall into the culverts and drainage ditches. They also played hell on a top-heavy vehicle's balance when taken too quickly. The truck tottered again, this time the left side lifting a good six inches. Kuro held his breath until he knew the truck made the turn, counting on the driver to be rattled by the near misses he'd taken.

Instead, the truck sped up again.

"*Shit.*" Kuro gripped the steering wheel with his left hand and passed his right thumb over the sensor built into the front of his modified center console. "You should've taken the fall, buddy."

He was too used to having protection, and despite being tagged out of the game, there was no way he was going to walk through the rest of his life as a sitting duck. There were too many scores to be settled and people he'd pissed off, even if he'd done his jobs under the watchful eye of his government. Angry people tended to strike out not at the puppet masters but rather the puppet, hitting the people they could reach, as if taking someone off the board would somehow cripple the shadows behind the curtain. He'd run deep, barely lifting his head above water or light, nearly secure in the knowledge he'd never been made until the very end, and even then his superiors wrote off his involvement as an embassy employee being in the right place at the wrong time.

The truck driver or whoever sent him definitely had Kuro in their sights, and the only way he was going to get an answer about who was pulling the strings would be if he and the driver came to an abrupt, final understanding.

The console flipped open, its smart switch activated by his thumbprint. He reached into the space and pulled out the fifth-gen Glock he'd picked up a few months ago, flicking a glance down at it to make sure it was primed to go. Keeping the gun down, he took the next turn, swinging wide so the truck could keep him in sight, then hugged the inner curve, counting on the bend to keep him hidden.

At some point the driver must have realized he couldn't keep up with the powerful Challenger on any straight stretch of road and took the one chance he had to ram the muscle car's back end. As Kuro lifted the Glock up, prepared for the truck to clip his fender, a gunshot shattered the Challenger's front and back windshields.

"Son of a *bitch.*" Shaking the tempered glass pebbles out of his hair, Kuro cut to the left, then slammed on his brakes, forcing the truck to shoot past him on the right. Aiming his gun out of one of the larger holes of his crackled front glass, he let off a shot.

It hit its mark.

The truck's right rear tire blew as it took the next outward curve, and already slightly out of control, the force of the exploding rubber threw the vehicle to the side. Its driver was probably panicking, especially since Kuro dropped the Challenger down to a low growl, easing back the throttle. The truck hit the dirt track on the side of the road. Then Kuro shot again, aiming at the man's silhouette outlined against the rear window.

The inside of the cab went muddy with red. Then the truck went over the edge of the hill, leaving shreds of rubber behind in its wake.

Kuro parked the Challenger in the turnoff and slowly got out of his car to view the carnage below. The utility truck was still rolling down the side of the sloping hill, tools bouncing out of its bed and scattering through the sagebrush. It landed on its side, scraping across the Laurel Canyon Park's asphalt lot, coming to rest against a cement-and-rock trash can set up against a sidewalk.

He could see the driver. The man had fallen out in the truck's tumble, and Kuro didn't need much more than a glance to know it was one of the men he'd shot at the night before. Sighing, he reached for his cell phone and put the Glock on the Challenger's glossy black hood.

She answered on one ring.

"Holly, I need you to pull everything you can on a former child star named Trey James Bishop." Kuro was always amazed at how silent the world became after a death, especially a violent one. He heard a squawk on the other side of the line and grinned despite everything. "No, I don't need a cleanup on aisle five. But what you can do for me is call the LAPD and tell them I've got some roadkill they need to scrape up off the ground. I'll be waiting for them at the Laurel Canyon Park. They can't miss me. I'll be the one holding my hands up in the air."

Five

THE SMELL of police stations haunted Trey in his sleep. The odor lay as a fetid undernote to the reek of burnt coffee, gun oil, and the musky cologne most cops wore. The air was kept cold, a glacial chill meant to do something, perhaps push a man's sanity over the edge because he couldn't get warm, shivering in his bones, much like fear taking over his body. Or maybe cops just burned from the inside out and needed the cold to keep their bodies going, slices of a demon's soul walking around with pitchforks they made out of accusations and prejudice.

Regardless of why a cop house was the way it was, Trey hated the smell. He'd had it in his nose often enough, usually while being walked in with his hands pulled behind his back in too-tight handcuffs, as if the police had something to prove by wrenching his shoulders out of joint. But the smell of cheap linoleum and cop house had nothing on the worst part of being walked through the gauntlet of badges... the eyes.

The eyes followed him, stabbing into Trey like barbed fish hooks baited with curiosity and suspicion. They haunted him, narrowed and accusing stares he could never shake loose. He felt them tugging at his flesh, piercing the glass veil separating the interrogation room from the observation niche behind a wall of one-way mirror.

There were people lurking there, probing shadows with nothing better to do than watch Kimber Bishop tear pieces of her baby brother off like marinated jerky, hanging them out to dry under the fierce, hot sun of her distrust and suspicion.

She certainly had the heat set up to eleven, having a cop show up on the doorstep of his carriage house at seven at night to escort him to the police station in the back of a squad car. There was never any question about Kimber playing favorites with her baby brother. She treated him no better than a common criminal, even when dragging him in to be asked a couple of questions.

Surprised the hell out of Trey when she stood there, saying nothing, her breathing slow and steady but her gaze landing on everything in the room but her younger brother. Kimber had a thin folder tucked under her arm, a flimsy blue paper thing worn around the edges and its tab covered by a sea of stickers, an illegible scrawl in black Sharpie across the most recent addition. Or at least Trey couldn't read what it said.

There was no warmth in the interrogation room. It wasn't meant to be comfortable. Not in any way, shape, or form. Maybe they used it for things other than prying information out of a reluctant person, but whoever threw together its walls and furniture wasn't focused on those rare instances. The walls were a pale puke, a hint of green in the lackluster beige paint. Something had happened near the door at some point, its smooth surface marred by irregular rounded pitting the size of a fist or perhaps a chin. A five-foot steel table sat in the dead center of the room, its metal legs bolted to the gray, tiled floor. Four utilitarian metal chairs sat arranged around the table, two on each side, their red vinyl backs and seats the only spot of color in the space.

Other than Kimber and Trey, but judging by his reflection in the wall-length mirror across of him and his sister's sallow complexion, he figured they were both now the exact same putty hue as the walls.

Then a man walked in and Trey realized that was who his sister was waiting for. Her demeanor shifted, the set of her face hardening into a stony mask not unlike the one their father wore when Trey was being dressed down for what the family thought was his latest fuckup.

"So this is the prodigal son?" the piece of meat wearing a finely tailored charcoal suit barked at Kimber. "Thought your family was supposed to be something, Bishop. Between you and him, it doesn't look like much."

It took everything Trey had not to flip the man off.

"Trey, this is Captain Garrett. He wants to ask you a few questions." Kimber didn't move from her perch against the wall, but her body tensed, her shoulders lifting up as she spoke. She didn't look happy, but Trey couldn't think of the last time he'd seen his sister so much as crack a smile, much less laugh. "Sir, we've got this room for another hour. After that, Narc's got it reserved for something they're running."

"They'll get the fucking room when I'm good and ready to give it to them," the cop growled back. "We don't get answers here and now, Central's going to yank this out from under us, and I've had enough of Book's assholes riding in like the damned cavalry. We get a jump on this and we make sure this case stays with us."

It was a cliché and a bit demeaning to say the man was built like a bull. That imagery came from a dark place in America's past, but there were some men for whom that label applied. This was definitely one of them. Minotaur came to mind. Actually, any other kind of mythological bovine with a thick neck and flared nose would do. All the man was missing was a labyrinth and a ball of thread. And from the disdainful look on his face, the cop wasn't auditioning Trey to be his Ariadne.

Garrett was older, his still-muscular body running to a downhill battle with age, and spongy, a too-pale ooze of skin over flaccid flesh. There was muscle wrapped tight around his bulky frame, but his fingers were puffy, and the gold watch peeking out from his cuff cut a little bit into his wrist when he moved his hand. His stride was a lope, his legs sweeping out as if to accommodate an enormous swinging ball sac between his thighs. There was a discreet gold cross pinning his bright red tie together, and it gleamed as brightly as the skin rippling over his bald head. He had a ghost of stubble along the back of his skull, the shadow of a receding hairline edging up over his pate. Judging by his thick blond eyebrows and nearly colorless blue eyes, Trey imagined he'd been a towheaded kid with freckles across an easily reddened nose.

His nose was still red, but Trey doubted it was from the sun. There was a meanness in his gaze, stropped to a razor sharpness by a sense the world owed him, and Trey somehow embodied every misstep and failed opportunity he'd been given.

Yet somehow this man was Kimber's superior. That much was evident when she rolled her shoulders back, nearly pressing them against the mirrored wall. As much as he and his sister butted heads, Trey didn't like seeing the man roll over her, so in true younger brother fashion, he took the first jab.

"I don't know what swamp you dragged yourself out of, but if you're going to walk among us humans, you should learn to treat people with respect," Trey drawled. "My sister is worth ten of you on her worst day. Maybe you should worry less about trying to prove you have a dick, and think more about how not to be one."

The cop's plump hands tightened into loose fists, the gold ring on his wedding finger straining to hold back his moving flesh. His lips thinned, a liver color slashed across his red-speckled face, and a flush rose up from his neck, coloring his cheeks before rippling across the top of his shaved head.

"They said you had a mouth on you," Garrett growled, slamming those fists into the table, leaning his weight on his hands and spitting wet flecks on Trey's face. "I'm thinking maybe that mouth of yours got you into trouble and now your big sister is trying to clean up another one of your messes."

"This would make a hell of a lot more sense if I knew why you dragged me down here," Trey replied, flicking his glance toward Kimber. "Bad enough you're playing games making me wait for an hour. Probably would have been better if you'd told me why I should be sweating beforehand instead of walking in here throwing your shit around. I'm guessing this has something to do with the dead guy I saw in Koreatown."

"Something. Just not *your* dead guy. Bishop, why don't you lay some of those photos down and see if your baby brother can figure out what we're talking about?" His eyes narrowed when Kimber held the file folder out to him rather than do what he'd ordered. Snatching the portfolio from her hand, he fixed a hard gaze on Trey. "Recognize this guy?"

Garrett dumped a handful of photos out onto the table, arranging them into a line in front of Trey's hands. They were glossy slick, but the man's face in the images was dull, his muscles slack and his skin a sickly gray. The one closest to Trey's fingers showed a splatter of dark brown marbling his left cheek, and for a brief second—up until he saw the next photo—Trey wondered why the man's eyes were mostly closed, a sliver of white showing beneath his pale lashes. Then he glanced over and caught sight of the man's profile, a good chunk of his head blown out on the left side, bits of bone and brain matter dribbling down his neck and across his bare shoulder.

Trey lost everything he'd eaten, emptying his stomach into the interrogation room's trash can.

Feeling as green as the walls, Trey jerked slightly when he felt a hand between his shoulder blades. Then Kimber murmured something into his ear. He couldn't make out what she was saying. Not through the rush of blood coming into his head. Nodding when she asked if he was okay, he swallowed hard. "Can I get some water?"

"Yeah, someone's going to bring you a bottle in a bit." His sister glanced up when the door opened. "Here. Why don't you sit up and breathe. I'll pull out the photo we need you to look at. Captain, I'd like to talk to you after we're done here."

Trey swallowed again, recognizing the cold edge in his oldest sister's voice. It was the same tone she'd used on him countless times before, one with the promise to skin him alive if he didn't do as she'd asked. Regardless of rank or her job, Kimber Bishop was going to have her say once Trey was out of earshot.

He pretended to be fascinated with the tile lines in the floor, studying the flecked patterns of sand stuck into the gray grout. Cracking open the water bottle took some effort, its cheap plastic twisting in his hand when he unscrewed the cap, but eventually Trey was able to wash the sick from his mouth. Taking another shallow sip, he turned back around, steeling himself to look at the images again.

There was only one photo left on the table, a close-up shot of the man's face. Only a few specks of brown showed on his cheek, but if Trey hadn't already seen the damage done to the side of his head, he'd have thought the man was asleep. Problem was, he couldn't *not* see what'd been done. Not anymore. Every time he blinked, his mind filled in the space around the image, sketching in lurid slashes of dried blood caked on broken flesh.

"Wouldn't think a guy who grew up on that shitty show you were on would get sick at the sight of blood. How many people did they gun down in that first episode? Fifteen? Twenty? Pretty graphic shit. Or did living the high life dull your senses?" The Captain sneered, and Trey didn't think it was possible, but his sister's face went even sourer.

"You know television's make-believe, right?" He lifted his chin, smirking back at Garrett. "Or did you really think they shot that many people to death in front of an eight-year-old kid?"

Garrett blinked, his Adam's apple bobbing and weaving over the clench of his buttoned-up shirt and too-tight tie. "Recognize him?"

Gingerly picking up the photo, Trey studied the man's rubbery face. Looking past the shock of his death, there were pieces of the man's brow and nose his mind latched on to. An uneven blue-black star was folded into the creases of his cheek, a blotchy companion to the ugly pink scar starting under his right eye to curve around down to his jaw. Trey's hands began to shake and he sucked in a breath, hoping the cold cop house stinky air would settle the pounding in his chest, but his nerves continued to roll with shock.

"Well, Harry?" Kimber prodded gently. "Do you recognize him?"

"It's Trey," he replied absently, his brain churning on automatic pilot.

The last time Trey saw the man in the photo, he'd been threatening Trey with a gun after dropping a dead man in the street. He'd fled in terror at the sight of the weapon, but the sheer evil in the man's expression lingered in Trey's thoughts. They resurfaced, coating his recent memories with an oily slickness, making it hard for Trey to gather his words.

"He's one of the guys who was carrying...." Trey clamped his mouth shut, then took another shuddering breath. "He's one of the men who shot at me. The one I thought was carrying a dead body."

"A dead man your father confirmed as being alive, right?" Garrett twisted his proverbial knife in further. "Or at least that's what the lieutenant here says. Could you be wrong? Like you were wrong with the other dead guy?"

"No." He shook his head, then slid the photo back over the table toward Garrett. "Unless there's another bald guy with that tattoo and scar. I remember seeing those right before I ran. Because, you know, he had a gun. And before you ask, no, I didn't know him, and I sure as hell didn't kill him. I never saw him before that night or after he and the other guy ran off."

"See, I find *that* kind of hard to believe, because I *know* who killed him. Seems like that ramen shop guy who allegedly saved your ass that night also murdered our friend here. He says the guy was trying to run him off the road, but somehow he ended up maneuvering his car to the back, then blew Mister Francis Bargle's head off while driving up Mulholland." A smug malevolence spread through Garrett's smirk, curling his lips up so far into his cheeks Trey wondered if the man owned a dog named Max. "So how about if we start from the beginning? Like at the point when you ran into some shit while trying to score a hit and run it down to the point where your sleaze of a boyfriend goes out and pops this guy for revenge?"

THE COPS took his gun.

Again.

And this time, Kuro was pretty sure it was going to be a long fucking time before he saw his Glock again. But as sick as he was of the LAPD taking possession of his weapons, he'd grown even sicker of seeing the department's Captain Garrett lumber in and out of the interrogation chill box they'd thrown him into. The man was an idiot, a blowhard who'd somehow stumbled on a golden path to a higher rank while clearly stepping on the necks of other people to get there. On one of the man's blundering forays into dubious fishing trips for information, he was accompanied by Lieutenant Bishop, the blonde detective who'd been on the scene the night he'd lost his first gun to the cops.

She was also Trey's sister, and Kuro bit the inside of his cheek to avoid asking her how he was doing. He shouldn't have cared. Shouldn't have let his focus wander off to the haunted shadows in Trey's wary eyes or the suspicion on his handsome face when he'd looked over at Kuro. For all he knew, those kicked-in-the-nuts and waiting-for-another-one expressions came from a life lived in front of a camera, with his every move captured and then dissected for public consumption, a fugu buffet prepped and served up by a score of incompetent chefs.

Kuro was also surprised to discover he wanted a taste of that particular dish, something much more shocking to his system than having to kill a man at seventy miles an hour. He'd given up on having anything more than a physical release with another man. Before his spectacular crash-and-burn on the international stage, he'd lived his life in the shadows, keeping his profile and his relationships as shallow as possible. It'd been the smart thing to do. His life hadn't been his own. He wasn't meant to have an ivy-covered cottage and white picket fence. God even doubled down on Kuro not living the suburbia dream by cranking his volume for other men up to eleven. There'd been no way in hell Kuro imagined he'd ever wake up next to another man, planning their Saturday afternoon over dim sum and hot tea, but there he sat in an ugly LAPD shakedown room, contemplating how to fit a very complicated Trey Bishop into his extremely simplistic life.

When Garrett started in on him again, Kuro stopped the man with a quiet whisper. "Either charge me with something or let me go. Just whatever it is, make up your mind, because the next thing I'm going to say to you is to ask for a phone call. And you're not going to like what happens after that."

"Are you threatening me, Jenkins?" The cop's nostrils flared, exposing a forest of close-cropped slightly ginger nose hairs hidden in each cavern. "Because to me, that sounds like a threat."

"Take it any way you like, Captain, but you need to shit or get off the pot. If you want to book me for something, I'm sitting right here. Instead, you're poking at me like you think you're going to get something else out of me." He leaned forward slowly, resting on his forearms, but the shift of his weight startled Garrett, who jerked his head back, his hand dropping to hover near his sidearm. "My story isn't going to change. Man fired on me and I maneuvered out of the way, returning fire. It was the second time this particular gentleman has tried to kill me, because even if he was after Trey Bishop the other night, he was aiming at *me*. Third time's the charm, Captain, and I wasn't going to let him have that third chance."

"I don't like you, Jenkins," Garrett spat, his words a rapid-fire stream he punctuated with a stab of his finger at Kuro's face. Kuro held steady, waiting to see if the cop would cross the line and strike him.

"Feeling's a bit mutual at this point," he replied. Someone was moving behind the mirrored partition set into the wall opposite of his seat, their shadow cutting through a bit of light coming from the hall. Garrett left the room a bit too dim for the reflective surface to catch fully, but up until a few seconds ago, Kuro would have sworn the observation niche was empty. "My associate called in the incident and I waited for the police to arrive, my hands on the hood of my car and my weapon stashed in the trunk. I informed the responding officers of its location and then did not resist them when they cuffed me. I've answered all of your questions, sitting here without a break or water for about six hours. At no point in this have I asked for a lawyer or not cooperated. So, Captain, ball's in your court. There's nothing else I can do or give you."

"I've got a dead man and a shootout in the middle of K-Town to explain to my boss, but I've got not a single damned thing to go on. You can answer one question for me." The cop straightened his cuffs, taking a step back from the table. "You can tell me why when I push for information about you, I get told it's none of my business. That you're not my problem."

"I'm not," Kuro conceded. "Not yet anyway. And I probably never will be. I'm the least of your worries right now. You've got a man on a slab, and somewhere out there, his partner's lurking doing God knows what. You've got a witness to a possible homicide who was shot at the other night, a witness I defended, and instead, you're in here trying to get me to admit I know more than I do. I don't know the man I killed today. First time I saw him was the other night when I came out of my shop and found him and another man shooting at one of my customers. Today, that man followed me and tried to kill me. So I tried to kill him right back. I just was better at it than he was. End of story. Again. Still. Now, are we going to head to a cell so I can be booked for whatever you want to cook up to keep me here, or are you going to let me go?"

Garrett opened his mouth to respond when a knock landed on the room's heavy door. Narrowing his eyes, he pointed at Kuro, gesturing him to continue to sit. Ambling over to the door, the man stuck his head out and Kuro caught a bit of heated whispering, then Trey Bishop's name being dropped into the middle of the conversation like a smoking match into a dumpster filled with dynamite.

"I'm not done—" The cop was cut off by more whispering. Then a deep voice boomed through the crack in the door.

"You're done, Garrett. Cut him loose before he asks for a lifeline, because I'm not stepping into that field of shit with you. I'm cutting Bishop loose too. Wrap up anything you need to put this to bed, but understand this, it goes to bed." The man's rolling voice dropped, a feathery brush of words barely audible above the clatter of the bullpen beyond the short hall. "We can't lock horns here. Man did all he was supposed to and a little bit beyond that. Have him sign for his effects and let him go. We know where to find him if we need him again."

"Sir—" Garrett protested.

"Sir, nothing. Cut him loose. You caught a wolf in that cat trap you laid out, and it's about to tear through that wire and eat your face. Be smart. Let it go."

Kuro said nothing when Garrett turned back around and closed the door behind him. The captain shuffled closer, much like a child caught cheating on a test. From the sounds of things, Holly'd been working behind the scenes, prying her way through LAPD's upper ranks and strong-arming people into doing what she wanted. He wondered how far she'd pushed, and a moment later, he got his answer.

"You can pick up your Glock later this month. Forensics is going to rush it through." Garrett barely parted his teeth to let his words out. "We're going to release you, but just so you know, I'm watching you, Jenkins. Don't leave the city without letting me know, and keep your nose clean, because the next time I find you in this kind of situation, I don't care who's holding that skeleton key, I'm dragging you right into a cell and slamming the door behind you."

LOS ANGELES was never ever truly dark. Its pulse beat in erratic flashes of traffic lights and passing cars, stealing the black from the sky. The cop house was lit up enough for him to stumble out of the front doors and immediately stop short at the edge of the sidewalk, struck speechless by the lean, handsome man resting his hip against a broad, low-slung black car. He was dressed from head to toe in the same ebony as the muscle car he stood against, much of his face lost in the smoky haze of shadows falling across his face.

No matter how far man evolved away from the animal he'd been once, some primal tickle of fear remained, a coded alarm set off by a person's nervous system, warning them of immense danger. The cook he'd watched dredge noodles through hot water was gone, replaced by a sleek jaguar of a man with glittering eyes and a faint smile with a whisper of teeth, a peek of white past his beautiful mouth heavy with the promise to bite if provoked.

And by the expression on his face, the ramen shop owner was beyond provoked. Trey mumbled a quick hello and wondered if he shouldn't bolt back inside and take up his sister's offer to drive him home. That thought faded away into dust when the ramen guy growled out Trey's name.

"Um, yeah?" He'd been hungry and tired when he'd stepped through the doors, but now his hunger lay in ashes someplace in his stomach and his throat was suddenly coated in thick sand, making it impossible for him to speak.

"Get in. I'll take you home." The man's growl deepened, unspooling a molten sensuality in its velvet folds. "And then you and I are going to have a very long fucking talk."

Six

"YOU WANT me to get into your car?" Trey backed up a few steps, mostly to give himself room to breathe. "So you can what? Kill me?"

"I've had you facedown and between my legs a night or so ago. If I wanted you dead, I'd have shot you then," he pointed out. "Now get in the damned Challenger and I'll take you home. I've already spent a couple of hours getting my windshields replaced. I'm tired of waiting."

"You don't even know where I live." The man rattled off his address, and Trey felt the blood drain out of his face. "How the hell do you know where I live?"

"You signed up for our newsletter and mail coupons. How many Trey Bishops do you think are out there who come into my place for ramen?" He glanced at his watch. "Tell me you have coffee at your place. The drive-thru near us is going to close in ten minutes. I'm going to need some bean juice. Something tells me we're going to be at this for a while."

"I don't think I even really know your name."

"Kuro Jenkins. Don't bother looking me up. I'm not that interesting." He sighed, rubbing at a spot above his nose. "I've also made you how many bowls of noodles? I've had plenty of opportunity to kill you, but here we are, standing in a parking lot while I'm trying to take you home and get some kind of sense of what the hell's going on here."

"Give me one good reason I should get into that car."

"Other than a free ride home?" Kuro countered. "Because I killed a man today. One of the guys who shot at you. He followed me up into the hills and tried to murder me, but it didn't turn out exactly as he planned. I want to know what's going on, and my gut tells me you're in the middle of it. First they shoot at you, now one's come for me. I want to know why."

"The cops don't believe I saw those guys trying to put a dead man into the back of their van. Even my own sister thinks I just pissed off a couple of drug dealers, but they've got it wrong. I've been clean since my last run in rehab." A couple of uniformed cops came out of the front door, chatting about food. Neither one of them glanced at Trey or the deadly man he'd somehow tangled with. "Wait, did you just say you killed that guy? The one they brought me in to ID?"

"Did you know him?" He tilted his head, studying Trey. "Because if you do—"

"No, I didn't know him. How many times do I have to say that before someone freaking believes me?" Exasperated, Trey paced closer, his simmering anger finally coming to a boil. It probably wasn't smart to tangle with a guy who'd just admitted to murdering someone a few hours ago, but Trey'd given up on common sense. Nothing he said appeared to matter, and he was tired of feeling helpless. "Those two guys wanted me dead, and not because I didn't pay them for drugs—which no one found on me, right? If I didn't see them doing something shitty, then why were they trying to shoot me?"

"Because you're annoying?"

As hot as the guy was, he was also beginning to get on Trey's nerves. Shaking his head, he said, "Give me one good reason why I should go with you."

His smile was slow, but it changed his face. He'd been handsome before, a sculpted god of a man dressed in black, as if he were Death coming to reap Trey's soul. With a smile—a damned peek-of-white-teeth smile—Kuro Jenkins was stunning, and Trey's heart tried to crawl out of his chest to get to the man, a resounding thump-thump-thump beginning under his rib cage.

"Because I believe you and the cops don't." Kuro pushed off of the car and Trey got a whiff of his cologne, a nerve-tingling blend of citrus and green tea with a heady kiss of masculine skin beneath it. "And since they don't, the only way you and I are going to get people to stop trying to kill us is if we figure out who's behind this… and stop them. So get in the car, Bishop. Sooner we get started on this, the sooner we can get started on other things that are a hell of a lot more interesting."

DESPITE THE late hour, getting across town was a nightmare. Friday night on the edge of Koreatown meant sitting in long streams of stereo-thumping cars and overloaded buses. Thousands were fighting to get home while even more were battling to go out, eager to shed the stress of a long work week with a little bit of play and debauchery.

Or a good bowl of ramen, Kuro reminded himself. Something they could pick up at the Tako Shop until two in the morning when his night crew would lock the place down and scrub it clean for the next shift. His stomach growled, reminding him he hadn't eaten since chewing a handful of bean sprouts that morning after prepping twenty pounds of char siu. Lunch hadn't happened. *Water* barely happened, and Kuro's hunger was making itself known, gnawing on the edges of his stomach.

Glancing over at the man sitting quietly in the seat next to him, Kuro cleared his throat. "Tell me you've got food in your fridge I can use to whip something up for us. If not, I can stop at the store before we get there. Didn't get any food today, and from what I can see, you need a bit in you too."

"I can't believe you can eat right now," Trey muttered under his breath. "And I can't believe I'm riding in a car with a guy who killed someone today. This can't be real. All of this. I probably ODed. Probably never even made it to rehab. I'm lying in some hospital bed, drooling, with my ass hanging out of a hospital gown so some sick perv orderly can wank off on me during his shift."

"You been storing up that little fantasy for a while, have you?" Kuro teased, not sure how Trey would take it. "Because that sounds particularly... specific."

"Nope. Just off the top of my head. Stick around. I'm sure I can come up with all kinds of shit just like that." Trey blinked slowly, leaning his temple against the Challenger's window. "And yeah, there's food. Sera fills the fridge every week hoping I'll get off my ass and cook something, but the joke's on her. I can barely boil water to make a Cup O'Noodles."

"Pretty sure I can make you something better than that." Kuro winced, shuddering at the memory of instant ramen on his tongue. "Even if it's just an omelet. If you've got eggs."

"Oh yeah, eggs I've got." He blinked again, his lashes throwing spiky shadows over his cheek. "It's common sense that I'm missing."

Traffic brought them to another standstill, idling through streams of steel and lights. Ahead a mobile road warning flashed arrows to the left, warning drivers they were coming up on a closed lane. As if Kuro needed reminding. There was a cascade of turn signals blinking in the blue-shadow-washed street, light-up salmons trying to jump the falls to safety.

Kuro took another peek at the man sitting next to him. He'd spent his life learning to read people, having to make split-second decisions on what their next action would be based on nothing more than a nose twitch or a blink. But he didn't need years of experience to read Trey Bishop. The dirty blond slumped into the Challenger's low-slung seat, molding his compactly muscled body into the leather curve. He sat with the stillness of a man burdened with fatigue and despair, and incredible sadness tugging down the corners of a mouth Kuro longed to kiss. He'd seen a smile on those lips, but it'd been wan, a distilled watercolor of fake delight laced with a generous helping of disdain.

Despite the tired expression on Trey's face, he looked young, the kind of young Kuro avoided like the plague. From what Aoki told him, there shouldn't have been any innocence on Trey Bishop's face, but it was there. Sitting firm alongside a blush of youth Kuro never remembered possessing himself. Trey Bishop had the kind of face handsome enough to clench at a man's balls, nearly androgynous with enough masculine strength to his features to be considered ugly on a woman but breathtaking on a man. There was an erotic rumpled air about the former child star, and Kuro's mind drifted to naughtier things than driving through Los Angeles. He wasn't one for fantasizing. He'd spent too much of his life in the reality of the world and its disgusting nature, but his brain obviously was tired of staying the course.

The man looked good on black leather. It didn't take much to imagine him stretched out on black satin, his thick gold-streaked hair spread out on musky sheets, eyes hooded with satisfaction and his long, slightly tanned body damp with sweat. Kuro could almost taste the heady salt he would pull up after following the length of Trey's ribs with his tongue. His imagination couldn't scrape up the sounds Trey would make when Kuro's mouth closed over him, but he was more than willing to get into a position where he could find out.

Problem was, Trey Bishop was trouble. He didn't need to retire from a dangerous lifetime of scary situations and even more frightening politics only to lose his head and life by getting involved with a man like Trey Bishop. Or at least that's what his common sense said.

The rest of him didn't agree.

"You said you believed me. Was this before or after that guy tried to kill you? Because I'm going to be honest, I wasn't sure I believed what I saw after everyone told me I was crazy. I don't have the greatest track records. Shit, there's a lot of times when people tell me I've done something in the past and I don't remember a damned thing about it," Trey murmured as someone in the line of cars began to honk, impatient with the slow-moving traffic. "And, as much as I hate to admit it, there's a couple of times my brain went down the rabbit-hole thing I took or drank, and what my mind cooked up seemed so real but it wasn't. You got no reason to believe me. I don't have reason to believe myself. So why are you throwing in with me on this? It's just bad news for you all around."

Trey's smoky gray gaze drifted back toward the street, the pink light from a bar's neon sign gilding his skin with a rose-gold glow. It was odd to see a patchwork quilt of resignation and determined resolve on a man's face, a conflict of spirit and experience doing battle in front of him.

"Maybe because I've spent my life fighting for the underdog," Kuro admitted cautiously. "Or maybe—just maybe—you're my particularly favorite brand of trouble."

TREY SAT at one of the tall stools near the kitchen's long island. He couldn't shake the feeling of déjà vu at seeing Kuro on the other side until he realized he'd sat at the ramen counter more than a few times, watching the then-silent man in black work his magic with a bowl of miso and freshly made noodles.

This time was different. There were still noodles, dehydrated ones newly liberated from orange plastic packets, but the seasoning foils that came with them were promptly tossed into the trash, their disposal accented by Kuro's disgusted hiss. Out of the cabinets came things Trey didn't even realize he'd had. Small plastic pots of concentrated stock were dug out from behind a jar of chili powder in the spice cabinet, as well as a small container of chili flakes. From somewhere in the fridge came one lone sweet potato, a handful of mushrooms, an unopened bag of baby carrots, half a packet of thickly sliced bacon, a few eggs, and a slightly limp bunch of green onions.

"I swear to God the only thing in there before you opened the door was a bottle of ketchup and some olives I got for martinis." Trey scowled. "And they weren't even my martinis. Where did all of that come from?"

"I didn't smuggle it in. That's one job I *won't* do." Kuro began doing something complicated with one of Trey's knives and the long steel thing Sera left in a drawer. The blade made snick-snick noises as Kuro ran the knife down the steel length, his strong fingers wrapped loosely around its black handle. "Why don't we get down to what we're here for... besides getting something to eat. Let's talk about what happened that night."

"Where do I start?" Kuro looked up, and Trey found himself drowning in the man's mesmerizing blue-flecked green eyes. It was akin to being caught in an ocean off the secluded beach in Hawai'i, the pull of a wave scented with salt and sunshine powerful enough to pick him up and slam him into the silken white sands. "I didn't ask for any of this. I was just trying to run off some shit going on in my head."

"Kind of shit?" The sweet potato didn't stand a chance with Kuro wielding a knife against it. From what Trey could see, he didn't even look down at the tuber as he sliced, lopping off identically wide rounds of its firm purple flesh. "It was three o'clock in the morning. What were you doing up then?"

"What were *you* doing up then?" Trey opened the carrots and fished one out. Nibbling on the end under Kuro's watchful glare, he pressed on. "Look, my crash-and-burn was played out on every television and magazine over the last eight years. I'm sober now. I was trying to stay that way."

"Up until someone told me about you, I had no idea." Kuro rescued the carrots from Trey's clutches and poured a dozen out onto the chopping board. After tossing the bag back at Trey, he made quick work of their plump orange bodies, slicing them on the diagonal. "It sounds like you had a rough time of it."

"You telling me you've never heard of *Down the Tracks*? It was the biggest thing on television next to that Korean War show." He sat back a little bit, trying to wrap his head around someone who hadn't caught at least a whisper of the gritty drama he'd spent so much of his life on. "It ran for twelve seasons. We dominated the airwaves. The finale was the most-watched thing in the history of television over the last twenty-five years."

"I was... busy." Kuro's explanation was cautious, a slow pour of honey over prickly bramble. "There wasn't much time for anything. Including television."

"You can't be that much older than I am. What? Four or five years? I started the show when I was eight. What the hell were you doing?"

Trey leaned back on the counter, resting his elbows on the hard stone. "You couldn't have been much more than twelve or thirteen. It was everywhere."

"Like I said," he replied with a shrug. "I was busy. Talk to me about that night. What were you doing out there?"

He didn't like talking about what led him to pounding the asphalt in the weary hours of a Los Angeles morning. In some ways it felt like a death wish, flinging himself out into the night with nothing more than his drug-starved brain and a growing desire to quench its thirst. He ran through some of LA's worst neighborhoods, or at least that's what people told him. Trey found if he didn't stop, he was left alone. No one bothered with the crazies in LA, and since no one but a crazy person would be running at two or three o'clock in the morning through its violence-haunted streets, Trey figured he was dialed up to eleven on the insanity scale. If only he hadn't run through that alley. If only those men hadn't dropped their plastic-wrapped corpse. And if only he hadn't recognized the man from years of staring at his smiling face in the photos on his father's walls.

But no one believed him. Not even his own sister. No one except the man standing across of him blending a bit of pancake mix with a lot of water in a blue CorningWare bowl he'd somehow inherited after a potluck. Trey was tired of the doubt and suspicion hanging over him. They were dark clouds following him, keeping the light off his shoulders and face. There was only so much pushback a man could take before he snapped, and Trey feared he would tumble back into the bottles he'd just climbed out of to get some relief from the pressure.

He couldn't do that. Not to himself. He would've said not to everyone who'd stood by him, but he'd burned a lot of those bridges, and the only one who had his back now was Sera, his father's ex-mistress and his best friend. Kuro represented something Trey never imagined he'd find. He was a clean slate. Ignorant of everything Trey'd done and his destructive past.

Kuro also was willing to help him, and the sheer relief of being believed in lifted Trey's soul. He was going to take a risk on the man who'd fed him and defended him. After all, Trey had already kicked more than a few gift horses in the mouth in his lifetime. He sure as hell wasn't going to look at this one's teeth too closely. He'd learned that lesson. One never knew when another horse would come by, and the one God delivered to his doorstep was possibly the hottest man Trey had ever seen.

Once he got past the sneaking suspicion Kuro could kill him with his pinkie finger.

Trey didn't think he would ever get past that.

"One of the things I picked up in rehab was whenever I wanted to take a drink or do drugs, I should distract myself. Sometimes reading a book works, but if things get too bad, I run." He grabbed another carrot, chewing on it as Kuro dredged the sweet potatoes in the milky batter, then slid them into a skillet with hot oil. "I was having a really shitty night with the shakes. I went all the way down to the freeway and came back up. I was getting tired, so I cut through the alley next to your shop, then across the back. That's when I ran into those guys on the next street. It was kind of like finding a spider in your bathtub. Okay, more like two cobras instead of a spider, because normally when I run into people doing something at that time of night, I just keep going."

"But that night you didn't." Kuro pushed at the battered sweet potatoes with a pair of long chopsticks Trey was certain he didn't own. His kitchen was turning into Mary Poppins's carpetbag, and if he wasn't already awestruck by the man's overwhelming competence, he'd wondered if he'd somehow wandered onto some magician's show. "You stopped. Why?"

"Because they felt like cobras. I don't know how else to explain it. There was something wrong about them. And I just stopped because it felt too dangerous. Or at least that's what it felt like afterwards. Right then and there? I wasn't thinking. I was just frozen in place." Bites of carrot he'd taken were turning to ash in his mouth, and Trey forced himself to swallow the gritty bits. "I probably would have turned around and gone the other way even if they hadn't dropped that guy onto the street. Something told me to get as far away from them as possible, but as soon as I saw them drawing their guns, it was like that's what my brain needed to see before it engaged."

"And you say you recognized the man?" He fished out the potatoes, putting them onto a plate covered in paper towels, then began another batch. Once he slid those into the oil, he picked up one of the cooked pieces and laid it on an empty plate in front of Trey. "Be careful. It'll be hot inside. Don't burn your mouth."

The man had fed him before, but this was intimate. Sure, Sera made him meals all the time, but the tumultuous current flowing between him and Kuro was nearly as sweet and hot as the tempura Trey gingerly bit into. He'd never been with anyone who cooked for him, and Trey was torn between wanting to fall in love or scraping back the emotions crawling up from inside of his depths, scared to discover he was attracted to the man solely because Kuro was being nice to him.

He also couldn't believe his kitchen actually had the ingredients to make what looked like a fantastic bowl of ramen.

"Yeah. He's someone my dad knows, but he's alive." Trey chewed, then swallowed, reaching for the glass of water he'd poured himself earlier. Kuro was right. It was hot, and he felt it burn all the way down to his stomach. "His name is Robert Mathers, and he owns a hell of a lot of companies. He also played golf with my dad the day I saw him lying dead on the street."

"Could you have been mistaken?" Kuro asked, fishing the rest of the potatoes out. The carrots underwent the same process, battered and then into the oil.

"No. When I'm sober—okay even when I'm not—I remember people's faces. I have to be pretty fucked-up to not know where I am or who I've seen and, not going to lie, there's quite a few blank spots in my brain because I've been pretty fucked-up," Trey confessed. "But my mind doesn't let go of things. That's my biggest problem. Once I've seen or heard something, it gets tucked away back somewhere. It might take me a while to recall where I've put it, but I always know. All I need sometimes is a little trigger. It's like I never get lost, because once I've been someplace, I always know where I am."

"Boy, I could've used you on quite a few trips I've taken," Kuro murmured, grinning up at Trey. "So, there's the dead guy who's not dead and another dead guy who shot at you and came after me. The cops aren't going to dig into what you saw that night, so we probably won't run into anyone with a badge while we try to figure this out."

"Are you seriously talking about investigating this?" Trey nearly choked on a piece of potato. "Shouldn't this be something we leave to the cops?"

"They're not going to do jack shit about this. They don't believe you, and other than both of us getting shot at, there isn't a murder to dig through. You said it yourself, the man you saw that night is alive and walking around playing golf." Kuro looked away, but not before Trey saw the fire in his eyes. "But there's still another man out there, and we don't know why his partner decided I needed to die. It's only a matter of time before he finds you too, and I'd really like that not to happen."

"How the hell are we going to find out any of this?" he asked. "I can't prove I even saw a dead guy. I *saw* Robert Mathers. And it's not like we can question the guy in the truck. You blew his head off."

"Let me ask around and find out who today's dead guy is. That will at least give us someplace to start. After that, I can see where that takes us." Kuro stopped fussing with the vegetables to give Trey a slight reassuring smile. "Remember when I told you I was too busy to watch television? Well, it's time for me to get busy again, because I really do love fighting for the underdog, and from where I'm standing, you need someone like me to fight for you."

Seven

"I WAS expecting you last night," Holly purred at Kuro as he climbed out of the Challenger. "Especially after I pulled all those strings to get you shaken loose."

The purr was deceiving, but then Holly always purred. She couldn't help it. It was in her nature, a beautiful package of danger and nurture, a conflicting bundle of trouble Kuro was very glad to have on his side.

Nearly as tall as he was, Holly was built along the lines of a 1940s gangster moll, complete with a filled-to-the-brim hourglass figure and legs up to her chin. Now in her midfifties, Holly hadn't changed a bit since the time he'd first met her, back when he was wet behind the ears and she assumed control over his life. Well, she'd changed somewhat. She was now missing her left eye. The cavernous hole left by the too-near-for-comfort sniper bullet was covered by a jaunty black eye patch, and her long blonde hair was now a smart bob cut short to curve around her sharp, fey features. Her blue gaze was still as cutting, a brilliant-cut sapphire not blunted at all by the lack of its twin, and she limped a little, the result of having her right kneecap blown out by a counteroperative she'd then taken out with a pair of shears.

She'd been his handler from the moment he'd picked up his first gun, and her retirement papers were on the chief's desk the day they turned Kuro out onto the streets. He'd traveled a bit after they'd black-inked his identity, rolling his stats back into society's registers, but Holly'd immediately taken up residence in her Brentwood chateau, surrounded by lush expansive gardens and a pair of Tibetan mastiffs she'd named Brutus and Fluffy. Kuro couldn't tell the dogs apart, and for all their fierce reputation, the most savage he'd seen them become was an intense wrestle over a pair of bunny slippers they'd found under Holly's bed. They each carried one around in their mouths at some point in the day, sopping bedraggled messes Holly refused to even acknowledge existed.

Kuro didn't know how she did it. Ignoring several hundred pounds of slavering fur carrying a mangled stuffed-bunny head in its mouth took a certain panache, and Holly dealt with the situation as she dealt with every wrinkle in Kuro's life, with grace and without a blink of her eye.

"I ended up taking Bishop home. They pulled him in at the same time they were shaking me down." Kuro closed the Challenger's door and eyed the two shambling mounds of fur quivering with excitement on the chateau's sweeping front steps. "Let's keep the puppies under control today, all right? I don't want a repeat of the last time I came to visit."

"They love you, that's all." Her smile was a thing of beauty, and Kuro knew from experience it held more than a tincture of treachery in its gleaming whiteness. "It's because they smell that cat of yours on you, and you know how they love cats."

"I'm pretty sure Yuki-onna would be as fond of them as I am." The one on the left dropped down, hunching next to Holly's heels, and not for the first time, Kuro wished he was carrying a weapon. He'd seen firsthand what a Tibetan mastiff could do to a man, and for all of Holly's assurances—and the dogs' oddly exuberant affection for him—Kuro wasn't convinced.

"I don't know why you don't like dogs."

"Those aren't dogs. They're killing machines you've raised as lap puppies, and one day, they're going to remember they can take a water buffalo down with a single pounce, and with my luck, that'll be the day I'm looking particularly like hamburger." Fluffy... or Brutus... finally broke his hold on his patience and bounded down the stairs, eating up the distance in a few short hops. The dog was on Kuro before he could blink, and he went down under the mass, hitting the hard cobblestone drive with a sickening thump he could feel up and down his spine. A second later he was blind, covered in fur and long viscous threads of dirt-speckled spittle. Shoving helplessly at the massive dog's chest, Kuro called out to his mentor, unable to dislodge her pet. "Swear to God, Holly, I'm going to shoot him."

"You wouldn't harm a hair on his pretty head. You love animals too much. Fluffy, come on. Let's go inside and get a treat." Holly turned, resting her hand on the other dog's head for support. "When you pick yourself up off the floor, come to the study. It's time you and I had a little talk."

Picking himself up was fairly easy. Getting into the chateau was a bit harder. The dogs haunted his every step, slamming into Kuro's legs as he tried to walk up the stairs. Holly was right. They were affectionate and, despite being totally unaware of their mass, playful and friendly. They just loved him way too much to make it easy to do anything like crossing a room without one of them being there to see what he was doing.

One thing he was grateful for—at least having the run of a multiacre estate surrounded by thick woods seemed like ample enough room for the dogs to work off their spare energy.

The chateau was a gorgeous aged burnished-ivory manor house, a thirteen-bedroom stretch of stone, windows, and blue shingles. Dovetailed stonework braced every corner and sill, the slightly lighter stonework curving into sturdy covered verandas on the east side of the building. Its cobblestoned drive was artistically laced with dollops of close-cropped grass, softening the hard dark round bricks, and its broad stairs leading up to the ten-foot-tall double doors glistening with flecks of mica, looking as if someone had scattered diamonds in Holly's wake. Several turrets competed for attention around the front and back, jostling a bristle of chimneys into place between the chateau's sloping roofs, as if fearful for the competition for the sky. If he hadn't known better, Kuro would have said Holly somehow plucked the chateau from the Aquitaine countryside and rearranged it among the gardens and various pools scattered about the estate. He'd have been fully fooled if it hadn't been for the neighbors' towering queen palms' fronds dusting at the top of the west side's tree canopy.

The chateau was an odd setting for his mentor. She'd never seemed like the French villa type of person, but then again, so many moments of their lives had been spent on the run through little alleys and in command centers filled with small-minded men and invasive technology. Retirement brought a different set of problems, odd ones to deal with after a lifetime of gunfire and death. Now Holly seemed content to whittle away her time in the estate's elaborate formal gardens, hidden behind a thick perimeter of impenetrable hedges and a tall, wide stone wall. Old habits died hard, though, especially for someone like Holly Michaels. Her security system was discreet, but Kuro recognized all of the signs of a deadly ring of protection around the area. If some idiot decided to breach the chateau's outer ring, the dogs would be the least of their worries.

And then, of course, there was always Holly to deal with, and since the woman taught him everything he knew, Kuro could easily imagine the drawn-out agony she'd have in store for anyone who crossed her.

The inside of the chateau was cool and silent. Closing the door left the outside world where it belonged, tucked away in its own false reality, churning away to provide the illusion of a safe existence for the countless millions who lived in the Los Angeles basin and beyond. Kuro knew better about that too. People existed behind a veil, a flimsy façade Kuro hadn't quite become accustomed to living in front of. Now with the trouble Trey Bishop brought to his front door, he was once again behind the curtain, working at the angles of a job, and he had no idea where the endgame was.

The dogs kept him company, but he'd lost Holly to the labyrinth of rooms. There were signs of the staff here and there, the sound of a vacuum being run somewhere and the soft buzz of a blender coming from the kitchen down the hall. The décor was a gentle wash of textures and soft colors, designed more for comfort, and in some cases, dusted with a light brush of tri-colored dog hair. Sunlight streamed through the broad french doors at the end of the long foyer, picking out the gold threads in the curving koa staircase leading to the second floor, and the back gardens appeared to be in full bloom, a dizzying palette of pinks and burgundies from the rosebushes Holly tended every day. Spots of yellow bobbed about the blooms, energetic bees zipping through the leaves much to the consternation of a gardener who batted at the small swarm with a Detroit Lions baseball cap.

A subtle push from Fluffy at the back of his thighs reminded Kuro about Holly waiting for him in her study. Then the dog bounded off, a nightmare of flowing fur dredged up from thousands of hair commercials.

His sneakers made very little noise on the polished honey-oak floors, but apparently it was enough to draw Holly's attention from the silver coffee service left behind by a ghostly silent maid who'd slipped out, having just deposited the serving tray on a curved-legged table set in front of a wall of french doors. Most were open, probably to let in the fragrant perfume of the formal rose gardens outside or, as Kuro guessed, to let the dogs roam freely, giving them access to the nearly three acres of trees, lawns, and a now-empty-of-fish pond after Holly discovered the mastiffs liked hunting and eating the delicate decorative google-eyed goldfish she'd once had in there.

He liked the study. It was a warm, welcoming place with huge soft couches, not unlike Holly's dogs, yet also someplace she pulled strings and maneuvered ruthless deals, cutting through people's lives with a gleeful disdain for rules. Of the three creatures in the room besides him, Holly was the most dangerous. The mastiffs, for the most part, were predictable, savage if provoked, but Holly was something much more deadly, a woman with a lot of connections and a very long memory.

Not for the first time in his life, Kuro was extremely glad Holly was fond of his continued existence.

"Sit down, sweetheart," Holly said, gesturing to the pair of plump love seats arranged into an L around the small table. "I'll pour and you can tell me about this little boy that's landed in your lap. And why I shouldn't have him killed for dragging you into this mess?"

"I was hoping you'd have something to tell me about him. All I have is a bunch of stories and gossip Aoki threw my way over chopped vegetables." Kuro took the teacup she held out to him, sniffing at the aromatic steam curling up from the hot brew. "Earl Grey with something else in it?"

"Other than cream? Yes. More of a different balance of the flavors but let's keep to the topic, the boy." She clinked a teaspoon on the rim of her cup, shaking off the last drops clinging to its bowl. "Well, hardly a boy. He's twenty-eight with a spectacular history of drug and alcohol abuse he picked up during a meteoric rise to stardom and then a crash down into the rocky crags below. A literal Icarus, burnt wings and all. What I don't understand is why you got involved with him to the point I have to pull strings to get you out of jail."

"That's what I'm here to find out," he admitted, reaching down to one of the dogs' heads when he plopped his chin on Kuro's thigh. A bit of spittle flecked his jeans, but the drying film was the price one paid for having tea with Holly. "There's baggage there, and I want to find out if the man I killed today is something Bishop's carrying with him or someone thrown into his path."

As fond as Holly was of him, Kuro was quite aware her pulling strings placed him further into her debt. Holly did nothing without an expectation of a favor later on. Sooner or later, he'd have to pay the devil her due, and having her pry into Trey Bishop's life was going to just add more to the tally sheet, but Aoki could only give him what was already out there. He needed more than what was on the table, and the only person he knew would ferret out the whats and whys of Trey's world was sitting across of him with a canary-swallowing cat smile on her elegant face.

"You know, of course, my darling boy," Holly purred over her cup's rim. "You are going to have to do me a teensy bit of work if I need it some day. Keeping you out of trouble is getting to be very expensive for me, especially since you blew the back of that man's head off. If you are going to go around executing people at high speeds, at least install a dash cam on that monstrosity you drive. More people would believe you were in danger if there's a recording of it."

"I know I owe you. Hell, I owe you my life ten times over, and that's lowballing it." He set his cup down, the tea souring in his stomach. The dog shifted, pushing into Kuro's leg, then flopped on his foot with a heavy *whoof*. "I just want to make sure I'm going to be around to pay you back."

"Don't lie to me, Kuro. I know you better than that," Holly shot back, an indelicate snort flaring her nostrils. "You feel something for the boy. Don't try to mask it with that thin veil of self-preservation you throw over yourself when you need to trick someone into thinking you're not a sentimental fool. You did this when Aoki was on the chopping block to be cut from the program and again when Samantha was caught. You *like* people. It just doesn't match the idea you have in your head about yourself if you admit it."

"Samantha was going to be executed," he pointed out. "I don't think extracting a fellow operative from an oubliette is being sentimental. She's not someone's Papillion."

"Girl is as stupid as one. There's only so much one can do to rescue a dumb animal that insists on running into traffic." Holly placed her cup down on the table, its foot rattling when it struck the saucer's lip. "Bishop is a lost cause. Don't let that paladin you keep buried down in your soul take over your heart. He's not worth your time, much less you. I didn't drag you out of the mud and polish you up for you to lose your head and life over a piece of trash, no matter how thick someone gilded it with gold."

He met her gaze, letting the heat of her simmering outrage roll over him. Something was going on, something he didn't understand, but he was in the thick of it, and Holly was driving her displeasure hard, whipping up her own personal Wild Hunt to ravage those in her way.

"I'm not letting anyone get to my head. Or anywhere else, for that matter." Insisting wouldn't help, but Kuro did it anyway, his voice lifting a bit. The dog at his feet whined, grumbling at Kuro's irritation, but soon settled back down. The other one at Holly's feet didn't so much as blink, snoring hard enough to ruffle the tassels on the table's decorative runner. "And what if I am? I'm out of the game, Holly. I'm done with leaping through fire and playing at being someone's pawn. I might owe you a favor or five hundred, but that doesn't mean I don't get to live my life."

"I just don't want to see you hurt, Kuro. I'm too old to be patching you up all over again."

"I'll be fine." The dog's head was back, spreading more spittle and hair over his jeans. "Just tell me what I've got in my rearview mirror so I know what I've got to do."

"Your boy Trey didn't just crash and burn. He bathed in a vat of kerosene, then set himself on fire." She refilled his cup, a fragrant lush amber stream coursing down the side of the bowl. "He's the youngest of a fourth-generation tycoon, a surprise baby at the tail end of Harrington Bishop the Second's long and dissolute life. The boy's mother was an entertainer of sorts, capturing the old man's eye, and my sources say when she turned up pregnant, old Harry had a DNA test done on the little bundle of joy. Because nothing says love like doubting if you got your wife pregnant."

"We've seen worse," he reminded her. "Remember that guy in Iceland?"

"The less I think of him the better." Holly shuddered. "Bishop Senior discovered he had a son and, well, promptly declared the boy the next Messiah and, well, his mother had other ideas. Harry Number Three has been a chew toy between those two since the beginning. Father wanted him to go into finance, and Mommy steered him into the limelight. Mommy won because your boy ended up behind the camera before he could walk."

"He's got a much older sister I know about. A cop. Pretty far away from the family's tycoon roots." He leaned forward, ignoring his fresh cup of tea. "Struck me as angry when she got to the scene. Tore into him almost as soon as she got out of the car. Had him corralled up tight. Like she needed to control him."

"He needs controlling. And she's got company. Besides Kimberly, there's two more much older sisters from Harry Two's previous marriages. Margaret and the unfortunately named Scooter work for the old man at the family's evil empire." Holly toed off her pump, using her stockinged foot to scratch at the sleeping mastiff's shoulders. The dog sighed contentedly, shifting over to show his belly. "From what I could gather up in what little time you gave me, Daddy made them work their way into those corner offices they have on the top floor, and the whispers around the tower are that if baby brother ever wanted to stroll through those sacred doors, the girls would have to find someplace else to park their staplers."

"Think the two guys were sent to take him out that night?" Kuro turned the possibility over in his head, tasting the angles. It was a shaky supposition but a definite possibility. "Maybe since he's crashed as an actor, he's making moves on their territory?"

"Darling, he didn't just crash. He's an urban legend. Trey Bishop is literally the poster child of how to destroy your life in a few short years. To be fair to the boy, he was put into the middle of a television show about drug dealers and vicious criminals when he was eight." Holly reached for her tea again, her sharp eyes settling on Kuro's neglected cup. "Drink something. I can get you coffee if you like."

Kuro picked up the cup, handling the delicate porcelain as gently as he could. "It was a show. All make-believe. Not like they were showing him how to shoot up heroin in between takes."

"It is always amazing how naïve you are despite everything I've dragged you through." Holly's lips curved into a beatific smile, the gold ring she wore on her pinkie finger flashing in the sunlight. "Trey Bishop was front and center for one of the most brutal shows depicting a criminal lifestyle. The cast lived the lifestyle. I can't tell you how many rehabs it supported over the years, but Trey Bishop wasn't its only victim. Simply the youngest."

"His story was he'd gone running because it helps him stay sober. I believe him on that, but I don't know him." Kuro made a face. "Odds of a user relapsing are high. Hard to shake that demon once it's got its hooks into you."

"Especially when they've been in and out of more than a handful like Trey Bishop has. He was fourteen the first time he was sent to find himself during the show's summer hiatus. His last stint was only a couple of years ago, and his father made it quite known if Trey didn't stay on the straight and narrow, as it were, the next time he landed in trouble, Harry the Second would wash his hands of him." The dog groaned again, pawing at Holly's still foot. She leaned over to pat it, thumping its broad chest. "So he's got a lot to lose if anyone found out he was buying drugs at three in the morning in the bowels of Koreatown. My money's on the whole thing is a story to cover up his tumble back down into the gutter and he's dancing as hard as he can because the red shoes he's got on are way too tight for his feet."

Kuro didn't like the sound of that. Not when his gut told him Trey hadn't been lying. Or at least not about that night. He'd been scared, terrified about being shot at, but Kuro had seen the confusion in the man's handsome face. He had no idea who those men were, and there was still the story about the dead man he'd seen them shoving into the back of a white van. "So there's a good chance his sister was right. The whole thing was a drug deal gone wrong?"

"I'd say yes, a very good chance, except for one small little thing."

"What's that?" Kuro leaned back in his chair, shuffling through the information streaming through his head.

"The Los Angeles Police Department just fished Robert Mathers's well-ventilated body out of the river not more than half an hour ago." Holly's purr was back, a deeper thrum to her melodic tones. "And *that* is the very man Trey Bishop told our boys in blue he saw dead and wrapped up like a stinking fish the night he was outrunning his demons."

Eight

"YOU'RE A fucking liar, Bishop," the bald detective spat at Trey from across the table. His fist slammed down, rattling the metal top, and its sturdy legs jumped slightly, shifting the table sideways. "Now I've got two dead guys and you're in the middle of it."

Trey had nothing left in him. Not another word. Not another breath. All he wanted to do was crawl in through his front door, lock the knob behind him after pulling in the welcome mat, and burrow under the covers of his unmade king-sized bed.

The world had other plans.

And they apparently included him once again sitting in a police station so his oldest sister could shake him down for information he didn't have. At least this time, she had the decency not to throw him into an interrogation room like he'd been the one who'd murdered their father's golf buddy.

She'd had him put in an office, not even doing the decent thing of picking him up herself. A hatchet-faced woman in crisp blues led him to the small square space and closed the door behind him with a final click Trey felt down into his teeth. There'd been no offer of something cold to drink or a reassuring murmur about his sister being with him in a few minutes. Just the door closing behind her and the soft rasp of the detectives' bullpen outside.

Garrett came through the door first, with Kimber hot on his heels. Trey couldn't read his sister's face. Not then. Not now. There was a coldness in her eyes, a glacial distance he'd seen too many times before. Trapped against the uncomfortable chair in the tiny space, Trey felt like a butterfly waiting for a pin to pierce through him to fix him into place.

It'd taken him a few minutes to realize he was sitting in Kimber's office when he'd first been led in. There was little by way of personal touches, mostly a discarded blazer hanging from a black office chair sitting behind a neatly organized desk and a few pictures fighting for space on a pair of bookshelves against the long wall next to the door.

A thin window sitting off-center to the right of the desk gave the room much-needed natural light, but the view left a lot to be desired, the rattle of an air-conditioning unit set nearly a foot away from the glass dominating most of the window's width.

The photos were a somber reminder of Trey's erased existence in his sister's life. Although, he amended, it wasn't just Kimber who'd thrown him out. Maggie and Scooter were captured standing next to Kimber, their frozen smiles sometimes strained, but they were at least there, standing up for their sister when she graduated from the police academy and possibly one of her college jaunts. Trey didn't know exactly *when* he was looking at. A trip to Italy seemed to be important, or at least the moment of Kimber standing in a gondola with the sunlight sparkling around her blonde hair had been snatched from time before it could disappear. Trey had been wondering who'd taken the photo when Garrett burst through with his bluster and accusations.

Accusations that included murder.

"Trey, you had a conversation with Dad about Mathers after you claim you saw his dead body being dropped on the street." Kimber sat on the edge of the desk, leaning back on her hands. Her body language was open, but her face was closed off, any hint of sympathy or emotion buried behind her cop mask. "We're just trying to figure out what happened. Because when you allegedly saw Mathers, he was alive."

"And now he's not," Garrett growled. "So your story comes off as hinky. Like maybe you were in on the planning of his murder, then chickened out. That's why those guys were shooting at you. Because you knew about what they were going to do. Then you went and set up that conversation with your father to cover your own ass."

"Why would I need to cover my own ass if the man was still alive?" Trey rubbed at the throbbing spot on his temple. The air in the cop house was dry, scented with unwashed human and coffee, a tried-and-true recipe for a headache. "I'm going to say this again—I saw what I thought was a dead man. He looked familiar to me, but I couldn't place where I'd seen him before. The next day when I was at Dad's office, I saw a photo of him on the wall and recognized him. That's when Dad told me who he was and that he was alive. That's all I know."

"And that little trip you took with Jenkins after we cut you loose?" The detective paced off the room, two long strides eating up the floor before he had to turn back around to face the desk. Kimber remained silent, even though Garrett gave her a ferocious scowl. "Any time you want to add something to this, Detective Bishop, just jump right on in. You're the one who spotted them leaving together."

"You were spying on me?" Trey tilted his head back, whistling up at the ceiling in slight exasperation. "Am I a suspect in this? Do I need a lawyer? I don't even know what you are trying to get at. The first time I heard of Mathers being dead was you accusing me of killing him. The officer who came to get me only said Kimber had more questions for me. I just don't have any answers."

"I wasn't spying on you," Kimber murmured. "I followed you to see if you needed a ride home. I was just coming outside when you got into Jenkins's car. You have to admit, Harry, you claim you don't know the man very well, but after he's in a shootout with two men you claim were carrying a dead body, he ends up being followed up Mulholland Drive by one of your attackers and kills him. Then, after I shake you loose, you climb into his vehicle."

"A vehicle we should have impounded, but funny thing about your friend, he's made out of Teflon. Everything and everyone just slides off of him. He or somebody he knows has a lot of juice." Garrett scratched at the silver stubble beginning to emerge on his jaw. "Since your daddy insists he's not going to dig you out of any more holes you fall into, that means you're going to bed with somebody else. Because you have a stink on you, Bishop, and people keep dropping like flies all around you. You know more than you're telling, and you're not going to see the light of day until I know what's going on."

Trey was about to begin another round of denials when a knock sounded on the door. A bright-eyed uniformed woman popped her head in, stage-whispering to Garrett that he was needed elsewhere. The man's forehead rippled with a conflicted frown. It didn't take a psychic to know he would have preferred to remain, spending his time stripping Trey of his sanity and possibly his mind, but he obviously thought better of it, telling the cop he'd be out shortly.

"See if you can get something out of your baby brother while I'm gone." Garrett stabbed at Trey's shoulder with a stiff finger. "You! Do you ever think about the shit you get into and how it affects your family? Your sister here is never going to get any further up the ladder because of the shitstorm you brought down on her. Do us all a favor and either finish killing yourself with a handful of pills or do the right thing and cough up some info. You owe her for all of the times she's stretched her neck out for you, only for her head to get cut off because you fucked up."

Garrett might as well have punched him in the face. The silence in the room when the senior detective closed the door behind him was ripe with past arguments and old anger. Rubbing at his knees, Trey shook his head, wishing he could undo the damage he'd brought down on everyone he cared for. His lifetime would never be long enough for him to make all of the apologies he owed people, and emotional restitution was useless if no one would let him make it. Glancing up at Kimber, he opened his mouth to say he was sorry, but his older sister tightened her lips into a thin line, then sighed.

She shifted against the desk, the leather holster she wore across her shoulders creaking when she moved. Kimber dressed better than most detectives, born into wealth and a mother who lived for Fashion Week, but there was no mistaking she was pure cop. Her wide-leg tweed trousers, mannish white button-up shirt, and black boots might've had designer labels, but she carried them on her body as if she was still wearing her uniform. Looking up at his sister, Trey realized he'd never seen his sister as anything other than an authority figure, another brick in the wall he'd slammed his head into countless times before.

"I thought maybe you'd finally got straightened out, you know?" Kimber rubbed at the same spot Trey did when he got a headache, and he couldn't help but smile, amused they shared something besides the patrician genetics of their sometimes self-centered father. "Don't grin at me. The famous Bishop charm doesn't work on me, remember? I know all of your tricks. I just don't know what your endgame is in this."

"Look, I get you don't believe me. I've done nothing to gain your trust back—"

"You never had it, Harry." Another sigh, and this time her words were razors slicing through Trey's heart. "You've been handed every chance in life and have done nothing with any of them. You've set fire to everything you touch and destroyed every accomplishment you've ever achieved. It's been like that since the day you were born. Like you were created solely to destroy our family, and once you got your wild up, you took that bit between your teeth and ran with it. I don't know why I even bother."

"I'm sober. Ever since I walked out of that rehab—*that last rehab*—I swore I would never go back to a place like it. I've worked on becoming healthier these past couple of years, and I know it may not seem like a lot, but I was finally at a place where I felt like I could do something again, be someone better than who I was, then this all happened." Trey felt his voice break, shattering beneath the weight of his emotions. "I wish I could take back everything. I do. Even if it's just so you believe me now, I'd give anything for that. I just don't know what to do, Kimber. I don't know what to say to you to make this right."

Someone outside laughed, a moment of jollity dancing through the ruins of Trey's life. It seemed unfair the world continued on around him while he struggled out of the quicksand he'd created for himself. Kimber was right. There'd been too many times when his family extended their hands out to him to pull Trey free of the quagmire, and he'd used their support to get out of trouble, then dove back in with a gleeful vengeance.

"I'm just so frustrated. There are times when I wondered if our lives wouldn't have been better off if I hadn't performed CPR on you that day. I think about it all the time. The taste of your vomit in my mouth. The sour stink of coke coming off your skin when I pressed at your chest." Kimber closed her eyes, turning away from him. "I couldn't get the smell of your death off of my hands, Harry. I couldn't tell the EMTs what you were on because you were lying in so much filth, I couldn't see what you'd taken that night or what you'd used the weeks before.

"Then Scooter lost her baby that night, and Mom was so angry at me," she whispered. "You know how superstitious she is. Because you can take the chicken herder out of her small village, but she carries that village around with her, holding on to her old beliefs. She started screaming at me in the ER, telling me the reason Scooter lost her little girl was because I pulled you back from death. A life for a life, she said. I'll never forget that. Because I stood there, crying for our sister's loss, and I couldn't even reassure myself that you were worth saving. Now, prove my mom wrong. Tell me everything you know about Robert Mathers's murder and let's give his family some closure."

IT TOOK nearly an hour for Trey to get to Koreatown from the police station. Sixty minutes spent bogged down in traffic and trapped in the back seat of an overly perfumed Toyota driven by a woman who spent more time on her phone than a telemarketer. With only a few miles left to go before they reached his bungalow, Trey tapped on the driver's shoulder and told her he was getting out.

A twenty-dollar bill took care of smoothing down her pissiness for having to cut the ride short, but it was worth it. Especially since Wilshire's bus-fume-filled air felt fresh and clean compared to what he'd been sucking in during the trip through a congested LA.

She'd let him out in front of the Tako Shop, an odd, serendipitous event Trey decided he couldn't ignore. The small twelve-seat ramen restaurant had a line waiting outside of its propped-open front door, and the delicious salty, savory aromas drifting out into the street brought a slavering lust to Trey's mouth. He'd been at the cop house for hours, going round and round with his sister and then again with Garrett, before finally asking them if he needed a lawyer.

That had shut them up.

There were whispers when he pushed through the small crowd on the sidewalk, hot mutterings and evil looks caught in his wake. There were words. Ugly words. Ugly enough to haunt his footsteps and chase him inside to the almost-too-warm confines of the cramped long shop.

A round-faced girl spoke to him from her perch at a podium near the door. She'd sat him before, usually leading him to a table in the middle before the shop's owner—*Kuro*—rumbled something at her in Korean or Japanese and he was taken to the back table where the employees usually ate. This time he stopped in the middle, a rock suddenly thrust into the stream of people trying to move in and out of the shop, and faced the prep area, where Kuro Jenkins stood behind the four-foot-tall glass panels separating the dining area from the ramen shop's cooking stations.

It struck Trey how loud the place was, a sudden flush of sound reaching his ears. People were bumping into him, nudging him aside to get past, but he paid them about as much mind as he did the girl by the door. He didn't know why he'd come in. He didn't know what he was looking for. There was a familiar itch along his spine and up the middle of his chest, but this time the monster crawling through his blood wasn't begging to be numbed by alcohol or drugs.

This time, it was crying out to be held.

He had no expectations of anything other than a bowl of noodles from Kuro Jenkins. The conversation they had in his bungalow had been mildly unsettling, a pull of attraction where Trey believed he was the only one tugging on that twisted rope. The food had been fantastic, but the conversation left him aching for more. It'd been a confusing night followed by a perplexing day, and he'd gone over every word Kuro said, looking for something warm to extinguish the coldness buried deep inside of him.

Trey meant nothing to Kuro Jenkins other than a complication in his life, bringing him death and chaos just like Trey brought to everyone's lives. He was about to turn around and leave when Kuro met his gaze and he fell into the mesmerizing trap of the man's blue-flecked green eyes.

From the moment he'd discovered he liked men, Trey reveled in tasting every single one who'd caught his eye. Finding sexual partners was easy. He was pretty, famous, and rich, the perfect storm of self-gratification and hedonism. There wasn't anything he hadn't tried, sometimes even more than once, and toward the end—before his final self-destructive crash—Trey couldn't even remember everything he'd gotten into. Or everyone.

So after a lifetime of men in designer clothes with their perfect teeth and beautiful hair, Trey shouldn't have found a rumpled Kuro Jenkins sexy.

But goddammit, he was.

His thick black hair was shaggy, unkempt inky black strands around his sharp-featured face, and there was a smear of something white along his strong jaw, a dusting of flour from the fresh noodles he shook out, then dropped into hot water for every bowl of ramen. A slightly soiled chef's apron covered him from his trim waist down to his knees, hiding a pair of powerful thighs wrapped in black jeans, but Trey knew what was behind the folded cotton panel tied around Kuro's muscular body. There was a strength to his corded forearms, and the bulge of his biceps flexed and strained the seams of his black T-shirt's short sleeves. A coiled elegance and simmering danger existed behind the taciturn, cool façade Kuro presented, and Trey caught a peek of it when Kuro's eyes went hot and fierce.

"Go sit down at the back table." Kuro's raspy baritone went thick with authority, hitting Trey hard. "Did you eat?"

"No." Trey wanted to say more, but the words wouldn't come, or at least it didn't seem like the place to dump out his frustrations about being in the middle of a police investigation and being choked to death by his family's disbelief. "I just came—"

"Back table." Kuro used a pair of long cooking chopsticks to stab at the air, pointing at the back of the shop where a darkened niche held a rickety round table and a pair of mismatched chairs. "Give me ten minutes."

Those ten minutes were fraught with anxiety. Everything Kimber said to Trey echoed back on him. Sitting in the shadowed corner, watching people eat and laugh dug deep into Trey's dawning understanding he would never be a part of his sisters' lives. Or never had been. Exasperated, he rubbed at his face, the brisk scratch of his palms on his cheeks rubbing away some of his self-pity.

"You're the one who set fire to the family," he reminded himself in a low whisper. "What did I expect? She's got no reason to believe me. Hell, I'm not too sure I believed me, but fuck! The guy's dead. They found him. And instead of buying my story, they—"

"Are you talking to yourself, or do you have one of those Bluetooth things hidden under your hair and you're on the phone?" Kuro nodded at the table, jerking his chin up. Holding a tray with two hot steaming bowls of ramen and bottles of water on it, he said, "Move your arms so I can set this down. Get some food in you, and if you want, we can talk, but let's get your belly full first. You look like shit."

"I feel like shit," he confessed softly. "I just didn't know where else to go. I know I'm not your problem but—"

"Hey, boss." The slightly pudgy kitchen manager hustled up to Kuro's side, his dark eyes flicking toward Trey's face. "I need you out back. There's something you've got to see."

"What?" Kuro carefully placed the tray on the table, but a bit of the broth spilled over one of the bowls, the swirled pink-and-white fish cake medallions set on top sloshing with the movement. "Can't it wait, Aoki?"

"I don't think so." The man shook his head, then mopped at the sweat beading his forehead with a bandanna he pulled out of his back pocket. "Somebody stuffed a dead man into our dumpster, and there's a note nailed to his forehead promising that this guy right here is next."

Nine

A LOT of people didn't understand Los Angeles. Many equated it with the plastic crinkle of Hollywood, but that really wasn't the city. New York shouted, screaming at its own armpit with a snarl that was mostly bluster and no bite. Its outer boroughs had charm, but Manhattan was an origami of steel and cardboard with neon runners along the edges. Boston just liked being an asshole, and San Francisco was a slice of old Europe with hints of Asia and the perfume of a smug superiority in the air.

Kuro liked all of those cities. He liked how they presented themselves and the treasures he could find on their streets, but Los Angeles held a magic of its own. A guy just had to know where to find it.

Too many let the California stereotype of a bubbleheaded blonde with big boobs stand in for the city's face. Los Angeles was anything but empty-headed. It murmured, a rattling chatter through its many neighborhoods, the language shifting and flowing from Spanish dialects to Korean to the uniquely patterned English of a SoCal speaker. Its inner core was rough, filthy with poverty and grime, while its outer rim sparkled with expensive mansions and white sandy beaches.

Every area had its own heartbeat, an immense gathering of sounds and colors wrapped up as an asphalt-and-steel present. But it was Koreatown that held Kuro's heart. He knew what to expect there. A little bit of dangerous edge from the young men walking its streets, bristling with resentment at their growing familial obligations or luxuriously carefree, ignorant of what awaits them. The women were the core of the neighborhood, a silent matriarchal presence where only the strong survived to lead families forward another generation. There were subtle battles for power in nearly every interaction Kuro came across, especially when running a restaurant.

But what he loved most of all about Koreatown was its blissful turning away when something happened. Kuro knew gossip ran strong, especially since he never showed any interest in the local women, but no one ever said anything to him, simply continuing a shallow friendly relationship before going on their way. It was probably also the most frustrating thing the police were going to have to run into, because no one in K-Town was going to give them the time of day. No one saw anything. No one would say anything.

A lot of that came from lessons learned during the LA riots, where the police did very little to defend Koreatown from looters and violence. The times were different then, but grudges ran hard and long, especially among the older Koreans. They'd armed themselves and waited, determined to defend the small scrap of America they'd fought to own. After the dust settled and the streets cleared, many sent their families down south to Orange County and the relative safety of Diamond Bar and Rowland Heights, but K-Town's population soon regained its strong numbers and expanded outward, swallowing up more territory from the surrounding neighborhoods.

Lieutenant Kimber Bishop and her people were reaping the rewards of dissentious seeds sown years ago, and from the sour look on her face, she wasn't too happy about the harvest.

"Why would I put a dead man wrapped in plastic in my own dumpster?" Kuro bit off the profanity he wanted to fling at the detective trying to crowd him against the ramen shop's back wall. "My crew takes the trash out every hour. It's not like they wouldn't notice. That's how they found him in the first place."

"That's what I'd like to know. Because it seems kind of funny one of your crew suddenly finds a dead body." The detective's attention shifted to a gaggle of uniformed police officers working through collecting statements from the ramen shop's customers. "It's the early hours of the dinner rush but no one sees anyone dumping this guy. Which is odd, considering there's a parking lot filled with your customers' cars right by the dumpster and they have to cut through the alleyway to get to the front door. Still, no one saw *anything*. So either I've got twenty-plus people who are legally blind or that guy was dumped there before your place got busy. Which is it?"

"Considering a couple of days ago, you didn't even believe *I'd* seen a dead guy, maybe no one wants to say they saw anything," Trey remarked, glancing at his sister, then up at Kuro's face. "I don't know what you want from him, Kimber. It seems like you keep hammering at the two of us instead of trying to figure out what's going on."

Kuro was sick of seeing cops. In all of the years he'd worked behind a shadowy curtain, he'd had little interactions with law enforcement. A lot of it had to do with being a part of his job, hard to be a covert operative when the local police had their eye on you—regardless of what country you are in—but mostly it came from his deep-seated dislike for people wearing a badge. He was going to have to put that away in order to deal with Lieutenant Kimber Bishop, but it was hard, especially since the first thing the woman did when she arrived on the scene was corner her little brother, demanding to know what he was doing there.

"That's because no one can believe a word that ever comes out of your mouth," the lieutenant snapped back. "If you told me it was dark outside at midnight, I would still look out the window to make sure I couldn't see the sun."

Trey flinched.

It was the type of flinch Kuro'd seen in people mired in emotional and physical violence. He'd seen it while working in the field, an instinctive reaction rolling off of a seasoned veteran slipping toward the edge of a forced retirement. Trey braced himself for his sister's presence, his shoulders stiffening and the fatigue in his face deepening the shadows beneath his eyes, his brilliantly stormy gray gaze going flat and dark.

Kuro hadn't wanted to get involved. *Didn't* want to get involved. He wasn't looking for sex or friendship, but there was something about Trey standing up to his sister despite the obvious beatdown he was expecting that invigorated a part of Kuro's soul he thought long dead. He could acknowledge his lust. God knew, he lusted every day while standing behind the glass panels at the shop, watching a parade of pretty boys go by, but there was something special about Trey. Or maybe, Kuro thought, he hadn't quite shaken off his white-knight-to-the-rescue tendencies. Either way, he was glad he'd thrown in his lot with Trey.

Not that it looked like Trey needed rescuing. He waded right into the conversation, backing Kuro up.

"What you are not listening to is me saying that's the guy I saw them drop that night. I recognize the plastic. It was hard to see at night, so I thought they were just dirty, but it's a pattern. They're shower curtains. The kind you would use in a hotel." Trey jostled in, edging his sister back with his shoulder. "Like the kind Sera puts into the bathrooms at the rentals. Heavy-duty so they can put up with a lot of people using them. Besides, that stink, it isn't just coming from the garbage. That guy has been dead for days. He couldn't have been in the dumpster that long. Somebody would've seen him before now."

"I've also been working the shop nonstop since four o'clock. There's always been somebody with me, and if you need to, I'm pretty sure we can go through credit card receipts and find customers who can verify I was there during the dinner rush." Kuro jerked his thumb toward the back door. "Shift details are on the walk-in. Trash detail is alternated between two or three runners working every night. It has to be pulled and dumped in the first ten minutes at the top of every hour, then they initial the space for that timeslot on that day's sheet. They can tell you the body wasn't there earlier. Aoki came and got me as soon as they found it."

"Look, I need to verify you were there. So don't go anywhere just yet," the lieutenant growled, shooting her brother a filthy look. "And Harry, I want to be able to find you if I need you again. I'll see about getting a uniform to drive you home."

"I'll be taking him home," Kuro replied sharply. It was an overt play of possession or at least establishing a connection between them. Kuro didn't know how Trey would take it, but he was tired of seeing the man being shoved around. "If he wants me to, that is. Just let us know when we're clear, because neither one of us had dinner and we just sat down when all of this dropped."

"You seem to be popping up every time I turn around, usually around Harry. Any reason for that?" The detective ignored Trey's exasperated hiss, turning slightly to edge her brother out. "I'm kind of curious about a guy like you suddenly showing up in his life. And now we find the dead man he allegedly saw that night in the dumpster outside of your shop. These kinds of things lead to a lot of questions."

"A guy like me?" Kuro cocked an eyebrow at her. "I own a ramen shop."

"You're licensed to own everything from a military tank and downwards," she said, stepping in closer. Her voice was low, practically a whisper, but the menace in it was clear. "But I can't get any information about you, even through unofficial channels. To me, that raises enough red flags to start the run of the bulls in Pamplona."

"I own a ramen shop. Everything else that's happened is shit your brother and I did not start," Kuro asserted. "But that doesn't mean I'm going to let anyone hang it on us, including you. I've got Trey's best interest in mind, because from where I stand, it looks like he needs somebody on his side of the road. And that doesn't seem like it's you. So unless you need us for something else, I'd like to find something to eat and take him back home, not necessarily in that order. You okay with that, Trey?"

"You seem to be under the impression that I went shopping since last time you were digging around in my fridge," Trey drawled. "There's nothing in there but a bottle of pickles and a lonely Diet Coke."

"Luckily, I own a restaurant. Once they let us back inside, I'll forage through the walk-in and see what I've got." Kuro caught the flush of red coloring Trey's cheeks. "If you don't mind me taking you home and feeding you. I did promise you dinner."

"It's good. Especially since she yanked me out of bed before I got something to eat." Trey shook off his sister's hand on his upper arm. "I'm tired, Kimber. I'm sick of looking at the inside of a police station when I haven't done anything wrong, and I'm really sick to death of you calling me Harry. I've never been called Harry. Our grandpa was called Harry. But most of all, I just want to go home and not have anyone wearing a badge try to pick my brain for something I don't have. So let us know when you're done and Kuro will take me home."

"I was thinking of taking you myself," Kimber replied, her eyes narrowing when she looked toward Kuro. "There's some personal stuff I want to talk to you about."

"In the words of our esteemed father, call my secretary and make an appointment." Trey stepped back from his sister, lengthening the space between them. "I'll see if I can fit your personal problems into my very busy schedule."

THE BUNGALOW was quiet. So was the main house. Lights were off in Sera's apartment on the top floor, something Trey expected since it was her yoga and drinks with the girls night. The neighborhood had an odd hush to it, as if it were holding its breath. Kuro's muscle car broke the silence, its throaty rumble echoing through the space between the buildings.

"So, I've got to ask," Kuro said as he got out of the Challenger, "do you not drive, or does your sister just like to play power games and load you into cop cars against your will?"

"My license was suspended for... well, a bunch of shit. I have a provisional that allows me to drive to and from jobs, but no one's going to hire me for their show, so there's a bunch of sports cars parked in the garage behind the bungalow," Trey replied, closing the heavy car door carefully. "There's a guy who comes out once a month to run them on the street for a little bit and check them out so they don't get screwed up while they're sitting there waiting for me to get my shit together. I've got a few more months before I can reapply to drive. I'm probably going to have to take driving lessons again. I don't think I even remember how to parallel park."

Trey waited for Kuro's reaction. Nothing came other than a slight shrug and the man pulling forward the driver's seat so he could get to the tote bags of groceries in the back. He didn't know how to respond to the lack of comment. Trey'd taken a lot of crap from his so-called friends at the time, but lack of license did nothing to slow down his partying. His lack of heartbeat did.

"You're going to have to open the door." Kuro's voice cut through Trey's melancholy thoughts. "Or I'm going to have to put down the bags to pick the lock. Either way, I'm going to get to a stove so I can make some dinner."

His smile warmed away the last of the ice left on Trey's soul. They had nothing in common other than a dead body and some bullets, but there was something there. Something inexplicable and unexplainable drawing Trey to the seemingly complicated and mysterious man who fed him at the drop of a hat. He knew nothing about Kuro Jenkins other than the man could make a mean bowl of ramen and knew his way around *karage* and *tonkatsu*, but for right now it was enough.

"Let me get the door," Trey said, jingling his keys. "I can at least promise you clean dishes and, if you want, some help chopping things."

"Considering the state of your knives when I first used them, I think it would be safer if you sat at the island and kept me company while I cooked." Kuro stepped up onto the front stoop behind Trey as he fit the key into the lock. "You can be my official taster and tell me where I've gone wrong."

"You're talking to a guy who grew up eating the orange powder out of the mac and cheese boxes while I was waiting for sets to be struck. My idea of cuisine usually came with an easy-open pop top and in colors not found in nature." Stepping into the bungalow, Trey caught a whiff of his shirt and wrinkled his nose. "Okay, this isn't meant to be sexual in any way, but I really need to shower. Do you mind if I take a few minutes and wash up?"

"Take your time. I'll reacquaint myself with your kitchen." Kuro set the tote bags down on the counter, looking around. "But fair warning, I find any of that orange cheesy powder and it's going into the trash."

"You won't," Trey promised. "But only because it comes in microwave cups now so it's all mixed in together."

The hot water felt glorious, and by the time Trey climbed out of the shower, he'd washed off all of the filth he'd rolled in during his time at the police station. Dealing with Kimber always made him feel small, an insignificant speck she would gladly flick off her fingernails if she could. He dealt with her more than he dealt with Maggie and Scooter, and while scrubbing himself off with a thick towel, he vowed to reach out to his other sisters, hoping to make some amends.

"Not like it's going to do any good," he grumbled to his knees, wiping them dry. "But if I don't, then I'm being the person they expect me to be, just another self-absorbed asshole."

Tugging on a pair of jeans and a stretched-out faded gray T-shirt he usually wore while attempting to paint, Trey braced himself for another confusing evening. The first time he had Kuro in his house, they'd talked about dead bodies and assaults. Then the man slipped out into the night, leaving a wake of frustration and sexual tension behind. This time, he brought both with him, along with enough groceries to feed a small army. Trey resigned himself to ending the night with a full belly and a hard cock, just like the last time.

Those expectations were partially met when he padded out of the bedroom to find Kuro humming to himself as he stirred something around in a pot on the stove, then turned around to begin tearing apart something lying on the peninsula's prep counter.

The sight of Kuro standing in his kitchen in low-slung jeans and bare feet did something to Trey's insides. It was too easy to imagine coming home to the long-legged man every day. Even easier to imagine him spread out over Trey on the king-sized mattress in his bedroom. A few seconds of erotic pleasure in watching Kuro suddenly became a domestic daydream with hot chocolate and a fire in the fireplace while cuddling on the couch. It was all too white picket fence and a couple of long-haired dachshunds for Trey, but… or maybe it had been something lurking in the back of his mind for a long time.

He *wanted* normal. He *wanted* Kuro Jenkins. But there was no way in hell the broad-shouldered, trim-hipped ramen master was normal, and

Trey couldn't see a future that had Kuro waiting by the door every night for him with a pair of slippers and an evening newspaper.

"Jesus fucking Christ," Trey swore under his breath. "I've become my father."

"What?" Kuro glanced over his shoulder at Trey. "What about your father?"

"Nothing important. He tends to lead his life with a want-take-have philosophy and damn everybody around him. I think I just realized I'm a lot like him, except without the ambition." Climbing up onto the barstool meant Trey didn't have to take in any more of Kuro's assessing look, but it was there when he settled in. "I haven't really done much with my life in the last two years. I don't count trying to stay sober as employment."

"Is there anything you want to do?" Kuro held up a piece of long triangular meat Trey couldn't identify. "And before you answer that, tell me you like duck. I've brought other stuff with me, but this was what I grabbed first. I can put it into the freezer with the rest of the meats I threw in there and grab something else. You can cook the duck breasts later."

"Well, it's no cheesy orange powder, but I'm sure I can choke it down." He grinned, leaning his elbows against the raised bar section of the peninsula, craning his neck to watch Kuro work on the lower slab. "And honestly, I have even less of an idea about how to cook duck than I do about what I want to do with the rest of my life. If it's not frozen and burrito-shaped, it's got to be in a Styrofoam cup and I can add water to it before throwing it into the microwave."

"You had food in the fridge the first time I came by. You're not that helpless." Kuro pulled a chopping board from someplace in the depths of the peninsula's cavernous storage and laid it on the counter. The knife he was using definitely hadn't come from Trey's kitchen, and there was an arrangement of spices and other things in bottles clustered at one end of the stone slab topping the prep area. "You're telling me you don't cook at all?"

"A little bit. I can make a mean assemble-your-own pizza, and if you count scrambled eggs with stuff thrown into it as an omelet, then I'm your guy. Usually Sera takes pity on me and cooks me something. She's my dad's ex-mistress or girlfriend, depending on who you ask. She runs the rentals in the big house. She was supposed to live here in the bungalow, but well, that's a long story. She likes living in the big house. I think she likes the noise. It's too quiet out here for her."

The duck meat was dark, a rich burgundy with a layer of white skin Kuro was scoring a latticework pattern into with his knife. Trey watched with interest, fascinated by Kuro's light, gentle touch. It wasn't hard to imagine his long, blunt-ended fingers running down Trey's sides or legs.

"I'm going to prep the breasts first and let the spices get into the meat. They don't take that long to cook, and can I tell you I am very glad Sera left you a seasoned cast-iron skillet, because it makes tonight's dinner a lot easier." Kuro began working on the other breast, running his knife along its skin. "So what do you want to talk about? Your dad's ex-mistress? You needing to figure out what to do with your life? Or should you and I get our heads together and figure out what's going on so we can get the cops off of your ass?"

Ten

"SO YOUR father has mistresses, including one who's your best friend, and your mother doesn't divorce him? But his other wives did?" Kuro's chopsticks stopped halfway to his mouth, a thin slice of duck dangling from their clenched-together ends. "I'd have dumped him as soon as I found out he was warming someone else's sheets."

"Dad can't afford it. His lawyers forgot to get Mom to sign a prenup, so one whisper of divorce and it'll be a bloodbath, so he works to keep her happy," Trey said with a shrug. "So far she's got the record for being married to him the longest, and I think they're content in their own way. I think they're friends with benefits. Dad falls in and out of love with every pretty woman who crosses his path, and I don't look too closely at Mom's male friends. It works for them, and I guess that's all that matters. At least they don't fight anymore."

It wasn't hot chocolate, but the crispy duck and fragrant fried rice more than made up for it. There was something fruity, sweet, and hot poured over the meat, a light drizzle of the sauce with enough of a punch to set the back of Trey's mouth tingling. Imaging that's what it'd be like to kiss Kuro, a hint of sugar with a lot of spice, he dipped his finger into the liquid, then placed the dollop on his tongue, savoring its taste.

"What's in the sauce?" Trey said around his fingertip. "It's good."

"Guava jam, garlic, and jalapenos," Kuro replied, expertly scooping up a bit of rice with his chopsticks. Trey envied the skill, but his pride came a far second to his hunger and he'd opted for the spoon to deal with the fried rice. "It's something I threw together once and liked it. Are we ever going to talk about the dead men or just rattle on about your dad's love life and the food?"

"I'm not sure what good it would do. I mean, I'm caught up in something I don't understand, and it's not like I can solve it. I'm an actor. And not even a good one anymore," he reminded Kuro. "I'm pretty sure the guy they found in the dumpster is the one I saw that night. But he looked exactly like my dad's friend Mathers, so I don't know what's going on there."

"Maybe they're not connected. Could be the guy in the plastic just looked like him."

"I'm going to say they looked exactly alike. I'm pretty good with faces. And I recognized him again in the photos." Trey shook his head, thinking back on the night he'd escaped the two gunmen. "And then there is that man who tried to kill you on Mulholland. How does he fit into it? And where's the other guy?"

"Good questions. And ones I want answered." Kuro put his bowl down on the coffee table, balancing his chopsticks across the rim. "And you're wrong about not being able to do something. So long as I don't get in the cops' way, it's not going to hurt to start asking around. One thing about Koreatown is no one sees anything unless the right person asks. A lot of people owe me favors. Someone had to know those guys. They have to be connected to somebody local or they wouldn't have been there that late at night."

"I was going to say don't you think the cops already asked around, but Kimber seemed to think I was making shit up."

His stomach was full, but Trey was reluctant to stop eating. It gave his hands something to do, and chasing a grain of rice around the bowl prevented him from getting lost in Kuro's eyes. It was bad enough he had to watch the man eat, tucking pieces of food past his delectable lips. There was going to have to be another cold shower in his near future and maybe even another run. Anything to get his mind off of his frustration and feeling helpless. Gently placing the nearly empty bowl on the table, he groaned slightly when his stomach ached when he stretched.

"What's going through your head right now?" Kuro asked softly.

Trey never gave much thought to happy endings or a life in suburbia. His life had been chaotic since he dropped from his mother. In the Bishop household, up was down and mothers were people who chased their dreams through him, pushing him onto stages and in front of cameras as soon as he could read a script. Now he was on the back end of a tumultuous twenty-plus years with little to show for it except for a bunch of money held in trust because the courts decided he couldn't manage things for a bit and a garage full of expensive cars he couldn't drive.

And of course, he couldn't forget the family he'd destroyed.

"You asked me what I wanted to do with my life. Honestly? I want to get the shit off of me," Trey was surprised to hear himself say, but once the words left his mouth, he heard the truth in them. Raking his hands through his hair, he leaned back into the corner of the couch and stared at Kuro, who was sitting partially sideways next to him. "I need to do something with my life. And I don't know if that means going back into acting or doing something else, but I can't just sit here and exist anymore.

"I fucked up everything with my family, and everyone who said they were my friend before I hit rock bottom was just using me. Now I've got Sera and...." He scraped through his acquaintances, looking for someone he knew he could call in a pinch. "Fuck, I just got Sera."

"You've got me." Kuro put a hand on Trey's knee, the heat of his body warming Trey's skin. "I'm going to be blunt here and say I really don't like the way your sister treats you. She might be family—even family who took a couple of hits from you—but I saw you that night. You were scared, and my gut tells me you had no idea what was going on. She should have had your back, even if that's not my place to say."

"That's because you don't know me. I put them through a lot, and I don't blame them for not trusting me," Trey confessed. "Kimber put her career on the line so many times to save my ass, and I repaid her by continuing to do shitty things."

"Wasn't that a couple of years ago? How long do you have to pay for your mistakes?" Kuro's thumb moved over his knee, stroking at the fold.

"What? Don't you have family?" Trey teased lightly. Between Kuro's low rumble and the sensation of his long, slow strokes across the rise of Trey's knee, he was having a hard time concentrating on anything but the swelling lust simmering in him. "It's what family does. They remember every bad thing that you've done from the moment you took your first breath until the day you take your last."

"Nope. I don't have family, but I know what you mean. There's quite a few people I count as relatives who never let me forget any time I screwed up." Kuro laughed, his deep, sexy chuckle setting Trey's blood on fire. "You met Aoki. He's worse than having three meddling aunties rolled up into one person. So, your sister aside, I'll dig into it."

"That's asking you to stick your neck out for me, and I think I've already brought down enough on you," he replied reluctantly. A part of him was eager to dig out the reasons he was trapped in the middle of one of Kimber's cases, mostly because it meant he'd be near Kuro, but common sense won out. Endangering an innocent ramen shop owner—

no matter how well armed—probably would add more negative points to his already soiled karmic rap sheet. "I mean, I appreciate it because I'm not—"

"It's what I used to do for a living. Before this," Kuro said, nodding toward the mostly empty bowls on the table. "And I'm in the middle of it whether you want me to be there or not. Someone came gunning for me, remember? For better or for worse, you and I are in this together. Might as well see it through, and after that, who knows?"

A few years ago, he would've leaned over and kissed Kuro, consequences be damned. Sitting across of one of the sexiest men he'd ever seen, Trey wondered where his daring personality had gone. He'd always been a risk taker, even when sober, but in washing his body free of toxins, it seemed like he'd also bleached away his courage and confidence.

"You know what's funny? The most fucked-up thing the universe can do to you is have you meet the right person at the wrong time," Trey whispered under his breath. "What if there is never a right time? Do you just say damn the torpedoes, full speed ahead?"

"There's going to be times in your life when you're standing on the edge of the cliff and you need to jump because if you don't, you're going to be trampled to death by the herd of horses running through the fields behind you." Kuro's thumb stopped and he leaned in, a concerned frown on his face. "I don't know what you're talking about, but if it's got anything to do with hunting down the people who got us into this mess, then I'm all for it."

"What if it's about me kissing you?" Trey asked softly. "See, the thing is I know you have guns. And I've had my face punched in for kissing the wrong guy more than a few times, but I'm wondering if you're really the wrong guy. And I'm not sure if I'm feeling this way just because you've been nice to me and it's been a fuck of a long time since anyone's been nice to me. Shit, I'm not even nice to myself, but I really want to kiss you and—"

"You know, you talk way too much," Kuro said, then stretched forward, resting his weight on his knee, and cupped Trey's face, his lips brushing against Trey's mouth. "One of us has got to jump off this cliff first. Might as well be me."

As kisses went, Trey definitely put it in his top ten. Perhaps even higher once the oxygen returned to his brain. He'd been right about how Kuro tasted. Even with the lingering hint of the spicy sauce on his tongue, there was a deeper hot sweetness drawn up between them when their mouths touched. It'd been a long time since he'd touched another man, and when Trey put his hands on Kuro's powerful shoulders, a delicious thrill ran up his spine.

Kuro's fingers along his jaw mimicked the erotic stroke of his tongue against Trey's lips. It was maddening, the hovering, then the slight dab of pressure against his mouth, and Trey parted his lips, wanting more. Instead, Kuro took his time, nibbling and stroking Trey's lips and face until his nerve endings felt like they were on fire. Kuro's right shoulder pressed into Trey's left, lightly pinning him down, but if anything, Trey felt freer than he had in a long time.

He tugged at Kuro's shirt, pulling it up so he could run his hands down the man's corded back. The touch seemed to inflame Kuro, because after a slight gasp, Kuro finally deepened their kiss.

It wasn't as if Trey had plans to breathe anytime soon. Especially not since the heart-stopping kiss seemed to steal his breath away.

Kuro lingered, drawing out every second in a sensual crawl. His hands moving along Trey's ribs were a slow torture. Kuro seemed to find every inch of Trey's body, a sensitive exploration of skin hidden beneath his clothes. He hadn't known how erotic being stroked through cotton could be. Or how intimate silence between two men kissing could heighten the experience.

His sexual encounters had always been loud and frenetic, as if racing toward climax was all that mattered. Kuro dealt with it differently. He seemed satisfied with prolonging their kiss, focusing most of his attention on Trey's mouth with brief skirting strokes of his hands down Trey's sides. He was about to burst when Kuro drifted to the seams running down Trey's thighs, his thumbs a skittish brush across Trey's lengthening dick.

Trey moaned into Kuro's mouth, plunging his tongue into the heat he tasted there before. They danced rather than fought, a curious occurrence for Trey. He wasn't used to the delicious give-and-take going on between them, and he had to admit he liked it. Still, the lust in him grew, and it wasn't going to be quenched until he felt Kuro deep inside of him.

He couldn't get enough of the man. Trey's hands didn't seem to be able to find a place they could stop. He needed to touch every inch of skin, even the scars he seemed to find beneath Kuro's shirt. They were small but inexplicable evidence of a hard life lived fast, or at least that's what Trey imagined. There was a thicker bundle of scar tissue near Kuro's shoulder, a tangle of something slick and hard running over toward his arm, and Kuro murmured something through their kiss when Trey's fingers found it.

"I'm going to have to do better about keeping you busy." Kuro laughed gently, lightly biting at Trey's lower lip. "I can't seem to get you focused on what's going on up here."

"I just want it all. All of you," Trey confessed, shifting against the couch. He liked the weight of Kuro's body against his. It felt comfortable, protective in ways he didn't understand. He should've felt trapped, struggling to breathe or at least needing to get free, but not this time. Not with this man. "I wouldn't mind getting you naked. And it's probably too soon to say that, but I thought I'd toss it out there. Just so you know where my head's at. In case you had any doubts."

"I have a lot of doubts, but none of them about you." Kuro moved, easing the press of his body away from Trey's. "Mostly I'm wondering if I can keep up with you. You're a hell of a lot younger with a hell of a lot less mileage."

"I've got a lot more mileage than you think." Trey snorted. "Some of it I even remember. But I get it. Slow isn't bad."

"Mostly. It's just right now, I'm kind of torn between dragging you into the bedroom or making you scream my name but here on the couch," Kuro whispered, his voice a lick of heat across Trey's skin. "But it's been a hell of a long time for me, and empty boasting doesn't impress anyone. I also don't have anything with me, and I'm not going to risk you like that."

He felt how aroused Kuro was. It was impossible to miss. The length of him was pressed against Trey's shin, and there was no mistaking his own response, especially since the jeans he'd put on after his shower were old and thin. He wanted to say fuck the consequences and everything else, but he knew better. It was only by the skin of his teeth he hadn't picked up something in the past, and there was always an underlying worry, no matter how many times he came back with clean blood tests.

The last time he'd been with somebody had been in rehab, a fumbling excuse for intercourse fueled mostly by his need to be touched rather than any affection for the guy he'd propositioned. There were murky things lurking in his past and he didn't want them near Kuro, but something told him he wasn't going to have a choice. There had to be honesty between them. If he was going to go forward with his life and not repeat his mistakes, Trey was going to have to embrace everything he'd been and everything he'd done.

Even if it amounted to nothing between him and Kuro, it was the only way Trey knew to prevent himself from sliding backward.

"I know there's other ways of having sex," Kuro said, settling back down. "But I'm not sure I trust myself to stop. Or trust you to stop. I think once we go down that path, neither one of us is going to come up for air until we wring each other dry."

"I don't think you're wrong," Trey agreed with a sigh. Pulling at his jeans gave him little relief, but it was at least enough to get him some room to adjust for his still-hard cock. "I liked the kiss, though."

"Kissing's fun. I've never gotten to do enough of it." A noise outside caught Kuro's attention and he stopped, tilting his head. "You expecting anyone?"

"Could be one of the guests turning around in my driveway. Sometimes that happens," he replied, tugging at Kuro's shirt. "What? You think someone's coming to kill me?"

"Someone tried to kill me." Kuro's reminder splashed a coldness over Trey. "We've still got another guy out there who knows what you look like and sure as hell knows about me. That and we don't know who's behind the guy left in my dumpster. Or if it's connected to your dad's friend. I think it is, but until we know what's going on, I'm not sure I like leaving you here. This place's too indefensible. There's too many people coming in and out of the property, too many strangers, and it butts up against too many of the properties. Easy enough to jump the fence to get you, and you're far enough away from the main house that nobody would hear you calling for help."

"So what? I'm supposed to move into a hotel? Come stay with you?" He laughed, imagining his father's face when he showed up on the doorstep with a suitcase. "Or better yet, I could always go crash with either one of my parents and cramp their style. They'd like that. I wouldn't have to worry about anyone trying to murder me. They'd kill me themselves."

This time, Trey heard the noise too, the soft roll of tires through the gravel outside of the bungalow. He was about to make some comment about it probably being hard to get around Kuro's Challenger when the noise stopped and the sound of a car door softly being closed followed close on the heels of the silence.

The relaxed, sexy man next to him slipped away, disappearing into a tight coil of danger and menace. If he didn't know better, Trey would've sworn Kuro became a different person, someone he wouldn't have recognized if he hadn't seen him in that alleyway a few nights ago.

"Any idea who that is?" Kuro hissed. "Did you say Sera was out? Could it be your sister?"

"No, Kimber wouldn't be here. Should still be on the scene, probably. And my other sisters have never been here." There was definitely someone there. Someone who was moving as stealthily as they could across loose gravel. "I don't know who that could be. Nobody shows up without calling except Sera."

"Get behind the couch," Kuro whispered. It was an order, harsh, cold words meant to be obeyed, but Trey opened his mouth to protest, only to be silenced by the icy look on Kuro's face. "*Now.*"

Trey got behind the couch.

Peeking around the corner would probably get him yelled at, but it was only a few feet away from the fireplace and its makeshift armory of fire-tending tools. He was fast, honed from a couple of years of running through some really shitty neighborhoods, but Trey knew he wouldn't be much good in a fight. He'd lived in a choreographed world, where every punch was telegraphed and someone else took the heavy blows.

"Again, right person, wrong time," Trey muttered to himself, calculating the distance between himself and the fireplace. "Come on, God, give me a fucking break."

Footsteps echoed across the walk, but they weren't the confident stride of someone coming to knock on the door. They came in fits and starts, the shuffle across the uneven stones near the side of the door. Kuro hunkered down, grabbing at the jacket he'd left on the wing chair near the peninsula. Glancing back, he scowled at Trey when he spotted him peering around the couch. Motioning furiously with his hand, Kuro silently ordered Trey to get back, his scowl going thunderous when Trey shook his head no.

"We'll talk about this later," Kuro mouthed at him. Pointing to the floor, his lips moved with great exaggeration. "Stay down."

The door was unlocked. Trey could see that from his position beside the couch. He never locked the door. Not until it was time to go to bed and he was sure Sera wasn't going to make a last-minute appearance looking for a cup of hot chocolate or a pint of ice cream buried in his freezer. The knob turned slowly, the door's hinges creaking slightly as it swung open. Kuro went flat against the back of it, keeping himself out of view, probably hoping the thick wooden door would give him some kind of protection.

It was dark outside, but there was enough illumination coming off of the dimmed recessed lighting set into the living room's ceiling for Trey to see the large gun held out in front of whoever stood in the doorway. The light didn't quite reach past the portal, but there was a hint of a silhouette framed in the space, and then a voice whispered in a staccato Russian accent.

"Stay back, sir," the woman whispered. "Let me clear the house."

If there was one thing Trey learned over the last few days, it was that gunfights were nothing like they appeared on television, even knowing most scenes were angled for maximum shock and to give the audience a decent view of the show's actors. Time didn't slow down, and there didn't seem to be as many monologues as the film industry led one to expect. But one thing remained true—guns were loud, and scary people were scary.

Luckily, Trey had one of those scary people on his side for a change, and Kuro came out fighting.

There was no delicacy in his punch. No hesitation over the fact that the person holding the gun in Trey's doorway was a woman or that he probably had at least forty pounds of muscle on her, judging by her silhouette. Her grunt as she took the hit was enough to get Trey moving toward the fireplace, his hands stretched out for the hook-looking thing on the far right of the rack.

The movement must have drawn the woman's attention, because the next thing he knew, Trey was staring down the barrel of her weapon and Kuro stood a few feet away, a deadly-looking gun pointed at the center of Tatiana's forehead. His father's redheaded assistant narrowed her eyes, and her aim drifted toward Kuro's chest.

"Kuro, stop!" Trey panted, rubbing at his knee where he barked it against the hearth. "I know her!"

"I know her too." Kuro didn't drop the gun. If anything, he grew more menacing, stepping in between Tatiana and Trey. "Hello, Boom Boom. Long time no see."

"Hello, Blackie," Tatiana said with a chilling smile. "Now, if you don't mind, drop your weapon, because as annoying as he is, I'm not going to let you kill my boss's son. And after you do that, you can tell me who sent you to assassinate him."

Eleven

"Last I heard you were stuck in a Turkish prison trying to carve your way out with a wooden spoon." Kuro cut across the living room, keeping Boom Boom in his sights. "Someone finally scraped up enough belly lint to get you out?"

Edging between her and Trey took only a few strides, and he caught a blur of movement behind her, a bit of shadow lurking in the darkness beyond. He was getting soft, no two ways about it. The moment he'd come into the house, he should have turned on the outside lights, flooding the area in the anticipation of someone coming in just like the Russian operative had done.

"Last I heard you were babysitting and got the tires blown out from under you," she retorted, keeping her gun steady on him. "I got out of the Turkish prison, but it seems like your tires are still blown out, yes?"

"Tell whoever you're with to come out and I won't blow your head off." Kuro couldn't risk glancing back at Trey, but he felt the man coming up behind him. "Get down. She—"

"Works for my father," Trey replied. "She's not going to kill me. She's had lots of chances to kill me before. Hell, she probably *wants* to kill me but my dad won't let her."

"You would not be wrong." The Russian woman took a step to the left, trying to ease around Kuro. "Are you okay? Has he harmed you?"

"He made me dinner. Seriously, I'm really kind of sick of guns, and the sprinklers are probably going to go off in a few minutes. I'm guessing my dad's outside wearing something expensive and dry-clean only." Trey's exasperated huff was enough to bring a smirk to Kuro's mouth. "Tatiana, put the fucking gun down and tell Dad he can come inside. If you're hungry, there's probably enough duck left. Dunno about the vegetables, but I'm pretty sure we can do something."

"The man's an assassin." Boom Boom eyed Kuro, a sharp, assessing gleam in her narrowed eyes. "He's here to kill you, Trey."

"I was an operative, never an assassin," he corrected her, keeping his gun up. They'd tangled more than a few times in the past, and if he remembered right, he was in the black on their tally marks. "Tell whoever is outside to come in. With their hands up."

"Jesus, the two of you!" Trey moved to get around Kuro, aiming for the door, but Kuro made a grab for him, snagging him by the waistband, holding him back. Boom Boom retaliated with a step forward, her gun lifting up as she closed the distance between them. Trey struggled, but Kuro was too strong for him, his stockinged feet sliding on the wood floor. "Dad! Can you just get in here, please?"

"Sir! Ignore that!" Tatiana raised her chin, shouting over her shoulder, but her gaze remained fixed on Kuro's face. She was waiting for him to telegraph his next move, probably wondering if she could take him, considering he was off balance by holding on to Trey and only having one hand on his gun. It's what he would've calculated, but it was hard to tell what was going on behind her ice-queen façade. "Blackie, let him go and then we can talk. But I'm not going to drop my weapon until I know he's safe."

Trey stopped pulling, but his frustration was as spicy hot as the jalapenos Kuro put in the duck sauce. Something was going to have to give. Judging by the shuffle of feet on the gravel outside, it sounded as if the person was uneasy, uncomfortable with waiting. They were too loud, with too much movement, and chances were, it really was Trey's father, but whether or not Boom Boom came in hot in the hopes of snagging his son was a reality Kuro couldn't afford to risk.

"Let's see the old man first," he offered. "It's been a *never* since we were on the same side. The only time you've ever had my back is when you were aiming at it."

"You killed my brother."

"Only after he tried to kill me first," he reminded her. "And that was after he tried to get me into bed. Your family doesn't take rejection well. Also, there was that small matter of a nuclear bomb I didn't want him to have. Or have you forgotten that little detail?"

"We weren't that close," Boom Boom replied, giving Kuro a lazy shrug. "If he'd been talking to the family, I would've told him not to bother seducing you. People who go to bed with you tend to die afterwards."

"Only the ones intending to fuck me over," Kuro responded. "I want to see his dad come in. After that, we take it from there."

"What is taking so long?" A deep, authoritative voice broke through the tension, the sound of leather loafers scraping through the dust on the cement walk outside. "Tatiana, either shoot the man and step over his body or put your gun down, but either way, I'm coming inside. The goddamned sprinklers went off and the back of my pants are soaked."

The doorway filled with a man who carried most of his weight in his chest. A barrel of muscle and a bit of middle-aged fat around his belly filled out a suit that probably cost more than Kuro's monthly take at the shop. There were bits of Trey here and there scattered about his face, but his features ran more toward centuries of country club breeding rather than Trey's aristocratic beauty. His hair had gone silver, a glistening thick metallic mane any man worth his salt would be proud to sport. He was an aging lion but still majestic and in charge of his pride. As he moved into the room with powerful strides, it became obvious where Kimber got her tough exterior. Trey's father suffered no one lightly, commanding the room with the force of his personality. The gleam of intelligence in his hard eyes warned Kuro he was someone to be reckoned with.

Kuro neither lowered his weapon nor let go of Trey.

"Trey? We good?" Kuro kept his lips as relaxed as he could as Boom Boom—Tatiana—dropped her arms, then holstered her gun. "Your call."

"Yeah," he muttered. "That's my dad. This is his assistant. Or at least I thought she was his assistant. I didn't think the corporate dress code extended to firearms. What the hell is going on?"

"What's going on is someone left Robert Mathers's hand in the front seat of my car a couple of hours ago with a warning that I'm next if I don't shut my son up." Harrington Bishop the Second flared his nostrils, pushing his shoulders back to take up even more space. "So what I want to know is what are you doing here with a man Tatiana swears is a killer, and what do you know that's so dangerous I'm getting death threats?"

THE BEER Kuro found in the back of the beverage refrigerator was Chinese and cold. Having sworn off alcohol, Trey apparently buried them behind sparkling water and sodas left over from a party thrown when he'd moved into the bungalow. Since Kuro never really considered beer could expire, he figured the Tsingtao was still good enough to drink, especially when being shared with a former Russian spy who'd apparently come in out of the cold and into a plush job with a Los Angeles mogul.

"You sure it's a good idea to leave them alone in the house?" Sitting on the Challenger's front fender with Boom Boom was a surreal experience, but it seemed to be the safest bet, considering he wasn't going to actually let her into the car. He passed her over a bottle he'd just popped the cap off, tucking the metal disc into his jacket pocket, then began working on opening the other with the lever on his keychain. "The old man didn't seem too happy. He the type to take a swing?"

"No. They have a very complicated relationship. Bishop Three is a waste of space for most of the family, but the boss says he has untapped potential. He just doesn't know what that potential is or how to get to it." The redhead sniffed at the bottle, wrinkling her nose, a gesture easy to see in the glow given off by the bungalow's front porch light. "Trey has let him down more times than there are stars in the sky, but it appears as if this time, sobriety has stuck. He still hasn't found something to do with his life, though, and the boss is getting antsy."

"I met the first daughter. She's… it's hard to say because I want to call her a bitch, but there's a lot of water under the bridge between them, and now that I've met the old man, I'd say she was actually just a chip off the stubborn block." The beer was cold, and from what Kuro could tell, the years it spent in the refrigerator hadn't affected it one bit. At another time in his life, he would have never drunk alcohol when there was a potential the night would go bad, but he lived in stranger times now. A beer seemed like a good place to start. "I haven't met the other two."

"Variations on the first. Scooter is a little bit more Earth Mother, but I think that just hides how much she's like her father. All three of them are very driven, ambitious women. Not at all like their brother." Tatiana shot him a look from under her eyelashes. "I thought you meant to use him. Looks like something different with you and him, though if you were planning on killing him, you wouldn't tell me."

"I wasn't planning on killing him but eventually, probably will sleep with him. Not that that's any of your business." He saluted her with the beer bottle. "For right now, I'm just trying to keep him alive. Tell me about the hand you found. The detective daughter didn't tell me Mathers was missing a hand."

"He's missing both of them. The boss recognized a ring on one of the fingers as Mathers's. Some family thing. Kimber reluctantly told us. It's not something they're letting out to the public." She hooked her heels into the space between the wheel well and the tire, resting her feet on the rubber. "She also told us about the dead body in your dumpster. Trey wasn't wrong. When Kimber showed the boss a picture of the dead man's face, he identified him as Mathers. So the boss's friend is the key to this whole thing, but I don't have a clue what the whole thing is."

"Me neither," he confessed. "Do they even know who the dumpster guy is? And why does he look like Mathers? Plastic surgery or relative? And was he killed because they thought he was Mathers, or were they planning to replace Mathers with him and something went south?"

"I was thinking the same thing. I tapped into some of my resources to see what I can get on Mathers." She gave him another look. "I burned bridges behind me, so I don't have the resources you probably do."

"If you're telling me you flipped, you know I can check that out, right?"

"I not only flipped, I sang." She took another sip of beer, wincing as she swallowed. "God, I wish this was vodka, but beggars can't be choosers."

He grinned, amused at the stereotypical response he'd come to expect from every Russian operative he'd known. "Why'd you flip? From what I understand, things are pretty good on your side of the fence for you."

"I had a mother who was getting sicker and sicker while they were using her to push me into assignments I didn't want to do. So I sang and she got to spend a year and a half in Fiji before passing away. That alone was worth everything." Tatiana glanced at his knee. "Are you as burned as people say you are? Rumor is they shot you to hell and back, crippling you, but you seem fine to me."

"I get a little stiff on cold mornings. There's a reason why I'm in LA." He gave her back one of her shrugs. "And there isn't a news agency that didn't have my face on its feed for two weeks after that extraction, so chances of me going under again went to zero, even if I could pull a hard job. This thing with Trey is easy. You being in the mix is hard. I don't want to have to watch my back knowing you're in my rearview mirror."

"I have no problem with you. I have a job to do and I like it. For the first time in my life, I own my own time." She still winced when she took a sip, but the beer seemed to be going down easier.

"I killed your brother, remember?"

"He had it coming." Her smile was a flash of white teeth, sharp enough to belong to a lioness. "I probably would have shot him myself eventually."

"I know how I got into the middle of this," Kuro said, returning her smile. "How did you end up going from blowing up buildings to working in one? And how did you wind up working for Trey's father?"

"The first one is a long story best told over better alcohol than this piss water," she muttered, holding the bottle up as if to examine its pale liquid. "And the second question has a very simple answer. Kimber Bishop is my girlfriend."

"DID THEY cut his hand off when he was alive or dead?" Trey asked from the kitchen as he sliced up some of the duck breast, trying to keep it as thin as he could.

The guava-jalapeno sauce was already warmed up, and the air fryer he used for crisping frozen french fries was once again churning away at its appointed task, a bottle of ketchup at the ready for when it dinged. Knowing his father wouldn't touch any of the vegetables, he nibbled on a spear of roasted asparagus as he cut, arranging the slices on a plate as he went. It didn't look as good as when Kuro did it, but Trey figured so long as it tasted nice, his father wouldn't care what it looked like, and it wasn't as if he was passing the food off as something he cooked.

"Do you honestly expect me to eat while we're having this conversation? And what difference does it make?" His father scowled as he studied one of Trey's paintings. "Two men are dead and I've been threatened. How or why they mutilated Robert isn't the question you should be asking. I'm more interested in what they are trying to keep quiet and how you're involved. Or better yet, is that man outside at the center of this and he's dragged you in?"

"Considering I was the one getting shot at and he defended me, Kuro couldn't have dragged me into anything." Pointing out the obvious to his father was something Trey was used to. The man never seemed too willing to see anything outside of the narrative he had in his head. "Should I even put asparagus on your plate or just leave it on the side so I can eat it?"

"If it's green, I don't want it," his father protested with a dark grumble. "My guts are fine. Stupid doctors don't know what they're talking about."

"Just because scotch is made out of barley doesn't mean it's got fiber," Trey remarked, putting the last of the duck onto the plate. The fryer dinged, announcing it was done with its potato-crisping task. After dumping the fries next to the slivered meat, he tucked the bottle of ketchup under his arm and brought the food over to his father sitting on the couch. "And before you complain, I'll move the asparagus onto my plate. I didn't see the point in dirtying another dish."

"You wouldn't have to worry about washing dishes if you were living up at the house." His father held his plate steady while Trey scooped the spears off. "You wouldn't have to worry about a lot of things."

"Drugs made me not worry about things, and look where that got me," he reminded his father. "'Sides, you and Mom would end up using me as a poker chip in that marriage game you two are playing. I'd rather not be played."

"Is that what you're doing with that man outside? Playing him?" His father stabbed a piece of duck with his fork, then sniffed at it. "What's the sauce made out of?"

"Guava and jalapeno. And I swear to God if you dip that into ketchup, I will hold you down when they come to kill you."

"I'm not an ignorant savage, Trey. Ketchup only belongs on hot dogs, french fries, and scrambled eggs." His father tucked a piece of the duck into his mouth, chewing thoughtfully. "Now answer me about the man, and then I want to talk to you about Robert."

"The man's name is Kuro Jenkins. I told you about him before. He's the guy who came out and shot at those men trying to kill me that night. Someone on his staff found Mathers's doppelgänger in the dumpster outside of his restaurant." The asparagus was still tasty, but Trey found it hard to get anything else into his stomach. "What about the threat you got? Besides the hand, was there a note?"

"Printed off of a computer. Nothing so exotic as a typewriter or letters cut out of a newspaper. That would've at least given them something to go on, or so your sister told me." His father studied a fry as if it held the answers to the universe's mysteries, then chewed through it. "Is this Kuro guy going to stick by your side through this, or should I have Tatiana cover you?"

"I'm fine. Or at least I think I am." He thought back about the kiss Kuro gave him, its tingling warmth lingering somewhere along his nerve endings. "Just so you know, I'm kind of interested in him."

"I'll have Tatiana run a background check."

"I think it's safe to say that they know each other, Dad. From the sounds of it, it looks like they have a history." He grinned at his father's frustrated huff. "Why did they kill Mathers? And why did they kill that other guy? And why do they need his hands? Does Kimber know any of that?"

"Didn't she tell you?" His father shot him a curious look. "That other man was Robert's twin brother, David. They haven't spoken in years, not after David embezzled twenty million dollars from the company they inherited from their father. The last thing Robert knew about his brother, he was living down in Venezuela, but it wasn't like he could get extradited, so the loss was written off and Robert rebuilt."

"You said Robert's golf game was off, right?" Trey leaned back, an idea percolating in his head. "Does that happen a lot?"

"Sometimes," his father replied. "Not often. Robert was a pretty steady player. He might have a few bad holes, but his game was usually on par, no pun intended. Why?"

"Because I'm wondering if the guy that you played golf with was really David and Robert was the one in the plastic that night," Trey conjectured, his mind working at the angles of the murders. "David already embezzled once. It would be pretty easy for him to step into his brother's place and start funneling money out of the business. Maybe they took Robert and David moved in, thinking he could make a quick score. Then something happened and Robert ended up dead."

"Then why would they kill David?" Harrington argued. "And why chop off his hands?"

"Because maybe David found out they killed Robert and that wasn't what he signed up for?" The argument was solidifying as he spoke. "The only reason they would want me to shut up would be because I saw the body that night and eventually recognized it as either Robert or David. I don't know what else it could be."

"They'd want to preserve Robert's fingerprints. Driver's license. Passport. Even some security boxes are fingerprint locked," Kuro interjected from the open door, leaning against its jamb. "Even identical twins have fingerprint variations like scars or puckering. Cutting off David's hands led police to believe they'd found Robert. Someone's thought this out and is getting tripped up because Trey saw Robert's body, and now they're trying to clean things up but it's not going very well for them."

"Probably would have gotten away with it if I didn't have my own ninja," Trey teased.

"Not a ninja." Kuro shook his head. "Or an assassin. Just so we're clear on that."

"This all seems more like one of those television shows you were on," his father replied. "Robert's business took more than a few hits over the past couple of years. He was asset rich but cash poor. If what you're saying was possible, David wouldn't have been able to get a lot out of their accounts. Robert was stretched pretty far. He was looking for investors to increase his cash flow."

"I don't know what else it could be," Trey said. "Now that they dumped the body—whoever it is—they don't have any need to come after me. Everything's already out in the open, right?"

"Except for who is pulling the strings," Kuro said as he came inside. "Did your father share with you one very important piece of this puzzle?"

"I hadn't gotten to it yet," Harrington muttered, putting his half-eaten plate of food down on the table. "Robert Mathers and I have been friends for years, and I don't know if you remember this, but he was one of the men I asked to be your godfather. I'd forgotten all about it until Kimber reminded me. It wasn't like I ever asked the man to do anything besides show up at the church that day, but he obviously remembered because he left you a good portion of his business. You're one of Robert Mathers's heirs."

"One of five, if I'm supposed to believe Boom Boom here," Kuro said, jerking his head back toward the redheaded woman coming up the path. "There are four people with a good enough motive to kill that we've got to worry about, and one of them might have set this whole train wreck into motion. So Trey, the question is, are you going to move into my place or am I going to bunk in here, because until this is all put to bed, you're a sitting duck, and I don't think I can let you out of my sight."

Twelve

"WORST PART about being gay?" Trey called out to Sera from his bedroom as he sorted his unfolded laundry onto the top of his dresser. He was angry about the night before and how his father, Tatiana, and even Kuro fought with him about moving out of the bungalow until everyone thought he was safe. There'd been no discussion with him, just around him, and it got Trey's back up, to the point where he kicked everyone out and told them he'd think about it in the morning. When morning came, he was still pissed off and grumpy because he knew they were right. "Guys are assholes, and there's no asshole detection software."

"I slept with your father, remember?" She sauntered into the sunny room, her arms filled with fresh bedding.

"So you know, then," he shot back, trying to suppress a shudder but not quite making it. Sera caught the lift of his shoulders and frowned at him. "Look, it's weird. I mean, my family's not normal, but I'm standing here with my best friend who slept with my dad and my mom pretends doesn't exist while I'm trying to decide if I should go take up the offer to go stay with a guy who owns a ramen shop but might have been an assassin for the government. Oh, and I find out my dad's assistant is actually his bodyguard and is my oldest sister's girlfriend, a sister who I didn't even know was a lesbian. My life has telenovela written all over it. All that's missing is a secret baby that I somehow fathered with a woman I've never met."

"Have you even ever slept with a woman?" Sera asked, plopping down to sit on the edge of his bed. She began doing that thing he never could understand but somehow folded a fitted sheet into a perfect square. "I mean, if that happened, then I would expect a secret baby."

"No one actually needs to sleep with the woman in order to have a secret baby. Don't you know that's how telenovelas are?" he sniped, digging through his laundry basket to find a match for the black-striped athletic sock he found clinging to a pair of his jeans. "It's right up there with me probably finding out I have amnesia and Kuro was my secret lover while I was a double agent in some European country that doesn't exist."

"I'm beginning to think you spent way too much time on the sets," she commented, snapping the sheet into shape. "Maybe you should get back into acting."

"There's no way in hell anyone would take a chance on me. Insurance would be too high, and if you remember, I torched my last set trailer." He found the errant sock, then realized they were different lengths. Sighing, he went back down into the pile, draping the shorter one over the edge so he didn't accidentally rediscover it. "I'm not a big enough name for anyone to be willing to take me on. Besides, it's been years since I was on a show, and I'm not so convinced I was that great of an actor."

"You won an Emmy. And you were a kid," Sera pointed out, bringing back a flood of memories Trey didn't want swamping his thoughts. "I don't know why you're putting away your clothes when it makes sense for you to be someplace safer than this bungalow. It's not like anyone can see this place from the main house, not with the trees, and it's too easy to get to. If there's someone trying to kill you, I'd feel better if you were someplace more secure."

"My choices are Kuro's apartment above the ramen shop or my parents' place." There was the beginning of a headache edging into Trey's left temple, a throbbing reminder he should either have more coffee or a handful of ibuprofen. "I was going to go to a hotel, but apparently the Russian ex-spy who sleeps with my sister and works for my father tells me the easiest place to kill someone is a hotel."

"Your parents would drive you insane within two days." With the sheet folded, Sera moved on to the pillow shams. "And you don't know this Kuro guy."

"Tatiana says staying with Kuro is probably the safest place I could be." He found another black-striped sock, then compared it to the other two, frustrated to discover it matched neither. "And I swear to fucking God, I'm going to throw away all of my socks and buy new ones in totally different colors. None of these damn things match."

"Leave them to the end and I'll help you." Sera snapped out another pillowcase, flattening it on the bed. "And I thought he and Tatiana were on different sides."

"They were. Their relationship is as complicated as mine is with my family." Giving up on the socks, Trey moved on to his T-shirts, the bulk of his wardrobe these days. "I like the guy. *A lot*. I just don't know if I'm willing to live in his back pocket while Kimber and the rest of LAPD tries to figure out if I'm in danger or not. Why the hell would Robert Mathers leave me a part of his business when I really didn't even know him?"

"He *was* your godfather." Sera cocked her head. "I mean, it's something."

"According to my mother, so was her ex-hairdresser, Sven." Trey rolled his eyes, chuckling. "He was the guy my dad suspected of being my father when my mom got pregnant. Well, him and two other guys. Harry the Second was kind of surprised when everything came back pointing to him. Not that my mom is a slut, but neither one of them are saints. She made him buy a diamond necklace as an apology, then asked everyone he accused her of sleeping with to be my godfather. He countered, and apparently I have four godfathers and three godmothers who I never knew anything about, including a dead guy whose twin brother may have switched places with him."

"Is anyone buying that besides you?" Sera laughed when Trey flipped her off. "So Kimber is not swallowing that theory of yours?"

"I'm not even sure if it matters, but someone killed them, and there had to be a reason for their murders. I'm waiting for someone to come up with the theory that I somehow did it because Mathers left me part of his business."

"I can't see that happening," she said, shaking her head. "You're already rich, even if you can't touch it."

"In the words of my father and practically everyone he knows, there's no such thing as too rich." The subject was beginning to depress him, and Trey still hadn't made up his mind about what he was going to do. It made sense to leave the bungalow, especially since his presence could bring down a bunch of trouble on Sera and whoever else was staying at the bigger house. Still, as idealistic as it sounded to crash at Kuro's place, he wasn't sure that was a good idea. "I know I can't stay here. I'm on borrowed time, because Tatiana threatened to plant heroin on me and call the cops if I didn't get myself someplace safe. Imagine me trying to explain *that* to Kimber."

"How much danger are you in, really?" Sera stood up, stacking the bedding she folded into a small tower. "With both Mathers brothers dead, what kind of threat are you? I don't see—"

The outer wall of the bungalow blew inward, sending a storm of wood and plaster through the bedroom. A beam struck Trey along the side of his head, pushing him down to his knees. The air seemed full of bullets, and he couldn't catch his breath with all of the dust in the air. Sparks flew from a cut electrical line as it was hit by something metal, and a whiff of smoke began to curl up through the gritty cloud. Fear got Trey moving, his knees aching, and a throbbing twist along his right arm warned him it might not hold his weight as he began crawling across the bedroom floor.

He needed to find Sera. He needed to see her alive and get her free of the chaos. It seemed like forever until he found the end of the bed and the pile of sheets she'd been holding.

She was lying on her back, her eyes closed and her white shirt slowly turning crimson around the holes punctured through her belly and chest. The air sparkled with a wave of plaster flecks, a cruel mimicry of the pink hologram glitter polish she'd painted on her nails. He couldn't tell if she was breathing, unable to see the rise and fall of her chest in the slightly shadowed niche she'd fallen in next to his bed. But she wasn't moving, and his stomach twisted down into a small ball of black pain, fear pushing him forward.

"No. No, no, no." Trey ducked behind the heavy platform frame, his hands bloodied from his crawl through the sharp debris. "Sera, we've got to go. Wake up."

Blood was everywhere, creeping across the floor like a thief, and Trey's heart stopped, his mind frozen by the metallic sting wafting up from the growing pools. Logic flew out the gaping hole in the wall, and he somehow seized on the notion that she'd be fine if only he could get her blood back into her, stop the wounds from oozing just a little bit, anything to help Sera hold on.

"Get in there," a man's voice shouted. His words sank through the fear wrapping around Trey's chilled body, starting a fire of frenzied panic at the back of Trey's skull. "Find him and—shit!"

A siren cut through the air, followed by another, their wails off sync but growing louder. It was difficult to tell how far away the emergency vehicles were or even *what* they were, ambulances or cops, but the sound of their approach was unmistakable.

"Go! Get back in!" Another voice, higher-pitched and panicked, screamed through the air, and the bungalow shook again with a barrage of gunfire, bursting sprays screaming past Trey's head, punching through the ceiling and far walls. "Come on. Leave the shells. Get in!"

He barely heard the screech of tires, but the hum of bullets seemed to stop. Trey somehow expected silence to descend, but the world crept in, small drops of sound working past the sudden crashes of broken walls and his tortured sobs. It didn't seem right to hear birdsong begin again so soon after the sun reemerged when whatever the shooters drove onto the property raced away, but the tweets and whistles were soon joined by a scream of sirens, the symphony of alarms warning people out of the way. His own staggered breaths deafened him to even the possibility of Sera's faint heartbeat.

There was no way he could hear anything when he pressed his ear against her breast, her blood slick and wet across his cheek. The distant memory of what to do for CPR haunted the edges of his thoughts and Trey jerked back up, wondering if he should press his folded hands on her chest and begin a steady beat to keep her alive until someone who knew what they were doing arrived. A press to her chest only pushed more blood from her wounds, and Trey grabbed at the bedding Sera'd been carrying before the wall was torn apart.

Pressing down on the wounds with the folded sheets, Trey bent his head and prayed, pushing as much of his heart into the murmur of hope pouring out of his mouth. The words burbling up from his soul probably made no sense. They didn't have to. Someone had to hear him. Someone had to put the life back into Sera's ashen, bloodied body and get her to open her eyes.

At least one more time. Trey needed to say he was sorry, tell her he loved her, and promise Sera everything would be okay.

She didn't wake up. Her skin did not bloom again with a rosy blush across her cheeks and her eyelashes did not flutter with the promise of opening, so Trey began again, pressing down harder on her wounds and begging her to stay with him.

Trey didn't know when the EMTs got to his side or even when they were able to break through his shock so he could hear them tell him to get back, to let them handle things. The silence was finally there, the numbness sinking in and sealing the world off behind a glistening wall of pain and terror. Trey blinked, looking up through a waterfall of tears at the Hispanic woman dressed in a blue uniform urging him to come with her, but he couldn't seem to move.

"Come on, honey." She seemed to whisper or maybe it just sounded that way with the echoing whoosh of his heartbeat slamming through his ears. "You can't help her now. One of the EMTs is going to look at you, but is there someone we can call? Someone who can meet you at the hospital?"

"Yeah," Trey grunted as a wave of pain ran down his right arm. "Kuro Jenkins. And when you get ahold of him, can you tell him I'm done with this shit? It's time to end this. One way or another."

IT WASN'T the first time Kuro had a ringside seat to the loss of someone's innocence. He knew Trey had seen more than his share of shit in his lifetime, but death was a different matter. Violent death brought a whole new awareness no one who'd ever seen it firsthand could explain. It was an assault on creation. The ultimate arrogance of man and the need to dominate and subjugate without purpose. Murder was a vicious circle, a rabid Jörmungandr set loose and in motion the first time blood was spilled for no other reason than to take a life.

Kuro could only hope that Trey was not poisoned by this particular ouroboros's venom. He'd seen that before, the black crawl of an insatiable revenge eating away at a man's reason. Trey's glassy-eyed stare was a concern, as was the seemingly deep disregard for the blood caking his hair or the light coating of plaster dust on his clothes. He moved slowly, as if every joint needed its own push to work and Trey only had so much energy to give to each limb.

The drive back from the hospital was accompanied by a heavy silence, one only broken by the infrequent hitch of Trey's occasional suppressed sob. His tears were dry by the time Kuro arrived, streaking the gritty film on his face, but as they got farther and farther away from the hospital, Trey's stony demeanor began to crack. His shoulders shook every so often, but Trey tightened his lips with each shudder, staring out of the Challenger's window, Wilshire's bright lights stealing shadows from his face.

He'd driven down to the hospital as soon as he heard, then paced the halls while Kimber and a couple of other detectives ran Trey through the wringer. A doctor cleared Trey physically but broached concerns about his psychological well-being, especially in light of his oft-documented addiction problem. His parents chimed in their own objections, taking time out of their pushing to reassure Kuro he wasn't needed at Trey's side.

It was nearly midnight at the time Trey was cut loose, and after a storm of rising arguments about what he should do, Trey told them all to fuck off and asked Kuro to take him home.

Yuki-onna was waiting for them at the top of the stairs, her sleek hairless body gleaming under the recessed lights. She was vocal, sounding off the typical yowling of a Sphynx cat who'd gone way too long without her evening meal. First she bitched and warbled at Kuro, scolding him as he climbed up the steps, then switched her attentions to Trey, hopping down the stairs to wind around his feet, purring and pleading as if she'd been severely abused and neglected.

"You have a cat." Trey spoke for the first time since getting into Kuro's car, and he stepped carefully, trying to avoid the lithe, serpentine feline tangling up his feet. "I never imagined you had a pet. Maybe some fish. Or a lizard."

"That's Yuki. Her full name is Yuki-onna." Kuro tried for a smile, but nothing seemed to reach past the dead flatness in Trey's eyes. "I named her that because she's white and has those two black spots over her eyes like the women used to style their brows in feudal Japan. Also, it's the name of a female snow demon that freezes her victims to death, then sucks their souls out of their mouths. Yuki is always freezing, and she's woken me up more than once by lying across of my face. Ignore her yelling. She'll shut up as soon as I get her some food."

"I don't mind. I like cats. I think." Trey looked around, but Kuro wasn't sure he was seeing anything other than the bloodshed he'd lived through earlier that day. "My mom's cat hated my guts but he hated everyone. He's the only one I've really been around."

While the ramen shop had been being worked on, he'd taken out most of the walls on the third floor, leaving the main area open from the street-facing wall all the way to the back, shoring up the ceiling with a recessed steel beam. From remaining space, he'd carved out a large master bedroom and bathroom, leaving the smaller room at the front to serve both as an office and a hidey-hole for the gun closet he'd built up in the middle. The exposed honey stone of the outer walls was several shades lighter than the caramel-hued oak planks running through the space, and while he'd spent a pretty penny on a chef's kitchen, he spent most of his time downstairs cooking, then crawling back up at the end of the day to crash.

The cat owned most of the high-ceilinged apartment, from her four-story cat tree to the dark gray sectionals she spent most of her time sleeping on. The bookshelves he lined the walls with were filled with everything he'd read and wanted to read, leaving enough room for a widescreen television he couldn't remember the last time he turned on. It was a comfortable apartment, with Koreatown's street noise seeping in through the double-hung sash windows, and smelled mostly of the herbs he had hanging from lines strung over the island separating the cooking area from the living room.

It was the first place Kuro ever truly lived in, a space he could call home where he could set his things down and not worry about how many egress points it had. Yuki had been a gift, a scrawny mewling naked thing Holly gave him as a housewarming present, and it was the first time Kuro could say he'd fallen in love.

Looking at Trey wandering around in a devastated silence made Kuro realize he probably had room in his heart for more than just Yuki.

"I know you probably don't feel like it, but you should get something to eat," Kuro broached. "I'll make you something light. Maybe some soup or noodles? How does that sound?"

There were other things he wanted to do. Things that included hunting down the men who brought such sorrow into Trey's life. There was a laundry list of slow, painful things he could do to them, a thousand ways to make the remaining hours left them a literal hell on earth. The only thing that stopped him was the brittle fragility of Trey's expression as he cradled Yuki against his chest, both of them nearly swallowed up by the sectional's deep pillows.

He couldn't fix lives. That was a truth Kuro knew very well. Once something was shattered, no amount of glue or spackle would make it right. He hadn't been around Trey long enough to know if words were comfort or if he needed silence to work through his thoughts, but the only way Kuro was going to learn was if he tried.

Sitting down on the couch seemed like such a small thing to do, but it was a start.

"I know this is going to sound crazy, especially coming from me, but it's okay to cry," Kuro offered up first. "She was a pretty big part of your life and someone took her from you. I promise you—"

"I don't want any promises, Kuro," Trey whispered, his eyes irritated and red from unshed tears. "I want to hurt someone, and I want to be sick because there's a hole inside of me where she was. They came after me and they got her instead. None of this makes any fucking sense, and Sera's dead because of it. I don't know what to do, but I want to punch something. I want to make somebody feel like I feel right now.

"She was all I had." He dug at his eye with the heel of his hand while scratching at Yuki's head with the other. "I fucking loved her more than I love my sisters. I mean, she was there every day, and I don't know if I can wake up tomorrow and not have her with me. Especially since I was the one who got her killed."

"You didn't get her killed, Trey. You didn't take a gun and shoot her. That's not on you. Don't ever think that." As much as he wanted Trey to believe that, saying it out loud wasn't going to make it happen.

There were dead bodies Kuro still carried around with him, tragedies he'd been a part of that were lodged into his conscience. Some were friends, but many were strangers, nameless people who'd died because he made a mistake. If there was one thing he wished he could give Trey, it would be that his dreams weren't haunted by the dead.

"I feel dirty inside. Maybe just filled with garbage. Everything is just so numb, but I can taste the stink on me." Trey closed his eyes, leaning his head down as Yuki scraped her chin against his cheek. "I know this is the wrong time and the wrong place, but I need to feel *something*, Kuro. Can we just go to bed? Can I just spend the night with you? So I'm not alone?"

"You're not alone, Trey," Kuro murmured as he leaned forward and kissed Trey's temple. "You've got me, and I'm not going anywhere."

Thirteen

WAKING UP with an exhausted Trey in his arms wasn't the worst experience in the world. Or at least not in Kuro's books. Sure, he'd have liked the circumstances to be different, a daybreak where he could roll over on top of the sleek, muscled man, rake his fingers through Trey's dirty-blond hair, and kiss him awake so he could spend a long time driving him back into a sweaty, contented sleep.

Not that Trey had been in any condition to do anything other than roll over after he passed out as soon as his head hit the pillows, his hair wet from the hot shower Kuro ran for him. Dressed in a pair of Kuro's old sweats and a T-shirt, he'd started off curled into a ball on the edge of the bed, only relaxing once Kuro climbed in next to him and wrapped his arms around Trey's shivering body.

Men needed to be held. At some point in their lives, they'd all been told it was unmanly to want someone to stroke their backs or be comforted by a tight embrace. There'd been little love in Kuro's childhood and even less once he picked up a gun and chose death as a way to make a living. The best thing he'd ever taken away from a lover was the realization men needed to be caressed as much—if not more—than a woman. It just took a real man to admit it and an even bigger man to ask for it.

Trey asking to be held the night before, openly admitting his needs, opened up Kuro's heart to him in a way nothing else could.

Asking showed a strength no one seemed to credit Trey with, but Kuro saw it. Despite being battered and badgered from all sides, Trey held up, struggling through the death of someone he loved while in the middle of a psychological war zone. He needed time to heal. Any idiot could see that, but his family didn't or weren't able to grasp that simple concept. He needed a little bit of freedom to breathe, and Kuro was determined to give it to him.

Along with finding out who wanted Trey dead and possibly taking care of the problem himself.

He dressed carefully, as if going on a job. There were certain pairs of black jeans with a little bit more give than regular denim, and he'd stashed them at the back of his closet, thinking he would never wear them again. They still fit, although he'd gained more muscle from working out at the boxing gym down the street, and he filled out the slightly loose black Kevlar-knit shirt he dug out from a stack beneath the peacoat he hadn't worn since he'd been back East. Working a kitchen and boxing was a good way to put on bulk, and it was going to be hard to remember he carried an extra fifteen pounds of muscle since the last time he did a job.

"Windows don't get skinnier, Blackie. Be careful of what you can fit through," he grumbled to himself, shoving his feet into a pair of black boots. Trey slept on, kept company by a slumbering Yuki sprawled out on Kuro's pillow. "Keep him company, girl. Daddy's going to turn on the cameras and the alarms. Then I'm going to go find out who's bringing shit to our front door."

Weapons were easy. He had a few disposable Glocks and a leather jacket loose and long enough to hide his shoulder holsters. Nothing was showing, he checked in a mirror, but Aoki still knew something was up as soon as Kuro came through the kitchen doors.

"What are you doing?" Aoki hissed, glancing over his shoulder at the kitchen crew prepping for the incoming lunch rush. "Did Holly pull you into something? Is she insane? You tapped out!"

Aoki crowded him back, lightly pushing Kuro into the dining room, the heavy plastic flap blocking the view to the kitchen catching on Aoki's shoulder before he shook it off. One of the sous chefs called out to Kuro, but Aoki waved him off, shouting they'd be back in a moment.

"I need you to run the shop for a bit," Kuro said, reaching under his jacket to adjust one of the holster straps. "Trey's upstairs. I'll have my cell phone on me. If he comes down, get some food in him. I left him a note not to leave, so if you can make sure that he stays put until I come back, I'd appreciate it. If he leaves, I want you to call me right away. Someone's got him in their crosshairs, and I don't want him to serve himself up on a silver platter."

"Are you sure it's not Boom Boom? It's kind of weird that she's in LA and working for his father." His friend rubbed at his forehead, familiar stress lines digging down into his skin. "Look at me! I'm sweating like a pig. It's like we're on the job again. I don't want to get shot at. The first five hundred times was enough."

"You were shot at twice," Kuro corrected. "And both times it was blue on blue. Which now I'm beginning to understand more and more. Yes, I'm pretty sure it's not Boom Boom. If she was going to kill him, she would've done it months ago. She's been working for his old man for a while now."

"Do you even know where you're going to start looking for these guys?" Aoki shuffled his feet, his frown deeper. "I mean, what have we got? The guy you killed up on Mulholland was driving a stolen car, but you got his name, even if the police can't seem to chase down anything on him. Did that Bluetooth snooping work for you when you were down there last night? Or did they show you paper?"

"It worked fine. Mostly I got shots from the bungalow. Nothing beyond that, but it shows me what shells they were using. Something they had is using 50s, so that at least narrows it down from something off the street," Kuro said, shaking his head. "I'm going to need help, because this kind of thing isn't what we do."

"Shit, does that mean what I think it means?" Aoki pulled back his lips into a fierce grimace. "It does, doesn't it? Did you tell Holly that you're going down there? Does she know what kind of shitstorm you're starting?"

"We don't work for Holly anymore, remember?" Kuro patted Aoki on the shoulder, reassuring his former communications tech. "And yes, I'm going to go see Pops, but she doesn't need to know that, does she?"

AS MUCH as Kuro found a kinship in the city of Los Angeles, there were places that even God didn't show his face. Amid glittering glass highrises and a wave of gentrification sat a determined squalor, stretches of streets littered with society's debris and deranged. Most of the storefronts were boarded up or were repurposed as places of worship and charity, with a few dots of civil service depots thrown in for good measure, but the only religion truly practiced was self-preservation, and as Kuro knew, survival of the fittest had no pantheon of saints.

The Challenger's throaty roar slowed down to a low purr when Kuro slid the car into a parking spot. Not many people would brave leaving their vehicle wedged in between two graffiti-covered buildings anchoring a busy corner in Skid Row, but the business he was heading into had a picture window overlooking the area, and given the reputation of the man he was coming to visit, his car would be safe.

Kuro just couldn't say the same thing about himself.

The weight of his guns against his ribs was only a small comfort when he walked through the barbershop's front door, the bell hanging over the jamb rattling an uneven chime. The men inside the dark, long shop were a diverse crowd, a spectrum of races and a scale of ages that went from midtwenties all the way to a skinny, hunched-over ninety-year-old man sitting on a barstool in front of a curtained doorway at the back of the shop. The air was hot, stirred to a lazy breeze by a phalanx of metal fans coated with clumps of greasy dust and hair. If anything, opening the front door let in a bit of the cooler wind whooshing down the street, but Kuro wasn't going to suggest they leave it open.

To a man, their faces were hard and worn, evidence of their rough lives ground into their skin and bodies. The elderly barber trimmed the back of his client's neck with a pair of clippers, his index and middle fingers missing their top two joints, but he moved the machine around with adroit skill, ignoring Kuro's presence. The others simply watched, no one stirring to intercept Kuro as he walked toward the old man sitting in front of the curtain.

His eyes were milkier than Kuro remembered, the corners burned yellow from years of sun damage, but his brown gaze was still as sharp as ever. His skin was glossy despite his age, wrinkled with deep crevices and nearly as dark as a cat's heart. His teeth were antiqued from years of smoking, the bulging squares an ill fit into his small mouth, but they were all his own. He boasted about that fact whenever given the chance. Preferring to dress in loose trousers, a button-up shirt, and red suspenders, he seemed as much a part of the shop as the cracked goldenrod floor tiles and the stench of the leatherworks next door.

No one knew his name. Everyone simply called him the old man, an ancient artifact of a time when the streets outside were vivid with life and on the edge of violence. The violence had come swiftly, carried on the shoulders of young men coming back from an unpopular war only to find themselves in the middle of civil unrest. It lingered at the edges of the street, pooling in the gutters like runoff from a rain the district couldn't seem to escape.

Kuro called him Cerberus, but never to his face. The old man was always armed, dangling a glistening silver revolver between his knees with a loose hold on its pearly stock. There were rumors he shot a man for breathing too hard, but that was a lie. He'd actually shot the man for snoring, offended at the disrespect to the barber the man showed for falling asleep during a haircut. That man had been the first body Kuro ever disposed of.

And he hadn't been the last.

The stench of unfiltered Camels greeted Kuro before he got within three feet of the old man, and he reverted back to a habit he'd had when he was younger, breathing through his mouth when approaching the shop's back area. Nodding once, Kuro cut straight to the point, "He back there?"

"Might not want to see you," the old man growled back, his breath ripe with cigarette smoke and cheap alcohol. "Considering you're too good for us now. Maybe you should go crawling back to that bitch that holds your leash. Get her to scratch that itch you've got going there."

"That come from Pops?" Kuro asked, cocking his head as he hooked his thumbs into his jeans' front pockets. "Or from you? Because if it's from you—"

"Get the fuck in here, boy," Pops shouted from the back. "Don't mess with the old man there."

Kuro ducked through the split curtain, schooling his face carefully to show no emotion. There were too many memories coming at him, triggered by the smell of comb cleaner, stale tobacco, and gun oil. He trailed his fingers along the chair rail running down the hall at his hip level, catching his thumb on a nail he knew was there but never seemed to avoid. It was a short walk, filled with nightmares and dead dreams. It was only a few strides, such a different experience than the first time he'd taken that walk toward the office at the end of the hall. The door was partially open, a slice of harsh fluorescent light cutting through the deep grays. Inside the office sat a man who was both Satan and Santa to him, and Kuro briefly questioned his sanity for coming back.

Trey's muffled, choking sob echoed in his thoughts, a whimpering cry he'd murmured in his sleep, mourning not only the loss of his friend but also, in essence, his illusion of safety. Kuro would never be able to get it back to him. That mimicry of innocence was long gone, but he could try to give Trey some peace, and the only way he was going to be able to do that was find someone who knew the city, someone who knew the games people played and the puppet masters who pulled the players' strings.

That person was Pops.

Kuro swung the door open, and it groaned with a loud creak, an early warning system a couple of good shots of oil would take care of, but none of Pops's enemies had the balls or the resources to get that far into the barbershop without someone taking them down. The squeal always sounded like a scream, a captured echo of everyone Pops fucked over. It terrified Kuro the first time he heard it. Now it was as much background noise as the old man with his glistening gun sitting in front of the curtain.

Pops hadn't changed. Sure, there was less hair on his head, and what there was now glistened silver, a patchy spread of kinky curls cropped short to his skull. His ethnicity always appeared fluid, a mixed-race child born to Los Angeles's gutters, but there were hints of Asian and black in his features, eyes shaped much like Kuro's but as black as night. He was still large, corpulent, and hanging over his bones in a loose wattle of pale sienna flesh, but there was a fatigue draped around him, an intense gravity dragging him down to the floor. Like always, Pops wore an oversized bowling shirt, a throwback to the days when knocking down pins constituted a good time on a Saturday night, and if Kuro looked around the massive Army-green metal desk Pops sat behind, he'd more than likely find the bright orange shirt was coupled with khaki trousers and a pair of Birkenstocks worn over a pair of ancient athletic socks.

Pops didn't get up to greet Kuro, but he hadn't expected the man to offer up his hand when he came to the door. It'd been too long since he'd walked down that hallway, time rushing past them quicker than water beneath the bridges Kuro burnt behind him. Still, he noticed a flicker of something in the man's dark eyes, and then Pops nodded toward the door.

"Close that," he barked, the intensity of his voice loud enough to rattle the narrow window on the outer wall. "I don't want anyone to overhear our business, because the only thing that I expect to hear out of your mouth is an apology, and I'm going to give you enough privacy for you to spit those words out. Consider it a gift that I'm sparing your dignity."

"I'm not here to apologize." Kuro resisted curling his lips up into a smile. "I came for information, and since that's what you're the best at gathering, I came knocking on your door."

"I should get the old man to come in here and shoot your fucking head off," Pops spat, struggling to get to his feet. His cheeks flushed pink with the effort, the edges of his mouth going white. He coughed, a wet, sticky sound moving up from his chest into the back of his throat. Rubbing at his shoulder blade, Pops glared at him. "You come in here—"

"Yeah, yeah, I come to you today—on the day of your cat's quinceañera—to ask you a favor," Kuro drawled, tilting back on his heels to stay out of spittle range. "This is business, Pops. Nothing more. Nothing less. You interested in hearing what I need, or should I just turn around and find someone else?"

Pops never had a poker face. It was the main reason he never gambled. Put a winning hand of cards in his grasp and he lit up like a kid given a free bicycle with a thousand dollars stuck into its spokes, so Kuro wasn't surprised when Pops's expressions ran through avarice and suspicion in under five seconds. Turning away would hurt Pops's wallet and eventually his reputation, when word got around his prodigal somewhat-son came into his place, then walked back out because he wouldn't do business with the man. Kuro figured he had about ten more seconds of standing in the office before he was going to be forced back out the door. He couldn't risk lingering long enough for people to believe he'd begged Pops to help and had been turned down. Cutting the conversation short himself would give Kuro the upper hand, definitely not what Pops wanted.

"How much are you willing to spend?" The man's eyes narrowed, his lips thinning in thought. "And don't jerk me around. You and I both know there's no way that bitch can get you local information like I can. That's got to be why you're here. You're chasing after something in the city."

"Five grand," Kuro offered, lowballing the deal. He was anxious, but this was a game he'd been taught to play. As anxious as he was to find the person behind the attacks, he couldn't let himself be taken by Pops, not if he needed to earn the man's respect and verifying the information would be clean and hard. On more than one occasion, he'd heard Pops slip someone more than a few half-truths, muddying the waters. "I need to know who was behind a kind of over-the-top house hit above K-Town.

Victim didn't see the vehicle but said it sounded big, and I've got word they used 50s, not something you find rolling off the street. Shit like this should be easy for you. Can't be a lot of players with that kind of firepower."

"You'd be surprised," Pops grumbled, easing down into his chair. It creaked beneath his weight, the hydraulic squealing in protest when he leaned into it, its back brushing up against the wall. "Lots of people in K-Town have firepower that big, and not all of it left over from the riots."

"How about if we settle on a price and then I can tell you the particulars?" he suggested, counting down the seconds he had left. If they didn't come to a deal soon, he'd have to walk to save face and maybe get into a tussle with the old man on the way out. "Price is fair. I'll give you an extra thousand if you actually give me the name of the guy who dropped the shooting."

"What? You don't think I could get the guy who directed it?" he snarled back, lifting his fleshy lips.

"Do we have a deal? Or do I head out the door?" Kuro pushed again.

"I'll take the six in cash. How long do I have?" Pops grunted, leaning on his elbows.

"Twenty-four hours. After that, offer's off the table. I've got to move fast on this. These don't seem to be the kind of guys that are going to sit around and wait."

"Pop me another thousand if I get it to you in twelve." Pops pushed back, edging closer to the deadline Kuro had in his head. "We both know why you're trying to shove this down my throat. You don't look good for the boys outside, and people are going to start saying you've gone soft."

"I leave a bullet in the front of your head and that kind of shit stops," he replied, rolling his shoulders back. "Old man didn't check me. I came in hot."

The deadline hit and Pops sagged, probably no longer certain about Kuro's reluctance to kill. There were too many years between them, too many psychological skirmishes when they butted heads and the moment Kuro decided to leave Pops behind, stepping up to take a badge and orders from Holly.

"Going to have to take the old man off the door," Pops mumbled. "He shouldn't have let you in carrying."

"No, he shouldn't have, but old habits die hard, even when you know better." Kuro leaned on the desk, spreading his hands across the façade of papers Pops used to hide his business dealings beneath. There would be calendars and contact numbers under the stacks, a meticulously arranged network of information very few would be able to piece together if they didn't know how Pops's mind worked. Kuro knew. He'd been tapped to take up that chair, and turning his back on that only sharpened the knife he plunged into Pops's chest. "I came to you because you're the best. I'm not here to pick up old arguments. I'm not here to wipe you out. I'm retired. I want to make ramen and just live my life. I don't want this. I don't need this. And whoever you have on deck should know they don't need to come after me just because I came to that door.

"But understand something, old man," he whispered, making sure that no one down the hall could hear him. Pops's pride and dignity needed to be respected and maintained. That was something he knew, or the house of cards in Skid Row would come tumbling down and he didn't know who would pick up its pieces. "Any of your boys get it into their head that they need to teach me a lesson or take me off the board, I will carve them up thinner than noodles and feed their guts to whoever is left behind. I don't want to start a war with you and yours, but I will if I even see someone in my rearview mirror. Now, five thousand. Another one G if you drop within twenty-four hours, and two G if you drop in twelve. Agreed?"

Pops stared up at him, judging Kuro's words. It was nearly five breaths before the man nodded, then stretched his hand out for Kuro to shake. "Agreed."

"Good," Kuro replied with a small smile, taking Pops's in a firm grip. "Let me show you what I'm looking at so you can figure out who you're looking for."

Fourteen

THERE WAS something warm on his face. It wasn't the sun. If anything, it blocked out the light. As Trey lay curled up on the very comfortable bed, silky linens wrapped around his aching body, the reality of the day before seeped out of the grogginess clouding his disorganized thoughts and suddenly hiding in the dark didn't seem like that bad of an idea. Then the warm heaviness along his shoulder and neck began to purr.

"Cat, I don't remember your name, but I've got to go pee," Trey mumbled, carefully turning over to dislodge the naked mole rat of a cat Kuro left him with. The thing rolled with him, reluctant to give up its perch before finally giving in to gravity, sliding off into a graceful stretch. "My bladder thanks you."

It felt late. He had no idea of the time, and his body didn't seem to want to move correctly. The day before left him bruised—physically and emotionally—and Trey stared at the folded pile of clothing left on the bathroom counter for a full minute before realizing they were his, washed and ready for him to wear.

The water was as hot as it was last night, and as cleansing. Standing under the powerful blast, Trey tilted his head back, then dropped to his knees, stricken by Sera's death. His sobs came hard, from someplace deep and dark inside of him, and Trey couldn't catch his breath, choking under the water and the memory of her blood on his hands.

"It's not fair," he whispered, his throat raw from crying. "I shouldn't have been there. She'd still be alive if I—"

He'd fucked up so many things in his life, consequences of his actions nipping at his tail every time he turned around, but this time seemed so unreal, so incredibly wrong. There had to be something he could do to change things, to find out who'd taken Sera's life and put her death on him.

"Okay. *Okay*. Get up." Trey grounded himself with a shuddering breath that tasted of tears and fresh water. "You can do something. You can figure this out. Because God knows, the fucking cops are going to do it. They probably think I arranged all of it just to get some attention. No one's going to help me but me. Get up off your ass and get going."

He felt every single one of the bruises on his body as he stood, and as Trey scrubbed at his skin with Kuro's soap, it also sank in he wasn't really alone. For some reason, Kuro pledged himself to Trey's cause and protection. It didn't take a rocket scientist to see Kuro Jenkins was a man of his word, and Trey sighed in relief.

"Don't know what I'm doing, but I'm pretty sure he does," Trey muttered, climbing out of the shower to find the naked white cat sitting on his clothes, grooming its long serpentine tail while holding it steady with a hooked paw. "Okay, it's not that I don't like cats, but you don't have any hair and your butt is smearing all over my jeans. I've got to wear those, and I've got to find your daddy because I need to do something about this."

The cat stopped its grooming, looking up at Trey with enormous green eyes. It studied him, listening intelligently while Trey urged it off his clothes while he dried himself off with the towel, but it didn't budge.

"Seriously. I've got to go." Trey reached for the cat, sliding his hands around its sleek body. It wasn't as naked as his mind was locked on to, more like a thinly flocked velveteen bunny after ten years of being dragged around by an affectionate child. "Don't purr at me. You know what you're doing."

They eventually came to a compromise after the cat jumped right back up following Trey gently putting her on the floor. Trey discovered the cat was female, and she agreed to sit on his clothes, mewing at him whenever he took something from the pile.

The shirt wasn't his.

It was a little bit too large, age-softened and black instead of dark blue, something he hadn't noticed with the cat sitting on top of it. The silkscreen on the front gave a shout-out to the Four Horsemen, a band Trey didn't know, and from the wear on the graphic, definitely vintage instead of a reproduced knockoff. The fabric smelled clean, a hint of softener and thankfully, no cat hair, an unthought-of bonus of having a naked feline around. It wasn't that he was allergic, but he and cats hadn't always gotten along, what with the constant war he battled with his mother's Persian while he was growing up. *That* cat hated him. It lurked in the corners of rooms, thundering across the floor to attack his legs and sometimes leap at his face if it could reach. The wrinkled white thing with a permanent scowl sat on the counter and simply kept him company, throwing out a deep purr whenever Trey made eye contact.

"Sorry I don't remember your name," he told the cat, scratching between her ears. "I'll get it from Kuro later. Or Blackie. Whatever *his* name is. There is a lot of shit I don't know about, cat, but I'm going to find out. Hold the fort."

The long flight of stairs had a door between the steps and the landing to the second-floor storeroom, and Trey was careful to lock up behind him. He didn't have a key but figured he could lurk in the back of the ramen shop if he came back before Kuro did. Armed with only his phone and a set of house keys to a home he couldn't return to, he was about to head down to the ground floor when he realized he hadn't texted Sera about not coming back to the bungalow the night before. His phone was already out of his pocket and his fingers poised to apologize when it struck him again that she was gone.

He staggered, leaning against the rail for support. The stairwell was tight, too boxed in for any air to move around, and the tall frosted windows on the outer walls were shut, keeping the wind and street noise out. He wanted to throw up, dragged down by the grief punching through his guts, but he'd had nothing to eat or drink other than… he couldn't remember when.

"You okay?" a dark stocky shape silhouetted against the opening at the bottom of the stairs called up to Trey. "Kuro said to make sure you got some food in you, but maybe we start with some soup?"

The man took a step up, and when the light hit his face, Trey recognized Aoki, Kuro's manager. Or at least he thought that's what the man was. Now he wasn't so certain. Kuro appeared to be tied up in things Trey suspected went deeper than guns in the past relationship with his father's personal bodyguard.

"I need to go out," Trey said, forcing himself down the rest of the stairs. His legs were shaky, unresponsive, but he refused to stop. A plan was beginning to form in the back of his head, something he could do to ferret out who wanted him dead, and Aoki was well-meaning but in the way. "Tell Kuro I'll be back."

"Oh no." Aoki scratched at the back of his head, raking through his short dark hair. "Kuro said you had to stay here."

"I'm not." He took another step down, drawing closer to the doorway. "Staying, that is. I need to talk to a few people, but I'll be back. The apartment door's locked, so everything up there should be safe, but I can't get back in. I don't know how long I'll be, but if you're not still around, can you tell the staff I can hang out at the employee table?"

"Kuro said for you to stay here." From the look on the man's face, he was deadly serious, as if Trey was insane for questioning Kuro's orders. "I can't just let you walk."

"He doesn't look like the kind of guy who'd kill you because I left," Trey said, trying to edge past the stockier man. While shorter, Aoki had a lot more heft on him and was practically immovable. "Actually, I don't really know what kind of guy he is. A couple of days ago, I thought he was just a good cook. Now I find out he's some kind of ninja with a noodle fetish, so you have to excuse me for not wanting to stick around just yet. I've got some stuff I've got to figure out, and the only way that's going to happen is if I talk to someone. Actually, a couple of someones, so you've got two choices—let me go or I'm going to go through you. You pick."

It was a gamble. Mostly because Trey knew he probably couldn't take Aoki in a fair fight. Or even an unfair fight. He knew next to nothing about hitting someone, other than what he'd learned watching stunt actors, so he didn't put much faith in his bluff. When Aoki looked him up and down, Trey bristled as much as he could, taking a frilled lizard approach to his threat, hoping mantling would help him out.

Something in him must have given Aoki pause, because the man grumbled under his breath, then sighed. "Let me get Frankie to cover for me and I'll get my keys. Last thing I want is having to tell the boss I let you go without a fight. If I come with you, at least someone might kill me before he gets back so I won't be around for him to tear me a new asshole."

"THERE IS no way in hell they are going to talk to us," Aoki grumbled loudly as Trey strode across the building lobby's polished marble floor. He glanced furtively about, his eyes bouncing quickly from the security guard counter to the bank of elevators directly across of the front doors. "Neither one of us is dressed for this place, and I'm wearing a ramen shop's T-shirt without carrying the delivery bag. Even a rookie knows if you're going to try to breach security dressed as a delivery guy, you have to be able to prove you're delivering food. If you don't have something on you, they will stop you before—"

"Sir?" one of the guards called out, coming around the end of the sleek wood counter set against the wall to the elevator corridor. He moved quickly, intercepting them before they could reach the elevator banks. "Can I help you with something?"

"No, thank you." He may have fallen pretty far from the expectations of the Bishop family tree, but Trey still clung to its branches, good manners and entitlement mentally beaten into him alongside French and how to choose a good wine. Even dressed in faded jeans and an outdated band T-shirt, Trey cloaked himself in the haughtiness every single one of his relatives carried as easily as breathing. "I am here to see my lawyers. Caldwell and Gilder. On the fifteenth floor, unless for some reason they've moved since last week?"

"I'll ring ahead." There was a challenge in the guard's eyes, and he reached for the phone next to him, picking up the receiver. He was calling Trey's bluff, a passive-aggressive pushing back Trey knew was coming. "Who shall I tell them to expect?"

"Harrington Bishop the Third. I've got my family's access code, so I don't need to be brought up," Trey replied, glancing back at Aoki. "Please tell them I'm bringing my personal assistant with me if they'd like to have two cups of coffee ready instead of one. Come on, Aoki. We've got a lot to do today. The sooner we have a talk with Gilder, the sooner we can get back."

The skyscraper was like many in Los Angeles, mostly glass and with panoramic views. The elevators hugged the outer wall on the south side of the building and were probably lock-coded against unauthorized access, but that was a gamble Trey was willing to take. He needed to talk to Mathers's lawyers, and while in Aoki's tiny convertible, he'd made a quick call to his father's office, asking for the name of the man who pretty much held Trey's life in his hands. Although he'd kept the call short, his father's administrative assistant was a talker and chattered everything she knew about Stuart Gilder while looking up his address.

From what the bubbly woman knew, Gilder was a shark who had his finger on the pulse of nearly everything Mathers did and had for years, which was exactly what Trey hoped to hear.

Nodding at the guard, Trey continued walking, expecting Aoki would catch up. He didn't stop to see if the guard actually rang up the offices. Nor did Trey care. He was through apologizing for what he'd done and his past mistakes. Someone took Sera away, killed her in his home, and the time for crawling around on his belly was long over.

Trey held the door for Aoki when the elevator slid open. Staring at a keypunch by the buttons, he shrugged and worked through a sequence of numbers, smiling to himself when the access light flared green and the Fifteen button turned on. Aoki snorted and settled against the wall, staring at the Los Angeles skyline through the elevator's windows.

"Good thing you knew the code." He grinned smugly. "Probably pissed that guard off. I mean, sure, we don't look like we belong here, but man, no need to be a snob about it. Damned good poker face you've got. And how'd you know your dad's done business with this guy?"

"Yeah, I've been here before, but I was kind of buzzed, but my dad's got habits. And the code's easy. I'd just use the same passcode he always uses." Trey shrugged when Aoki's mouth dropped open. "It's always my birthday. He's weird that way. He's got lawyers on staff, but the best way to make sure the good lawyers can't sue you is to have them on retainer. You should see the suits he's got around his poker table. I've been nose-deep in lawyers since I could see over the table and deal out chips."

"Never would've imagined you to be a poker player." Aoki chuckled. "You look too—"

"Naïve? All-American?" Trey had his own laugh at the thought. "I spent my formative years on the set with some of the biggest assholes in the world, and those were the good guys. First thing they did was teach me how to play poker. Second thing they did was teach me how to fix a drink. If I can't bluff my way past a security guard, I think I'd be kicked out of SAG. On second thought, they might've already kicked me out. I haven't checked. I did decide to find my balls again, and I'm sick of someone punching at them, so let's hope somebody at the lawyers' office will talk to me about Mathers."

"That the dead guy we found in the dumpster? Or the other one?" Aoki rolled his eyes. "Because I'm having a hard time keeping track."

"Hold that thought, because I've got a few questions about that," Trey replied, taking a deep breath when the elevator dinged their arrival.

"Okay, we got past the guard. Now let's see if we can get past the bigger monster, the receptionist."

It went far easier and smoother than Trey expected. The woman at the desk either recognized his name or the guard calling ahead gave the office enough time to scramble up some information, because a few moments after his feet hit the law office's lobby, they were escorted into a meeting room and asked if they wanted coffee.

The Caldwell-Gilder meeting room was a cookie-cutter knockoff of a gentlemen's club, much like many meeting rooms Trey associated with his father and his ilk. Dark mahogany paneling and forest-green paint dominated the walls, with overstuffed tufted burgundy leather chairs in artful arrangements around low tables on a scatter of old Oriental rugs. The setting was at odds with the floor-to-ceiling windows overlooking downtown Los Angeles, but the outside environment was obviously not taken into consideration when decorating. Trey knew from experience people like his father felt more comfortable in the stodgy trappings from an older time, eras where they held a firm grip on their industry and the people beneath them.

"I feel like there should be a tarp in the middle of the room," Aoki said, shoving his hands into his jeans' pockets. "And I don't want to touch anything. This is the kind of place that charges you for how much air you breathe."

"You are not wrong," he agreed. "But God knows, I put my lawyers through the wringer more than a few times."

"Well, technically, Mister Bishop, I suppose one could say I'm a new lawyer for you to put through the wringer, although I sincerely hope not. If you retain our services, of course." An older man entered the room, but he looked miles away from the clean-cut, gray-haired men in expensive suits Trey thought of whenever the word lawyer popped up in his head. Most of the firms his father engaged were tried-and-true old boys' networks where most business was conducted at the golf course or at the bar in a country club. This man, if possible, looked even rattier than they did.

He was about Trey's father's age, and his hair was definitely silver, but it ran long, gathered up into a ponytail that hung over one shoulder. The sneakers on his feet were expensive, but they'd obviously been used for hiking or something to drag them through red clay, because they were stained and scuffed. His T-shirt possibly could've been blue at some point but had since faded to a nondescript gray and sported a few holes along his belly. He looked fit despite having climbed firmly into his sixties, having a lean, ripcord body not unlike Trey's, his exposed arm muscles rippling as he reached out with one hand.

"Stuart Gilder, attorney at law and keeper of secrets. It's good to meet you, Mister Bishop." He grinned as he shook Trey's hand, then pivoted to clasp Aoki's before motioning toward the chairs. "I suppose you're here to talk to me about your inheritance."

His smile was blinding white, and everything about Stuart Gilder was meant to be disarmingly congenial, a smooth sweetness to his voice and a hint of reassurance in his manner. Trey trusted him as far as he could throw him, but he didn't know the man, and stewing in the trouble Mathers seemed to have put him in, Gilder was the only one who possibly had answers. Or at least someone he could ask.

"Actually, I'm not here about my inheritance. If anything, I'd like to give it back, because it seems like someone's trying to kill me and I'm not sure why," Trey said, settling down into one of the chairs. "I don't know how much you are aware of what's happened, but I lost a really good friend yesterday, and I think her death is connected to all of this money, or maybe just Mathers."

"If you don't mind me talking in front of your boyfriend," Gilder replied, nodding his head at Aoki, "I'll be glad to answer any of your questions."

"Oh, he's not my—" Trey started to protest.

"I'm just here to keep him alive, because the guy who probably is his boyfriend or going to be—I'm really not sure and I haven't asked— would skin me if anything happens to him," Aoki interrupted. "I'm already pretty sure I'm going to get my ass kicked for even bringing him here, but at least this way I can keep an eye on him, and if I'm lucky, they'll kill me instead of him so the boss can't get to me first."

"Are you in some kind of trouble, Mister Bishop?" Gilder reached behind him and pulled out a cell phone. "If you're being held or threatened—"

"It's not like that. If anything, Kuro's done his best to keep me alive, and lately, I don't seem to have enough common sense not to look up when it rains." Trey leaned forward in his chair, resting his elbows on his knees. "I need to talk to you about how Mathers died. Robert, not David. Or maybe both. I don't know."

"Explain to me what you need and I'll try to help you," the lawyer offered, putting away his phone. "But I don't know what I can tell you."

"A few nights ago, I saw two men carrying what I thought was a rolled-up rug but that turned out to be a dead body who I recognized as somebody I knew, but I didn't know who it was. Then I saw Robert Mathers's picture on Dad's wall, but he told me Robert was alive, because they played golf together that day," Trey explained, working through everything clouding his head to find the details he needed. "Later on, one of the guys I saw that night tried to kill Kuro, who defended me when they shot at me. Then a couple of days later, I think, they find Robert Mathers stabbed to death, but that's not the guy I saw that night. Or I don't think so. Because the guy I saw that night was found in the dumpster behind Kuro's shop the other day while I was there.

"Then yesterday, a bunch of guys shot up my bungalow and killed my best friend, Sera. They were probably trying to kill me but they got her instead, and none of this makes any sense, because I can't even identify the other guy who shot at me and I don't know who murdered Robert or David. Dad told me David was a dot on the horizon and no one saw him for years, but he shows up dead in Los Angeles?" Trey shook his head, unable to find his way out of the maze of conflicting information. "David was Robert's twin, right? Maybe they killed David thinking he was Robert? And why didn't anyone think I saw David when I said I recognized the dead guy as Robert?"

"Probably because they were fraternal twins," Gilder remarked, then paused as the assistant who'd led them into the room returned with a tray of coffee cups and cookies. Thanking her, he waited until she left the room before motioning for them to help themselves, picking up the mug to sip at the black brew. "If you put them side by side when they were younger, you could tell them apart. As they got older, it looks like genetics drew them closer. I was the one who identified David's body.

"His hair was cut the same as Robert's, and he'd gained enough weight around his face and belly until, if I hadn't known better, I would've sworn I was looking at Robert, but fingerprints don't lie and neither do teeth." Gilder aged in front of Trey's eyes, sagging in on himself. The lines in his tanned, vibrant face grew deeper and his skin turned ashen. "David's front teeth were false, implants he had put in after Robert punched him during the fight they had over the business. His front teeth were white and the rest of them were yellowed. That's how I knew it was David in the dumpster. Well, that and they'd already found Robert. The police are on it. I think your sister is on the case, isn't she?"

"She's not necessarily sharing information," Trey replied. "I'm just trying to make sense out of what's happening and who's after me. I didn't even know Robert. I don't know why he left me anything. I mean, he was my godfather, but I didn't even recognize the man. He was just one of my dad's friends hanging on the wall with other people."

Trey's cell phone went off, an oddly cheerful tune singing about the wonders of a fruity oaty bar. Glancing at the screen, he groaned, then showed the phone to Aoki.

"Don't tell him I'm here." Aoki waved his hands in front of his chest, a blur of fingers and panic. "No! You have to tell him I'm here or he'll kill me for letting you walk out of the shop. Shit! I don't even have a gun."

Gilder looked panicked, but Trey shook his head and said, "It's okay. It's just Kuro."

"It's just Kuro?" Aoki exclaimed. "You don't know him. I'm going to be shredding carrots and daikon for the next two years. I'll be lucky if he even lets me make broth after this. He's going to bust me down to checking chopsticks for splinters."

"It won't be that bad," Trey said, answering the call. "Hello?"

"Where are you?" Kuro barked at him across the line. The man who held a gun on Tatiana in the front room of his bungalow was back, stepping over the gentle soul who'd made him duck breast and left him with a bald cat for company after holding him through the night. "Is Aoki there with you? I told him to keep you at the apartment. Instead I find both of you and his car gone."

"Yes, he's right next to me. The car's downstairs in the parking garage. I couldn't fit it in the elevator, so it couldn't come up with us. And if you have forgotten, what you told him to do was pretty much kidnapping," Trey retorted. "Or didn't they go over that in the super secret ninja school you went to?"

"Technically, that's illegal confinement, but you should've followed my orders."

"If you haven't noticed, I'm kind of allergic to following orders," he growled back. "You could've left me a note. Maybe a text telling me why I needed to stay there? And that I don't appreciate—"

"I'm coming to get you because I need to know you're safe," Kuro cut him off. His voice gentled, rolling softly through Trey's ruffled temper. "And I found something out about the dead body in the dumpster. That wasn't David Mathers. That was Robert, and from what my people tell me, it looks like he's been dead and on ice for years."

Fifteen

KURO WAS spoiling for a fight.

He recognized the signs. The tightness of his gums around his teeth. The twisting clench of his guts and the pull of his balls up into the hollow between his thighs. Most of the time these signs crawled out of his body when adrenaline hit his blood and bullets were flying.

Never when he was angry at a man sitting next to him in the car.

Kuro was also scared to death.

Fear wasn't a new sensation. Only the insane and sociopaths never tasted the sour lick of fear through their lungs and up their throat. Anticipatory fear was the worst. There were too many variables, too many possibilities for things to go wrong, and the human mind had an endless capacity for imagination, dredging up even the most fantastical of disasters, packaging them in easily believable bites.

He just didn't understand why he was afraid. Or rather, why he was afraid for Trey.

Losing people was a part of the business. It'd been a while since he'd had to step over the body of someone he knew to complete a mission, but he'd done it so many times before, Trey falling to whatever mess was swirling around him shouldn't have even rippled Kuro's calm.

Yet it did.

He didn't like the idea of Trey's body going cold. Even worse, he hated the thought of something happening and not knowing where Trey had gone or where he lay. And it seemed like his fear manifested in a tight anger, a barbed-wire spiderweb wrapped tightly around his chest.

Trey wore his grief on his face, purple shadows smeared beneath his sad eyes even as his restrained anger worked to seep out. Kuro didn't have to be a mind reader to know Trey was pissed off. It rolled off of him in waves, slamming against Kuro's own agitation and working right back in on top of them, a continuous storm of emotion they'd bottled up as if it were a message to be thrown into the sea.

For all its roominess, the Challenger was a shitty place to have an argument. The car needed Kuro's full attention, but so did Trey. The surface streets were touch and go, a barely moving stream of brake lights and rolled-up windows. Even as congested as Los Angeles's arteries could get, Kuro was always amazed at how silent it was. There might be a boom-boom-boom of a bass line thumping through a lowered import's massive speakers or the odd caterwauling of someone singing along to a song about shiny knives and being unable to kill the beast, but there were rarely any horns honked.

At midafternoon, it was later than he liked, but there was no helping it. Between losing Trey and traffic, a fifteen-minute drive became nearly an hour and a half, or so his mapping application told him. He was about to offer to stop at a drive-through to get Trey something to eat or drink when Trey cleared his throat.

"I don't work for you." Trey's opening gambit was curt and to the point. "And I'm not going to be put behind the kiddie gate with Aoki set up as a watchdog. I'm grateful for your help, and you've pulled my ass out of a couple of really shitty situations, but that doesn't give you the right—"

"I'm sorry," Kuro ground out between his teeth. The Challenger roared when he pressed his foot down on the gas, giving the car enough to get past a slowing bus. "I came back to the ramen shop to find you and you weren't there. I lost my mind a little bit. I thought maybe somebody grabbed you."

"And what? Aoki went after them?" Sarcasm sharpened Trey's words into spinning razors through Kuro's apology. "I haven't known him long, but I'm guessing he's not the action hero kind of guy. I don't see him crawling on top of a white horse to go save the day. *Or* me."

"That's not fair to him," he replied, wincing even as he defended his friend. He hated lying, and Trey wasn't wrong. Aoki was more likely to hide behind the trash can lid than use it as a shield to protect others but still was a good man. "He would try to do something. I don't know what, but he would try."

"Okay. Agreed. I am being shitty about him because I'm pissed off at you." The grumble beneath Trey's breath was in French, a burbling spit of water on hot cast iron. Kuro didn't catch it all, but what he did hear wasn't complimentary. "You didn't have to come get me like I was some kid that got suspended from school."

"I came to get you because I thought you'd want to go with me to talk to this guy about the Mathers brothers. Especially since, while we've got the brothers swapped, our theory still holds. Someone needed Robert's identity to carry through on this long con, and David probably overstepped. At some point Robert's body probably began to break down and it couldn't be used anymore. I don't know for sure, but the guy we're meeting might be able to confirm some of this." It was an olive branch, a twisted, malnourished one, but an olive branch just the same. "He's got some backdoor information and maybe a name we can follow up on. The amount of firepower used at your place is pretty huge, but it was a messy hit. Don't know if there's anything we can learn there, but that's another maybe."

"Kimber said there's no way they can trace the guns that were used."

"No. Too many weapons out there that can use that kind of ammo, but the amount they used is what we're going to go on. It's either someone who bought a little over a long period of time or a whole bunch at once. Guns are easy to get, but these days, sometimes finding ammo is like digging up hen's teeth." Kuro glanced down at the GPS screen on his phone, calculating how long it would take them to get to East Hollywood in the thickening traffic. "The guy we're going to meet skims information. Normally, I would go through someone else, but the local source here and I rubbed each other the wrong way, so he sent me up directly. No phones. No emails. No recordings. Has to be face-to-face, and whatever's said has got to be remembered. I don't even know if we'll be allowed to write it down."

"So why do you want me around for this?" he asked, turning slightly in the seat to give Kuro a skeptical look. "Not like I can shoot a gun or interrogate people. Shit, I can't even get my damned family to believe me when I tell them I've seen a dead guy on the side of the road."

"Because you remember things and you might hear something different than I do. You have a different perspective. It's kind of like triangulating a conversation. We'll each listen to the same thing and come away with something different." Kuro shrugged, then said something he never thought he would say to someone he'd only *really* known for a week or so. "Besides, I trust you. I don't know why, but I trust the fuck out of you."

EAST HOLLYWOOD was exactly as Kuro remembered it, filled with lost tourists dragged down from miles of walking the strip thinking there was something else to see if they just went a little farther down. It was far away from the bustle of streets across of the Roosevelt and what used to be Mann's Chinese Theater. Down at the other end near the tangle of the 101's onramps and slightly run-down buildings, there were no out-of-work actors pretending to be superheroes and charging ten dollars to stand for a photo. Instead, they were skirting the edges of Thai Town, coming up to one of the Red Line's busiest stops. In the middle of the afternoon, the Metro station was filled with mostly kids, but Kuro had a description of the young man he needed to talk to.

He just needed another set of eyes, and luckily, there was one sitting right next to him.

"I'm going to circle around to see if I can get a parking spot," he said, clicking on his turn signal and pulling halfway into the intersection. "The guy we're looking for is Thai but has dyed bright red hair. Pops says it's long, like down his back long, but he might have pulled it up. Can you watch for him?"

"Is this supposed to be your informant?" Trey leaned forward in his seat. "Are they supposed to be inconspicuous? Are you sure he's still going to be around? It took us a long time to get over here."

Kuro was grateful Trey was at least talking to him, although he wasn't sure if everything was okay. He wasn't used to people questioning his decisions, even after he retired. The stop-and-go traffic reminded him his leg wasn't in peak condition, his thigh muscles seizing up when he shifted in his seat, and something twinged along his back, either recalcitrant scar tissue or he'd slept wrong and now was paying for it.

He wasn't even in his forties and he was already falling apart.

"He hangs out here. They call him Rooster, but I don't know if that's because of the hair or maybe he just laughs funny." Kuro snorted, thinking of some of the nicknames he'd encountered over the years.

"Like Tatiana calling you Blackie?" Trey asked pointedly. "Don't think that because of all this shit that's going on, I haven't forgotten about you and her reenacting the Kobayashi Maru in my living room."

"That had no resolvable solution unless you cheated. We came to terms very quickly—relatively—and nobody died. It's always a good day when nobody dies." If Kuro could have stopped time and rewound it a few seconds, he would've used it to punch himself in the face. Trey's expression went from curious and still pissed off to shattered, then closed down to a tight mask. After cursing himself out, he muttered, "I'm sorry. That was a shitty thing to say. I know Sera meant a lot to you, and sometimes it's easier for me to joke about death than—"

"No, I get it. Gallows humor and all that crap." Trey's lips lifted in a small smile. "She'd have liked you. Mostly because you cook. I never got to take her into your shop, but I brought stuff home. So you fed her a couple of times, even if you didn't know it."

"Sometimes that's the best gift life can give you," Kuro murmured, spotting an opening on the street he could fit the Challenger into. "Sharing a meal with somebody you like or love is usually the best memory you can have. Glad you had that."

"Me too," Trey replied, then grinned, pointing toward the back of the building, where a gaggle of teenagers gathered in loose groups. "I think that's him over there."

Kuro took a quick glance while he maneuvered the car into place, catching sight of a slender Asian man holding court beneath an overhang. His gestures were wild, and his face churned into different exaggerated expressions, setting off a wave of laughter among the teens gathered around him. From what Pops told him, they'd definitely found Rooster.

"And we couldn't talk to him on the phone?" Trey got out, shutting the door behind him.

"Hard to shove cash through the phone, and believe it or not, people who take bribes for information don't take credit cards or online payments. Something about trail of evidence," Kuro teased. "Come on. Let's go find out what the cops won't tell us. Not that I don't think your sister's working hard enough, it's just that she's got rules she has to follow. I don't."

Rooster looked up at them, and his expression shifted from playful to a hard mask. Detaching himself from the crowd, he walked over to a trash can tucked deeper under the covered walk, then lurked in the deep shadows to lean against the wall. He was probably in his twenties, but he'd played up his youthful Thai looks by dressing down, wearing what Kuro believed to be the uniform of the disaffected Los Angeles teen, in a pair of baggy jeans, an eye-bleeding yellow T-shirt with a nonsensical slogan written in bad Japanese, and a backward LA Dodgers ball cap on a fall of stoplight-red hair.

It was like someone had a handful of hard candy and brought it to life as their own private Pinocchio.

"Rooster?" Kuro called out. "Pops sent me."

"Shit, don't use my name." He looked about nervously, shifting from one foot to the next.

"You think everyone here doesn't already know your name?" Jerking his head back toward the crowd Rooster just left, Kuro scoffed.

"Hey, I know you," the young Thai man said when they came in close. "You're that guy on the show. Shit, the kid who blew that biker's head off and no one knew until the end. Broke my mom's mind. She thought your mom did it. Thought you died. Didn't you OD or something?"

"Or something," Trey mumbled, his discomfort visibly growing when Rooster laughed.

"No, it's cool. Gimme a selfie before you go." He smirked, nodding at Kuro. "That's insane. You see the show? It was crazy nuts."

"No, but I wasn't in the country, probably," Kuro drawled. "And the selfie's probably a bad idea. What you've got to give me is connected to him, and you don't want that tied to you, yeah?"

"Crap. You're right." He spat on the ground, his tough posturing softened by his too-pretty features. After digging through his pockets, Rooster came up with a small flash drive. Holding it out to Kuro, he grunted under his breath, "Everything I got from my girl's on here. Don't know all what's on it, but she gave me a heads-up it's about those murdered guys. Told me one of them was in the freezer so long his legs were, like, cooked through. Got all mushy when they thawed him out."

"Meat gets like that. Ice crystals break down the tissues sometimes if he was taken out of a freezer and left out for a long time, then put back in," Kuro murmured, sliding the drive into his pocket. Trey looked like he was going to be sick, so Kuro gently pushed him toward the nearly overflowing trash can. The slim envelope in his pocket made a brief appearance, as he passed it over to Rooster in a quick slide when their hands touched again. "Sure that's enough?"

"Yeah, no one else is going to ask for that, so it's not like there's competition. I'm going to get what I can." Rooster shrugged. "Dude, if you're going to hurl, don't get anything on my shoes. These are some bucks, and I can't replace them."

"Pops said you knew more than what you just coughed up," Kuro pressed. "What's on here? What am I going to be looking at when I open this up? You can't tell me someone sent you files and you didn't dig through them. Or else, how would you know you couldn't shop it around to someone else?"

"I've got an in down at the morgue, so she shoots me some of the interesting shit, figuring I can either upload it to one of the shock sites to sell or sometimes give people a heads-up if something shitty is coming their way. No chance I'd be able to farm this one out without it coming back to my girl. It's just too fucking weird." Rooster at least looked a bit chagrined at being caught out. Considering some of the assholes Kuro had worked with before, the kid seemed decent, despite needing his clothes dialed up to eleven. Sighing, he shrugged, then said, "This one's got those guys down there kind of confused. The other guy they found— not the Iceman but the guy from the river area? She said they started to cut him open and found plastic surgery shit underneath his skin. Like he had work done on his face. They think the newer dead guy had surgery to look like freezer guy, but they don't know who did it."

Kuro was getting a better idea of what happened but only the barest hint of who could be behind the attacks. After thanking Rooster, he headed back to the car with Trey in tow, keeping his thoughts to himself until they were almost to the car.

"So, let me see if I've got this straight," Trey said, his long legs keeping pace with Kuro's stride. "It sounds like someone killed Robert Mathers and his brother had surgery to look more like him. Then David stepped in to replace him and they shoved Robert's body into the freezer someplace. Does that sound right? How could you get away with that? Fingerprints and everything… that kind of shit only works in soap operas."

"There's ways to get around that. And from the sound of it, there seems to be enough money to splice in David's vitals over Robert's." Kuro opened up the Challenger, flicking the power lock up to unlock Trey's door. "The question is, when did the switch happen and who else knew about it? Let's get back to the loft and take a look at what's on the drive. I have a feeling it's going to be a very long night, and I want to get you someplace safe."

"Didn't we already have the discussion about you not ordering me around?" Trey growled, raking his fingers through his hair, clearly frustrated.

"It's not an order. I just want to have you someplace where I know if someone's going to come after you, I'm going to be able to take them out," Kuro said, starting the engine. "They were moving Robert for some reason. I don't know why they didn't dispose of the body to begin with, but you were there and caught them. I'm going to guess your sister is digging up information on any building in the area that has a deep freezer."

"Like a restaurant?" Trey chewed on his lower lip for a second. "Shit, *you* have a restaurant. You can't swing a cat in K-Town without hitting at least five."

"Yeah, that's the problem, but people will talk to me who won't give the cops the time of day." He eased the classic muscle car into traffic, falling in behind a red Metro bus. "We've got two leads to follow, the freezer and the plastic surgeon who did the work. With any luck, one of those will lead to the guy pulling the strings."

"And who killed Sera," Trey whispered. His grief flared through his voice, tempered by an anger Kuro understood well. "I really don't give a shit about them coming after me, but she was the only one in my life who… stood by me. After everything I've done, I don't blame my family for turning their backs on me and doubting me, but how long am I supposed to pay for that? I figured there was nothing I could do and I didn't deserve forgiveness, but Sera—she gave me a clean slate. I owe her everything for helping me get my head straight. I could be as sober as fuck, but it screwed with my mind so much when everything got clear but I was alone. She made me feel… less alone."

"Well, like I've said before, you've got me now," Kuro murmured, patting Trey's leg briefly. "And I'm pretty sure between the two of us, we'll be able to figure this out and hand this asshole over to the cops."

"Or die trying?" Trey teased.

"Yeah, let's try to avoid that," Kuro shot back. "I'd at least want to be able to get farther than a kiss with you before someone blows my head off."

HE WANTED a drink.

Actually, what Trey really wanted was the sour bite of cocaine in his nose and along his gums after he rubbed his finger across whatever slick surface he'd used to break down the load to pick up whatever minute grains were left there. In a pinch, heroin would do, but he knew from experience and other users that he would have to scale down the hit dramatically. It'd been too long and his system no longer had the buildup of drugs in it, so any heroin he injected wouldn't have to fight through any resistance.

Booze would work too. He actually preferred it because it gave him something to do with his hands over an extended period of time. It also had the bonus of lasting longer and numbing his brain to the point of erasing everything and everyone around him. He couldn't go for a run or call up Sera to talk out the burn in his blood. Her death struck him again, digging into him and chasing the stream of perverted want coursing through his body. Booze sounded really *fucking* good.

So instead, he watched Kuro cook.

It was almost becoming a habit. Trey perched on a stool next to a kitchen island opposite of Kuro as he worked. This time it was the loft's kitchen, with a much bigger selection of food and what appeared to be enough knives to equip a Roman army. There were spices and leafy things which eventually were going to become something, but Trey didn't know what. Sniffing at a jar of yellowish powder proved to be a mistake when he caught a full whiff of dust in his nose.

Suddenly, cocaine didn't seem like a good idea. Breathing again didn't seem like a good idea.

Choking, Trey asked, "What is that? It smells like someone punching you in the face."

"It's garam masala. It's strong because I make it myself so everything's bright and fresh," Kuro said, giving Trey one of his unbelievably sexy, lopsided smiles. "I buy the spices from a woman down at the market and grind them up. You're probably smelling the cinnamon and nutmeg. Maybe the black pepper too. I tend to go heavy on those."

"What are you making?" Trey stretched out his arms, feeling the tightness along his shoulders. Bruises were still coming up in places he hadn't realized he'd hit, and the emptiness in his chest seemed to throb and ebb without any rhyme or reason. Getting off the stool, he asked, "And how can I help?"

"I'm making chicken *makhani* because it's fairly fast, and if you want, you can make rice." Kuro nodded toward a squat, round appliance sitting in a corner of the kitchen. "I've only got Calrose, because well, that's just what *I* like, but if you like something else, I can probably get somebody to grab some."

"First, you're going to have to explain to me how to make rice, especially if you want me to use *that*." Trey pulled out the appliance and lifted its glass lid to look inside. "I'm guessing this is a rice cooker."

"Yeah, and it's very easy to use. Rice is in the cabinet below. Measure out three cups—there's a black cup in the container—then rinse it a little bit. Try to get a lot of the cloudy water out, but you don't have to be exacting about it. You just want to rinse that one. Some rice you actually have to pick through, but that just takes too long sometimes."

He found the rice and rinsed, swishing his hand through the grains and water. Draining it carefully under Kuro's supervision, he looked at the other man with suspicion when he got the next bit of instruction. "So, wait. I'm supposed to put in enough water and what?"

"Make sure the rice is level, then put your index finger into the pot until the tip touches the rice. The water should come up to the first-joint line. If there's too much, pour some out." Kuro chuckled, blending cream and yogurt together while minced shallots and chopped sweet onions were cooking in a skillet on the stove. "Then put the pot back into the rice cooker, put the lid on, and push the button down."

"How do you know it's the same amount of water for everyone? People's fingers are different." The water seemed to be tricky, and he had to add a little bit more after he'd poured too much out.

"Trust me. People have been doing that for centuries. Or at least however long rice cookers have been around." Kuro set the cream-yogurt aside, then began to add butter and spices to the pan. The fragrant hit of spices made Trey's mouth water, and he almost forgot to push down the button on the cooker. "This has got to simmer for about twenty minutes after I have everything together, so rice will be done at about the same time. Then we can eat."

"What do you want to do while we wait?" Trey's hands were suddenly clammy, and he wiped them on his jeans, aware of the heat coming off of Kuro's body as he moved around the kitchen, brushing past Trey to get something in a cabinet. "I don't know if I can look through any more of those reports. There's just too much... death."

"I'm sure I can find something to take your mind off of that," Kuro murmured, squeezing past Trey again. The stretch of Kuro's T-shirt across his back and shoulders did something funny to Trey's stomach, but watching the play of muscles beneath the pulled cotton warmed the kernel of coldness in the center of his chest. "Why don't you grab a couple of sodas from the drink fridge and we can go kick back on the couch while this cooks?"

"There's beer in there too." Trey studied the refrigerator's contents, a bit overwhelmed at the selection. "You should have one if you want. Don't *not* drink it because I'm here."

"See, I don't agree." Kuro gave the pan one last stir, then covered it. "I plan on kissing you at some point, and the last thing I want you to taste on me is alcohol. May not be today. May not be for a while, but I'm not going to do that to you. Even though right now I can tell you really want to take a drink. So you got a couch, a very needy cat, and me to keep you company while you power through that. And if you're very lucky, you might even get dinner out of it. Providing you didn't fuck up the rice."

Sixteen

"TELL ME about why Tatiana calls you Blackie and why you call her Boom Boom." Trey scraped the last of the chicken makhani and rice onto his spoon, gathering up as much of the sauce as he could. "Or do you have to kill me if you tell me?"

It was probably a mistake to stay with Kuro. Trey was dealing with the grief of losing Sera, the fear of someone trying to kill him, and balancing his attraction to the tall, dark, and handsome man sitting next to him. He was probably looking at Kuro through rose-colored glasses because Trey had to pick hard to find faults. The man was damn sexy, all lean muscle and broad shoulders with a careless mane of black hair and startling blue-flecked green eyes... all of which seemed designed to hit Trey's buttons.

He'd lusted after Kuro for a long time, but the ramen shop counter kept them apart, giving Trey space to fantasize without truly knowing the man. Up close, Kuro was devastating, a balm to his rattled nerves despite being a little bossy.

Okay, a lot bossy, but Trey understood why. He was in over his head and Kuro knew his way around dangerous situations. After everything died down, he didn't know where they were going to be or if Kuro would fade back into the background, leaving Trey alone. While promises were made, Trey's experiences told him they were also often broken. He'd shattered quite a few of them himself, so he was torn between exploring the fascinating man life threw in his path and keeping his hands to himself, leaving him to nurse the grief and emptiness inside of him.

But Trey was... hurting, and Kuro made him feel a hell of a lot better.

"My full name is Kurotsuki." Yuki the cat hopped over the back of the couch to sniff at Kuro's hair. He reached back to scratch between her ears, starting her rumbling purr. She'd eaten the piece of chicken he'd held back for her, letting Trey feed her bit by bit until her belly bulged, but now it looked like she was back for more. "Kuro means black or dark. So a few people who were on the other side of the fence started calling me Blackie and it stuck in some places."

"So how did Boom Boom happen?" Trey lifted his arm, turning sideways to face Kuro as Yuki began to roam down the length of the couch. "Because for as long as I've known her, she's been very cold and judgmental, but as soon as she spotted you, it was like fireworks."

"Tatiana can blow up anything. She's a master at it. There is a technique to explosives. Anyone can devastate an area with a large payload, but it takes someone who knows what they're doing to contain the damage," Kuro replied. "She disappeared about seven months before I rolled out, but she was working less and less over the years. I'm surprised to see her here but not shocked she landed on her feet. If she's out and isn't dragging any baggage, then good for her. I'd just watch your back, because you never know when someone like her is going to slide back in."

"She seemed alarmed to see you." Trey thought back to that night when his belly was full of good food and then suddenly filled with terror. "She called you an assassin. Said you killed her brother."

"The first is untrue, and her brother deserved killing," Kuro countered thoughtfully, his fingers finding the tip of Trey's ear beneath his hair, skimming down its curve. "And I wasn't in as deep cover as she was, but it wasn't like what I did for a living was broadcasted across the news. Not until the end, then a lot of well-placed bullets and a wall of photographers pushed me out. I can't tell you a lot, but I can reassure you I was never sent specifically to murder someone. Have I killed people? Yeah. I just did last week. But never murder. No one's ever asked me to do that, and I never will."

"Would you ever go back if they let you?"

"Oh fuck no." Kuro shook his head, chuckling. "I'm kind of scarred up. Day-to-day stuff, not a problem unless I overdo it, but pushing the limits would probably get me killed. Besides, I'm getting too old for that kind of work. Jumping out of planes and stealth missions are best left to people young and stupid enough not to realize Death's tapping them on the shoulder."

Kuro's fingers stilled, withdrawing from Trey's hair. He smoothed out the strands, then let his hand drop away, and Trey felt its loss deeper than he should have. He'd wanted to lean into the man's hand, anchoring himself against Kuro's solidness. He didn't know how to tell him how much he needed to be touched or how confused he was by Kuro's tenderness.

His thoughts were as muddled as his heart. Trey didn't know if he was pushing himself closer to Kuro because he'd lost Sera or was building on his already growing attraction toward someone who liked him for who he was and not what he could do for them.

"I don't want to take advantage of you," Kuro murmured, leaning his shoulder against the couch, facing Trey. "You're in a bad place right now, and I've never really dated. Life just never had room for it, and it's not like I don't want you—because I do—it's just that I don't want you to feel like I'm stepping into... I don't even know what I'm saying here. I'm torn between wanting to take you to bed and make you forget everything that's happened to you over the last couple of weeks and sleeping out here on the couch because you probably need some space, some breathing room to help you sort things out."

"Are you saying you don't trust yourself with me?" Trey tried to tease, but Kuro's expression turned somber.

"I never want you to feel like you can't be safe with me," he said. "I will never force myself on you. I'll never take from you. If ever you decide to be with me, it's because that's where you want to be."

"What if that's where I want to be tonight? And maybe tomorrow?" He pulled his legs up and sat with them crossed, facing Kuro. Every acting coach had schooled him about body language, about how sitting cross-legged or with his arms over his chest would put up a barrier between two people, signaling there was a wall, but it was a comfortable way to sit, and Trey placed one hand on Kuro's upper arm, running his palm over the bulge of muscle beneath Kuro's sleeve. "I got Sera killed—"

"That is not true," Kuro interrupted. "Between the two of us, if anyone can decide who's responsible for someone's death, it's me. I've had a lot more experience in that. You were there, but you didn't get her killed. You didn't order those guys to pull those triggers, and you didn't drive them onto your property. Whoever arranged that to happen, *that's* the person we're trying to find. Not you. Them."

"I *feel* responsible," Trey protested lightly, distracted by Kuro's thumb making circles on his left knee. "I miss her. I almost texted her to tell her about what you were making me for dinner because she'd be so jealous. And I feel really broken inside because I don't just want you, I *need* you. If anyone's taking advantage, it's me. Until you held me last night…. God, I can't tell you the last time somebody touched me. Not like that. Not like you. I felt like you *wanted* to hold me. And it felt so damned good. Can you blame me for wanting more?"

THEY WERE probably making a mistake, but Trey didn't care. He threw off his worries much quicker than he shed his clothes. Regrets were more than likely to make an appearance at breakfast the next day, a large bowl of sour next to his coffee, but tonight, Trey was going to live in the now.

Mostly because tomorrow might be his last with the way things were looking, and if he was going to die, it would be with a smile on his face and knowing he'd given someone at least a little bit of pleasure before he went. The fact that he liked Kuro went a long way into knowing he'd made the right decision.

It was hard to get undressed. Not because he didn't want Kuro. Far from it. No, the man was a damned distraction, and Trey itched to get his hands on him. He'd peeled off his borrowed T-shirt, tossing it on the bed. Then his attention wandered, captured by the sight of Kuro tugging his shirt out of the waistband of his jeans. The lights in the bedroom were dimmed, but K-Town's flashing, multicolored neon chaos pushed its way in, pouring dribbles of magenta and blue in through the exposed windows, their heavy blackout curtains held by wrought iron hooks.

His sexual past was… volatile, and he'd been with some of the most beautiful men the world had to offer, but Kuro Jenkins was in a league of his own.

Trey embraced the moment he lost control of his desire. His fingers were on his jeans' zipper when Kuro pulled his T-shirt up, snagging its opening on his chin, and for a brief mouthwatering second, he stood silhouetted against the windows framing the deepening night outside and the aged milk-honey brick walls.

He'd taken up painting as a way to pass the time, and now Trey mourned his lack of talent. Or at least the kind of talent developed enough to capture the grace and power of Kuro's lean body. His torso wasn't perfect despite his honed muscles and golden skin. There were vicious scars along his ribs, long stretches of shiny, pale skin following the curve of his side. Puckered starbursts peppered one side of his chest and up over his shoulder joint, pulling at his skin as he moved. When the shirt finally pulled free, Trey was struck by the intensity in Kuro's face and the simmering heat in his hooded eyes.

"Told you," he murmured through the rush of white noise coming in off the street. "Not a very pretty sight."

"I think you're fucking gorgeous." Trey closed the distance between them, his jeans open but forgotten. "Way past pretty. Straight into... beautiful."

Sleeping around Hollywood and on set brought a lot of pretty into Trey's life, but Kuro looked... *real.*

It was a body that looked lived-in, young and supple but wearing more than a few miles. Even if he hadn't known about Kuro's life before the ramen shop, seeing his naked torso would've told Trey there were stories beneath that skin. He traced the twisted stars on Kuro's chest, his finger connecting them into a constellation only they could share. Trey didn't get very far before Kuro snagged his wrist, drawing Trey's hand up to his mouth, then kissing the palm of his hand.

"Are you sure?" Kuro's voice dropped deep, a slice of midnight velvet running over Trey's skin.

He shivered, stepping in closer to hook his fingers into Kuro's loosened waistband and tug the other man's jeans down until they rested on his hips. The deep V-cut of muscles below Kuro's abdomen begged to be kissed, as did the powerful indent of his asscheeks, flexing when Trey explored them, his hands cupping Kuro's taut rear end.

"Never been so sure in my life," Trey whispered back. "So you know, I don't want this to be just for today or tomorrow. And it's not because I'm grateful to you for saving my ass. It's not because you make me feel safe. It's because I like being with you and I feel like I am someone again, even if it's someone I don't know really well."

"Then let me introduce you to a very brave, strong, compassionate, and pretty nice guy I know," Kuro said, dropping his head down to brush his lips against Trey's mouth. "He's had a kind of shitty life and has made a couple mistakes—"

"A fuck ton more than a couple," he snorted.

"Okay, a fuck ton of mistakes," Kuro murmured, then drank from Trey's mouth until he was breathless. "And he's a little lost right now, but I can't wait to see where he goes as he finds himself. Because I think I kind of like him a lot."

KURO'S MOUTH left Trey gasping for air. He was flat on his back, spread over Kuro's enormous bed and gripping the bedsheets in his clenched fists, begging for release yet wishing it would never arrive. His stomach was wet with beads of sweat, a drop growing heavy enough to trickle down his side, finding a depression between two of his ribs. His cock was cold now, pulled out of the warmth of Kuro's mouth and then frosted with puffs of air blown through Kuro's pressed-together lips. He clenched in his asscheeks, silently willing Kuro to stretch them out further with his fingers, but Trey couldn't find his voice, lost in the turbulent ocean of sensations Kuro dragged up out of his body.

He regretted nothing. And felt everything. Since the moment Kuro stripped him naked, then lowered him to the bed, Trey gave in to what his body needed—the touch of someone who cared about him. If there was one thing he knew for sure—other than he wanted to come so badly but couldn't because there was more to do, more to explore—he knew Kuro wanted him in his life.

That tidbit of knowledge humbled Trey more than Kuro telling him he deserved to be pleasured until he screamed.

He'd already screamed at least four or five times, and when they'd started, he nearly bit through his lip, scared somebody downstairs in the ramen shop would hear him. After fifteen minutes of Kuro's exploration of his body, Trey no longer gave a shit who heard him.

"Kuro…." Trey arched, feeling the warmth of Kuro's lips near his shaft. "I need you, man. Like really bad."

It wasn't poetry. He couldn't sing an aria proclaiming the glory of Kuro's existence, and he wasn't able to write a sonnet in his lover's honor. Trey could only plead and moan, wishing he had words to explain how on the edge he felt. It was more than Kuro touching him. He'd taken his own sweet time going over Kuro's body, leaving more than his share of purpling bites down Kuro's spine, and the back of his throat ached, stretched out from him pressing the head of Kuro's cock into the depths of his mouth, taking it in as far as he could and a little bit beyond.

Trey had the taste of Kuro on his tongue, a salty, bitter sweetness with a hint of spice and a lot of promise.

And he wanted more.

Until only moments ago, he didn't know how erotic it was to have a lover's teeth scrape gently across his taint or run fingernails up and down the inside of his thighs. Kuro awakened his body, pulling him out of the numb malaise he'd been living in. Reaching for Kuro, he tugged at the man's arms, urging him up.

"Busy down here." Kuro shook his head, licking around the base of Trey's shaft. He shifted the angle of his fingers, his incredibly long stretch brushing up against the too-sensitive spot nestled in Trey's body. "Unless you want me to stop doing this."

"I'd rather you be doing that with something else," Trey admitted. His voice was a little rough and he couldn't seem to get his tongue to work properly, but Kuro definitely understood him. There was another brush against his core. Then Kuro slid his fingers free, leaving Trey empty and aching. "God, I am not going to last long."

"We've got all night." Kuro got up onto his knees, then stretched across the bed, grabbing the lube and condoms they'd left by the pillows. "Of course, I'm never going to be able to go buy anything from that corner store anymore, because nothing is as embarrassing as putting a box of condoms and a small tube of lubricant on the counter in front of an eighty-five-year-old Korean auntie who normally tells me to put on a sweater because it's cold outside."

"If you think about it, it's sort of like another kind of sweater," Trey teased, laughing when Kuro growled at him. "Come on, or do you need me to open that up for you? Because they kind of remind me of those flavor packets you get in instant ramen, and I know you don't have any experience opening those, whereas I'm a master."

"Who the hell says whereas?" Kuro stopped trying to open the condom's foil pouch, looking down at Trey with intense curiosity. "I don't think I've ever said that in my life."

"I was raised on television show sets and lawyers," he reminded him. "I'm practically fluent in Latin and doublespeak at this point."

"Well, let's see if I can make you lose your mind and a few of those fifty-cent words you keep throwing around." Kuro slapped the empty foil wrapper onto Trey's stomach. Resting on his knees between Trey's spread thighs, he slid his hands beneath Trey's knees, slowly pulling his legs up until his shins lay on Kuro's hips. "Here. Take care of this for me. It's been a long time. I've got to figure out how the bubble gum I got from that works."

Kuro must have worked everything out, because a moment after Trey tossed the condom wrapper onto the nightstand next to the bed, he felt the push of Kuro's cockhead against his rim. The lubricant dribbled down his crack was warm, but the gentle glide of Kuro's dickhead brought a welcome burn.

Trey gasped when Kuro slid into him, the slow push dragging along his tender rim. Then in half a breath, they were fitted against each other, Kuro's arms sliding around Trey's shoulders, his weight balanced on his knees while Trey let out a small groan, adjusting to the press of Kuro's cock deep in his body.

"Any time it's too much," Kuro murmured, his lips ghosting over Trey's throat, "tell me—"

"Like I'm ever going to let you go," Trey said, biting at Kuro's earlobe. "Jesus, I can feel you up in my throat."

He held on, digging his fingers into Kuro's arms, and pushed his shoulders into the pile of pillows at his back, bracing himself against Kuro's long, hard thrusts. They found their pace after a few rolls of their hips, Kuro laughing in silky chuckles when Trey nearly pulled off of him when they couldn't find a beat. Sliding a hand beneath the small of Trey's back, Kuro guided him into a slow canter, their bodies moving in sync.

Trey lost the world. It slid away from him in a fall of stars and sounds, drowned out by his own heaving pants and Kuro's deep, low purrs. Los Angeles fell away. The busy street outside of the open windows faded into a muted hush, a whisper of dragonfly wings on a steady wind. Nothing mattered outside of their bodies rocking against each other, the slap of damp skin and the occasional murmured cry when Kuro shifted and Trey broke through his control, riding the shot of sparks curling up from his core.

Kuro's fingers were in his hair and his mouth on Trey's lips when a lightning ember began to flow up from Trey's balls to settle into his stomach, his cock beginning to tighten in its skin. He was afraid to touch himself, already feeling the tingle of prickles at the head of his shaft and the sticky wet of a drop of cum spreading over his belly. His cock was trapped between their bodies, their motions bringing Kuro's hips and abdomen grinding down on Trey's length.

Another roll and Trey couldn't stop himself from arching his back, desperate not to lose the sensation of Kuro's weight against his cock.

Sharp teeth on his throat sliced through his hold on his own release and Trey fumbled to find his burgeoning length, but Kuro was there first, those damnable, talented long fingers closing on him and stroking up in time to Kuro's thrusts.

The tickle of Kuro's hair on his chest was enough to jerk Trey back to reality and focus on the man giving him pleasure. Squeezing down on Kuro's plunging shaft drew a throaty growl out of Kuro's parted lips and he rose up onto his knees, riding Trey's writhing body while pulling on his erection. He drove deep, alternating his angles until Trey could no longer see straight. It was too much, too soon, and the sparks burst free, crackling through Trey's entire body, a fierce storm breaking loose of his control.

He came, clenching his teeth hard enough to make his head ring, but Trey couldn't—wouldn't—let go of Kuro. He dug in, working his hips up to meet Kuro's now erratic rhythm. He found a length of throat to lick, then a bit of collarbone to chew on while Kuro stiffened, his body shaking as he poured out his release into Trey's heat.

The reverberations didn't stop. Trey felt no desire to crawl out from under Kuro's weight and take a shower or a hit off of powder scraped across a mirror. The night crept back into the room, tiptoeing softly around the neon flashes, the burst of a car engine gaining speed and the mix of chatter punched up with gleeful laughter when a crowd of people passed by them on the sidewalk three stories below.

Trey didn't know what to do with the peace beating feebly inside of him. He was almost afraid of the silence, afraid of the lack of pain. He'd carried so much weight and anguish for so long, the freedom of his spirit was too light, too brilliant for him to embrace it as his own. He was so free of his burdens, a strong wind could have picked him up, plucking him from the bed and carrying him into the night sky without him noticing.

But he didn't want to leave. Kuro was wrapped around him, all long legs and arms, breathing softly into Trey's ear. They lay side by side in an awkward half-spooning position much too comfortable for Trey to break. He was sticky and damp from sweat, aching in places he hadn't for years and sensitive to the touch in others. Kuro's fingers were roaming over Trey's body, stroking at tender skin throbbing from a bite, then delicately running a fingernail across Trey's nipple, bringing up another ache Trey could get used to.

"Can I just lie here forever?" Trey mumbled, not caring if Kuro heard the truth in his words or would dismiss them as sex-drugged rambling. "You make it so it doesn't hurt when I breathe. I can't remember—"

"You don't have to remember," Kuro said, closing his mouth over Trey's. The kiss was nearly as intimate as the sex they'd shared, an exchange of body and soul deepened by the emotion behind it. When Kuro pulled back, Trey sucked in as much air as he could, hating that he had to breathe but relieved at the touch of Kuro's lips on his. "I'm not asking you to forget where you've been, but look forward to where you're going to go. And most of all, let me celebrate where you are."

Seventeen

KURO'S FIRST sip of coffee in the morning was always a religious experience.

He'd always enjoyed food. Even the basest of junk foods held a certain fascination. But coffee was one of his true loves. In a pinch, the sour, bitter, oily brew found at a corner convenience store would do, but if he had a choice, he sought out medium-dark roasts with a chocolaty undertone and a caramel finish. He had his favorites, a Ka'u-grown, family-owned coffee packaged in a gold-foiled bag with a picture of the owners' grandchildren on it, as well as a commercially produced blend named after another coffee lover, a former Army officer. There were others in his curated collection, but those were his two favorites, the ones he reached for when life was going fantastically well or horribly bad.

Waking up next to Trey started the day off as the former.

Watching Holly come up the stairs from his formerly locked front door turned his day to the latter.

The coffee, however, remained as delicious as it had been at the first sip, and he took a third simply to piss Holly off and make her wait for his attention.

"Most people knock," Kuro said above the rim of his coffee cup. "Some even call ahead."

Yuki met her at the top of the steps, sniffing at the toes of her boots. Holly bent over, scratching at the cat's head, finding the spot between her ears that made Yuki drool. The woman was dressed for a murder or to seduce, black leather pants with ebony riding boots paired with a white T-shirt and a bloodred leather jacket. No one in their right mind would believe she was up to any good, and Kuro knew her too well to assume she was there for his continued well-being. Still, it was good to see her outside of the stone walls she'd been hiding behind, even if she'd probably come to stick a knife in his back.

It was too much to hope that she'd come to remove one.

"I locked the door behind me." She matched Yuki's purr, scooping the cat up and cradling her against her chest. Yuki rubbed her cheek against Holly's shoulder, leaving a glistening trail of spit on the glossy leather. "And I do so adore your cat."

"Evil often recognizes other evil," Kuro replied, saluting her with his cup. "Do you want some? Or would you rather I brew you some tea?"

"Coffee is good. I can trust what you've made is decent, unlike some people I know." Holly slowly crossed the floor, her boot heels beating a sharp tattoo on the wood.

Gracefully lowering herself onto the couch, she twisted to face Kuro, turning her blind eye away from him. The seam of her prosthetic limb left an embossed line in her snug pants, breaking the fabric's sleek fit, but if he hadn't known she'd lost that part of her leg, he wouldn't have noticed anything from her gait. She was a master at hiding her weaknesses, and exploiting them in others. Keeping silent would be the smartest course of action, but Kuro also couldn't resist poking holes in Holly's rigid dignity.

"I don't have belladonna. Will creamer do?" Kuro added two spoonfuls of sugar to the coffee he'd poured into a dragon-shaped mug he'd gotten from a farmers' market in Half Moon Bay. He took her derisive snort as a yes and lightened the brew to the color of his skin. "Did you ever think maybe I had company?"

She waited until he joined her on the couch before answering, taking the cup from him. "I *know* you have company. I keep track of a lot of things in the city, including you."

"I don't work for you anymore," he reminded her. "In case you forgot."

"That could change. I wish you hadn't come to Los Angeles. Having you so close by makes me miss the game." She shifted Yuki to her lap, stroking the cat's flanks. "I was especially concerned when I heard you circled your way around the front door of a certain crime lord's establishment. It made me realize how out of touch I was with what is happening in your life."

"Once again, I don't work for you." He valued her friendship and the mentoring she'd given him along the way, but Holly always had an eye for what was going on behind the scene, and retirement didn't seem to be sticking. He knew the calculating gleam in her eye, having become entangled in more than one mission because she had to pull a certain string or influence a particular outcome. "Pops has his finger on the city's pulse and, sad to say, a lot of connections you don't have. Someone is trying to kill Trey. They've already killed his best friend, a godfather he didn't know, and that man's twin brother."

"I can help you," she offered with a smile Kuro trusted as much as he believed Yuki would leave a slab of raw salmon untouched if it was lying on his kitchen counter. "And doesn't he have a sister who is a police officer? Shouldn't the LAPD be working on this?"

"You and I both know the cops are only going to operate within a certain set of rules," he murmured as Yuki slid off of Holly's lap and swam across the couch to him. "For example, if they find out who is doing this—who is behind this—they will arrest them and we will have to wait for justice. I, on the other hand, have a more permanent, immediate solution."

She studied him, the tilt of her chin forcing her face up to grab at the morning light coming through the windows. "You've never killed for me."

"I worked for you. If you needed someone dead, you'd do it yourself," he pointed out. "Right now, my good nature is being tested, and I'm not so sure I would deal with whoever is terrorizing him in a very humane manner."

He blinked, delving into the depths of his feelings toward Trey. Broken and humbled, Trey still possessed a ferocity and will he admired, taking in the condemnation of his family while nursing his past wounds. He wanted to see more of Trey's smiles, hear him laugh, and most of all, be there when Trey decided he'd had enough of his family's demeaning abuse and struck out to find his own way. Last night had been a gift, a sliver of serenity they'd shared under warm blankets and laughter. Despite the chaos surrounding them now, Kuro wanted more of that peacefulness, days and even years more than the few hours he'd gathered up around him last night.

"Is he worth it? Because if you commit murder, I won't be able to protect you," Holly said flatly. "There's only so much influence I have, and I'm not sure you're worth me calling in any more favors."

"I don't plan on killing anyone. Not yet anyway, but if I'm in a situation like the one they put Trey in the other day, I'm not going to say no to bloodshed." Kuro tsked. "Is that why you came here? To tell me you're pissed off at me?"

"I'm not angry at you, darling," she replied in a husky drawl. "I'm disappointed in you. I know how much it cost you to go to that man and—"

"If I owe someone something, you would rather it be you?"

"You are not wrong." She smiled. "But mostly, it showed me how lackadaisical I've become. You didn't feel as if you could come to me. That I wouldn't be able to find what you need. I didn't realize how much that would sting. How much a part of my presence in that sphere is so closely aligned with my identity."

"Pops is local. This is where you live but not where you have ears on the street." Kuro moved his cup away from his curious cat when Yuki started sniffing at his coffee. "I needed to get more information than what the cops would share with me. I don't want to go into this thing blind, and the LAPD has this rule about confidentiality. So I reached out to see what I would find."

"To a coxcomb of a young man named Rooster," Holly said, chuckling when Kuro shook his head. "If I put my mind to it, I can find out anything. And I've decided I'm bored. As much as I love the puppies and the gardens, I'm not... challenged. I'm becoming a museum piece, something people come to admire and study for their research. That's going to change. I need to stretch back out, darling, so I've decided to dabble a little bit. For instance, your little friend Rooster? He works for me now. Exclusively."

"Pops is not going to like you picking off his resources, Holly." It was a very careful line he had to walk, leaving himself open to Holly's friendship because he cared about her but not so available she would drag him into whatever machinations tickled her fancy. "And what are you planning on doing with all of this?"

"For one, keep myself entertained," Holly replied, leaning over to pat him on his knee. "Secondly, I meant what I said about not liking you having to reach out to him. You've come so far from there. There is no reason for you to go back, not when I can give you what you need with a little effort on my part."

"I love you. You know I do, but you and I both know your little efforts cost sometimes way too much," Kuro pointed out. "I want to put this matter with Trey to bed and go back to making ramen. I'm too old and damaged to be jumping out of moving cars and having gunfights. There's other things I'd rather be doing, and I've already put in my time."

"I'm not asking you to do jobs, but I would like to have you on board as a consultant," she said.

"Aoki is off limits," Kuro warned her. "I don't want you getting him killed."

"Agreed." Holly held her hand out. "Can we shake on this?"

"I haven't agreed to anything." He took her hand, kissing her fingers, then letting them go. "You didn't just come here to tell me you were going to breach your retirement. What's going on?"

"I'll admit I got very interested when I got ahold of your informant and he shared with me the information he'd gathered for you." Holly waved off Kuro's irritated hiss. "You are a fool if you think he didn't have a copy made of the data he gave you."

"No. I would expect that, but I don't know why you felt like you needed to dig through it." Kuro glanced back toward the bedroom door, keeping his voice low to let Trey sleep. "From what I gathered, Robert Mathers has been dead for a very long time. The body was thawed out and refrozen several times, so that tells me it was either stored very improperly or—"

"Someone needed fingerprints or DNA over the years," she interjected. "Since he and David weren't identical twins, their prints wouldn't match."

"I'm going to guess the allegedly big blowout argument with David was a cover for Robert's murder. There was a security report lodged about David beating Robert rather badly, requiring facial surgery." Kuro dug through his memory, recalling the coroner's initial findings. "Things started looking suspicious when the frostbitten body looked like it had Robert's fingerprints but the other showed evidence of the plastic surgery. That's when it all started to unravel."

"So it's safe to say David has been living as Robert for years now, but we still do not know who killed David." Holly tapped at the rim of her cup. "There has to be another person in this mix. Someone who helped David slide into Robert's life and who set their hell hounds after Trey because he saw Robert's body as it was being moved."

"They probably assumed he knew who Robert was because his father was Robert's friend."

"Couldn't be that good of a friend if he hadn't noticed David stepped in." Holly tilted her head, her lips turned up into a ghost of a smile. "But I think Harrington Bishop the Second's relationship with

Robert Mathers was all for show. Casual and only frequent enough to be remarked upon. At that level of wealth, one has to maintain appearances, solidify connections whenever you can."

"What makes you think Mathers and Trey's father weren't really friends?" Kuro cocked his head. "Robert left Trey a fairly hefty inheritance, but Trey never saw him. What else would be the reason he would do that unless he was honoring his role as Bishop's friend and Trey's godfather?"

"Because Robert Mathers was Trey Bishop's true biological father." Holly purred with satisfaction when Kuro sucked in his breath in shock. "And there is a very funny little clause in Robert's will that states if he should have any offspring, legitimate or otherwise, all terms of his will become void and that child or children inherit the whole lot. We are talking over five hundred million dollars, darling. More than enough incentive to make sure Trey Bishop doesn't live another day."

"So LET me get this straight." Kimber rubbed at her temple, her hand on her hip, pushing her jacket back and revealing the gun at her side. "You think Dad isn't your father and Robert Mathers is?"

"Um, yeah, according to... people," Trey replied, coming out of the kitchen with a mug of black tea for his sister. "Maybe. Allegedly. I don't know. Kuro, help me out here."

"Yes, Mr. Jenkins, help my brother out here," she snapped, taking the steaming cup. "Because I was there when the whole *this isn't my baby* changed into the second coming of Christ. The DNA tests came back as proof Dad was Trey's father. I was *there* when they opened the envelope. My father celebrated like he'd found Bigfoot, the lost gold of the Incas, and discovered time travel, when a few seconds before, he was ready to toss the baby out with the bathwater along with the whore who'd brought it into the house. His words. Not mine."

From his vantage point, perched on the couch's wide arm, Kuro debated his options. It was his experience people didn't like outsiders to meddle in family affairs. That was pretty much a worldwide philosophy, but he knew Trey well enough to know he was hurt and angry when his jaw tightened at Kimber's careless statement. He waited a beat, listening for Trey's objection, then realized Trey probably no longer heard the toxic poison in his sister's words. Trey said nothing, his reaction quickly buried beneath a stony mask.

"I'll thank you to keep that kind of shit to yourself when you're in my house." Kuro slid into the conversation, meeting Kimber's stare as she turned around to face him. "I'm talking about the whole Trey is a cuckoo in the nest crap and then the dig about him being your dad's favorite. It's bad enough your family trots out that story in public, but it seems to me you blame Trey for how your father behaves. You're punishing him for things outside of his control. If you've got a problem with your father, take it up with him, but you shouldn't beat up on Trey because you've got daddy issues."

"I did fuck up a lot," Trey interjected, probably trying to keep the peace, but Kuro wasn't going to be diverted. "She's not wrong on that. I've got a lot of crow to eat. Like Thor drinking from Utgaroa-Loki's horn levels of crow to eat."

"First, I get that. And you're trying to fix things. Or at least trying to fix yourself," he said, holding Kimber's attention. "I wasn't there for it. I don't know what you all went through, but I haven't been around for very long and I'm already sick of all of you holding him over the coals. I can't demand anything from him. I don't have the right or the inclination to tell him not to see his family, but I can demand you don't treat him like shit while in my house. If you can't agree to that, I can show you where the door is."

"You *don't* have any fucking right." Kimber Bishop went stiff and her jaw clenched, much like Trey's did a few seconds before. Turning away from Kuro, her glare shifted to her brother. "What you've done to this family—"

"I'm not saying he hasn't done shit to your family, but you shovel a lot of it right back," Kuro interrupted, crossing his arms over his chest. Trey was only a few inches away, and he wanted to reach out, to touch him and reassure Trey, but Kimber would take that as a sign of weakness, probably doubling down on her brother. Maybe. Kuro didn't know, but he didn't want to take that chance. "You can do whatever you want outside my front door, but not in here. Now, do you want to get past all of this baggage you keep flinging at him and we talk about what we've learned, or does this conversation have to happen elsewhere?"

"Oh please don't," a woman's voice called out from the stairwell, partially broken from her hard breathing. "I just climbed these damned steps. I would've called ahead, but no one is picking up their phone, and I had to get the address from the Black Widow."

"Don't call her that," Kimber growled. "We talked about that."

"If the spandex fits," the woman grumbled, stepping into the loft. "You couldn't find a room on the ground floor? Do you know how hard it is to climb stairs in three-inch stilettos?"

"The Black Widow?" Kuro muttered at Trey, wondering why Aoki was letting everyone and his mother upstairs. "And who's that?"

"I spout off about Norse mythology and you don't even blink, but drop something about pop culture and you draw a blank?" Trey whispered back. "Tatiana. That's the Black Widow."

"Boom Boom?" He frowned. "She's never been married."

"Scooter and Maggie call her that and Natasha. Like Moose and Squirrel?" Trey shook his head when Kuro gave him a perplexed look. "It's a joke, but I don't think they realize how accurate it is. You know, female Russian spies who want to take over the world? Where did you grow up? Under a rock?"

"It just took me a moment." The woman was headed straight for them, and Kuro's hand itched, his mind instinctively longing for a weapon. He stood up, about to block her path when Trey's hand touched the small of his back.

"This is my sister Scooter." Trey allowed himself to be dragged into a hug, squeaking near the end of it. He was visibly uncomfortable, squirming around in his sister's embrace much like Yuki oozed when it was time to cut her nails. "Scooter, let go. Can't breathe."

"Let me look at you. It's been forever and a day since you've been to the house," the woman said, releasing Trey. "You're too skinny."

Scooter Bishop was practically a clone of her older sister, with a burnished-gold skin that didn't come from sitting in the sun. Her hips and chest were a little fuller than Kimber's, but her lush curves did nothing to soften her intimidating presence. Her legs were long and muscular, the hem of her gray tweed pencil skirt exposing most of her calves, and the tucked-in white button-up shirt was cinched tight with a broad red leather belt. Her hair was longer than Kimber's, frosted to a light gold, but she'd applied her makeup with a skillful hand, playing up her enormous gray eyes while leaving her skin dewy. There were more laugh lines around her mouth, but Kuro wasn't fooled. She may have projected a warmer image than her older sister, Kimber, but he knew Scooter Bishop was a cutthroat, ruthless businesswoman who'd cut her teeth on her father's business when she was just a teenager.

The long, assessing look she gave him solidified Kuro's belief she was a wolf wrapped up in a fuzzy sheepskin, her warm nature meant to blend her in with the flock.

"Why are you here?" Trey asked, edging away from his sister until his shoulder touched Kuro's. "I thought you were in Europe."

"I was. I came back when I heard about Sera." Scooter reached for Trey but let her hand drop onto his shoulder rather than embrace him again. The lines Kuro noticed before grew shadows as they deepened into creases. Scooter was either truly worried or Trey wasn't the only actor in the family. "I know I haven't been as present as I should be—"

"You've got your own family to worry about," Kimber ground out. "And why *are* you here? What do you hope to accomplish? This is an active investigation—"

"Which involves our baby brother," she shot back.

"You walked away from him before," their older sister replied. "We all did. Remember? No more coddling him—"

"This isn't coddling, and we agreed we wouldn't enable his addictions, not toss him to the wolves. And right now, Kimber, there's a shit-ton of wolves." Scooter took a step toward Kimber, squaring her shoulders. "That's something that hit me when Dad called to tell me what was going on over here. We're all very good about keeping our distance because it's easy, but right now, when he's in the middle of something like this, that's when we should be propping him up."

"Bullshit," Kimber snorted. "What do you *really* want? Dad offer you a promotion if you show your solidarity? Where's Margaret? Still in Asia, or is she flying in on her own broomstick to grab at the ruby slippers too?"

"You know what your problem is, Kimber? You never move forward. Once someone does something wrong, you cut them out like they're cancer instead of trying to deal with things like an adult," Scooter scoffed. "No wonder Dad doesn't want you to be a part of the company."

"Okay, I do not believe *any* of this shit." Trey shouted them down, taking a deep breath when both his sisters glanced at him. "Look, I'm not going to pretend we've ever been close, but right now, the only thing I need is for someone to find out who's trying to kill me. Scooter, I don't think you can help with that. Fuck, I'm not sure *Kimber* can help with that, because the entire damned police force seems to think I brought this down on myself."

"Can we get back to what I walked in on? Who thinks Robert Mathers is Trey's father?" Scooter reached down to unhook a heel strap, stepping out of the shoe once it was loose. She did the other, balancing on her toes while keeping her eyes on Kimber. "They proved he's Dad's. Twice!"

"It's a rumor that was started years ago, and apparently Mathers—Robert—didn't believe the test," Trey replied. "Someone Kuro knows dug up the gossip and threw it into the ring as to why someone wants to kill me. Robert Mathers left a bit in his will about everything going to his offspring if he dies."

"So someone believes the rumors," Kimber mulled. "I would suspect David, but he's dead."

"Who else would have gotten a part of the estate?" Kuro asked. "Because they were moving Robert for a reason. They couldn't keep him much longer. Too much ice damage to his body. They would have been trying to dispose of him when Trey saw the body on the street."

"How do you know about the damage to his body?" Kimber tilted her chin up, narrowing her eyes.

"Can we just accept I do and work on what needs to be dealt with first?" He jerked his head toward Trey. "Let's get your brother out of someone's dead pool and then we can talk about boundaries. Especially since I'm hoping that once this whole thing blows over, I won't ever have to be a part of something like this again."

"How many times do you think I'm going to be framed for murder and put on a hit list?" Trey grumbled under his breath. "This is like living in a soap opera."

"Honey, with you, it's always one thing or another," Scooter piped up. "Not to be a downer, but if there's a fleck of mud on the road, you fall in it."

"Okay, fair enough, but this time isn't on me." Trey appeared ready to argue, then sighed. "Who inherits if I die? My beneficiaries or someone else? Wouldn't that be who we look at first?"

"Well, I have an answer for you about that. It's why I came over to begin with," Kimber said, stopping Scooter from interrupting by holding her hand up in her sister's face. "I got a call today from Mathers's lawyer.

Most of the estate that's not given directly to someone rolls into a trust—which we knew from what Gilder told Dad from the beginning—but it took the firm some time to separate out who got what amount. Mathers definitely had a thing for Dad, because Harry… Trey… isn't the only Bishop in Mathers's golden book. He left a big chunk of change to all of us, as well as a few others. Everything stays in the trust. It's doled out in percentages. Trey's just got the biggest share."

"So if he dies, the percentages shift?" Scooter whistled under her breath. "Well hell, that changes things. *A lot.*"

"Yep, because now, not only are the three of us targets for whoever is after Trey," Kimber drawled, shoving her hands into her jacket pockets, "we're also now all murder suspects."

Eighteen

TWO DAYS after Scooter descended on him, Trey was climbing the loft's walls.

"Look, it's not that I don't appreciate not being murdered," he said, measuring two cups of rice out, then dumping it into the pot. "It's just that... I want my life back."

"Your life's exactly what we're trying to save here. Shouldn't be much longer," Kuro replied, not looking up from the onion he was turning into a pile of minced white squares with a knife too sharp for Trey to even think about holding, much less use. There was a pause. Then Kuro shrugged. "I think."

Measuring the water out, Trey snuck a peek at Kuro's index finger, silently guessing its length. Kuro assured him the water thing was valid and the rice had turned out okay the first time he'd done it, but Trey still had his doubts. Staring down into the milky water, he did what he'd been doing since he'd first run into Kuro after spotting Mathers's body—all of his trust and faith with the man holding a weapon.

He put in enough water until it touched the first-joint line of his index finger, then set the rice to cook.

"On the majority of people, that joint is an inch long. So the water level tends to be pretty consistent. Let me get these onions going with some garlic first, then we can brown the meat." Kuro took a flat-edged scraper and skillfully slid the onion bits into the tall-sided skillet he had warming on the stove. At a loss of what to do, Trey took up his now customary position at the barstool on the opposite side of the island to watch. There was an elaborate smash-and-mince dance Kuro did with garlic cloves before they joined the onion in the now sizzling pan. "It'll take a little while for the flavors to blend, but the rice will stay warm, unless you want to eat it cold."

"I don't even know what you're making," Trey confessed.

"Chili. I like it over rice with shredded cheese, sour cream, and chopped raw onion," Kuro replied as he reached for a thin green pepper.

"I'm trying to remember if you ordered your ramen spicy or not. Most of the time you go with miso with kakuni. I can always leave it out and add some Chinese chili oil to mine."

"I don't order the spicy ramen because it doesn't come with kakuni. My life is always made better from braised pork belly. I don't mind hot, but I don't like it too hot. I want to taste the food." He leaned forward, resting his elbows on the counter. "I like the kimchi you guys have downstairs. It's like the right level of heat. The cabbage one, not the cucumber, because that's not really hot."

"Okay, one pepper it is." Kuro began to deseed the pepper, nodding at the skillet. "Can you reach that to stir it?"

"Like mix-stir or just push around? I don't cook. Well, what I do really well is heat up things." He took a flat wooden spoon off the counter and began to move the onions and garlic about. "Like this?"

"Perfect." The pepper seemed to need more concentration than the onions and garlic, because Kuro's eyes were fixed firmly on the chopping board. "I'm going to ask this because I don't know if you would bring it up, so I'm going to. Are you feeling too crowded? And I don't want you to feel like you're obligated to share a bed with me, even if it is just to sleep. I know the first couple of nights you were shaky, but if things have changed, I want you to tell me. The couch is comfortable. I've slept there more than a few times."

"You are the only part of the craziness making this whole piece-of-shit thing bearable. Well, you and Yuki," he murmured, smiling when the cat meowed from her spot on the windowsill at the sound of her name. Putting the spoon down, Trey shrugged. "I just feel like I'm in a prison or a really crappy rehab facility because I can't go outside. I miss stupid things like the blue cup I use for coffee in the morning. Then I remember Sera sometimes and I just want to cry."

"I don't want you to feel pressured."

"I don't feel pressured. I feel like you're the only thing holding me together, and that's a lot of shit to put on you," he confessed in a low whisper. "Maybe you should feel more like I've shoved myself into your life and now you're stuck with me and you don't know how to tell me to get out."

"I don't want you to go. I like having you here, and I really don't want to let you loose into the wild while someone's trying to take you out," Kuro said with a grin, adding the minced pepper to the sizzling pan. "And it's not like I haven't wondered how things would be with you every single time you've come in for a bowl of ramen. I just wasn't looking for any connections with anyone. I never thought I would, but I like it between us. It feels good. Easier than I thought it would be."

"Even with all of the car chases and gunfights?" He tried to keep a teasing tone in his words, but the truth refused to be boxed in by humor. "It's been a shitty couple of weeks for you."

"Are you kidding?" Kuro said, gesturing with the knife he'd used on the peppers. "In my old line of work, this is just a typical Tuesday."

Trey was trying to ignore the burn in his blood, the rushing need to be numbed to the point of senselessness or taken right to the edge of not caring. Sex with Kuro had been comfort, a need he still nursed in his belly, but the addiction was something else, a wicked pull he wasn't always strong enough to resist.

"Everything is kind of at a standstill," Kuro pointed out. "Kimber is having to look at everyone in your family as a suspect, and Mathers's lawyer says he's still working out the logistics of the will. I don't know anything about inheritance and how long it takes to settle those kinds of things, but from what everyone says, an estate of this size takes a while."

"I don't even want the money," he muttered, scrubbing his face with his hands. "I want to ask Dad about Mathers and why he thought I was his kid. Mom slipped off to Europe and she's not answering me, but that's normal. I keep leaving messages for Dad, but I'm getting the runaround. Tatiana says he's busy. I think he doesn't want to deal with this."

"Is there any validity to Kimber's suspicions about your other sisters?" Kuro added. "Margaret is Kimber's full sister, correct?"

"Yeah. Dad had three batches with three wives. Kimber and Margaret, then Scooter. I was a *very* big surprise." Trey leaned back a bit as Kuro began to debone what looked like a piece of meat he'd gotten off of a dinosaur. "Scooter's always been hot and cold, but Margaret and Kimber weren't too happy when I showed up. There's always a lot of tension, and I didn't help things by fucking up my life. I think Kimber tries because she's the oldest and she went her own way, so maybe there's a little guilt because she turned her back on Dad's business."

"Did he expect all of you to go work for him?" Kuro stopped slicing, his expression growing thoughtful. "I know that kind of pressure, but sometimes you have to walk away from it in order to be your own person."

"That's kind of what Kimber said. I don't know Margaret very well. She stays very far away from me, even when I was a kid. Do I think they would kill me? No, not really but I think if I showed up at the office tomorrow and told Dad I was ready to have a desk, they'd be the first ones to sharpen the knives." He chuckled. "Well, not Kimber. She's not driven by money, and her mom came into the marriage already rich and left it richer. Scooter's mom is kind of a hippie, but I think that's sort of an act. She's got this whole organic, natural beauty line business, and she's pretty ruthless."

"And your mom?"

"My mom is *still* the current wife, so she's pretty much got her cake and eats it too." He'd long given up expecting Joy Bishop to be maternal, and any hurt he felt now was buried beneath years of disappointment. After spending so much of his life trying to earn her love and respect, Trey knew his mother simply was incapable of giving it to anyone besides herself. "I've got a few cousins scattered around, but I don't know them. I wonder if David had any kids. Because if Robert and David inherited the business from their father, shouldn't it flow down to both brothers' families?"

"That's probably something Kimber's chasing down." The meat had now been turned into strips, Kuro gracefully manipulating the dark red flesh with sweeping cuts. "How about if I throw this all into a Crock-Pot and you and I go on a very long run?"

"I think that's what I need," Trey confessed, exhaling hard. "Just feeling really cooped up."

"I can tell. You keep rubbing at your arms, so I'm guessing you need to burn off more than just a little energy," Kuro said, looking up. "I want you to promise me something. I don't ever want you to feel like you should be ashamed of being an addict. You got coping mechanisms in place to help you deal with wanting drugs and alcohol. Those are good things to have, and if you need to do them, just tell me. I'm here to support you, even during the times when you're feeling a little on edge. Talk to me. Tell me. Okay?"

"I didn't even realize I was doing it," he sighed. "It's a bad habit I picked up. It's like I'm trying to scratch the itch in my blood. I don't like calling attention to who I was, and I guess I'm not used to sharing what's going on in my head anymore. Not since I had to attend group therapy."

"Well, it's a good sign for me to pick up on, because it says you need to work it off. And I'm always up for a good run." Kuro added the chunks of meat into the skillet. "Let me just throw this all together and go get a gun, then we can head out."

"Really? We're going to go running with a gun?" Trey scoffed. "Didn't they take yours? How many do you have?"

"A lot less since your sister keeps taking them away from me," Kuro shot back. "First, I'm not taking you out without being armed because someone is trying to kill you. And I'm going to have as many guns as I need because there is a whole lot of other stuff I still want to feed you, so I'm going to do whatever it takes to make sure you're here to make rice for me."

"WE ARE running in circles," Trey complained, panting a bit from the hard pace Kuro set. "Not exactly the kind of jogging experience I was looking for."

Before his sneakers hit the track, Trey thought he was in pretty good shape. Then Kuro began to run alongside of him and that perception was blown out of the water. He thought he would have to set a slower pace, knowing Kuro's hip was damaged and his body was scarred, but within a few minutes, Trey had to lengthen his stride to keep up.

To make matters worse, the bastard was wearing long cotton pants and wasn't even breathing hard.

The fitness center was one of the million sleek buildings in Los Angeles featuring rows of weight machines and other torture devices scattered about two floors of toned, hard bodies working off the croutons of their lunchtime salads. They'd been hustled in through a back door off of the parking structure, taken past a room full of women doing hot yoga, the windows steamed up like a sauna. The man who met them at the garage was heavily muscled, his body barely contained by a pair of Lycra pants and a T-shirt emblazoned with the gym's logo, and he paced around the freight elevator, glancing up at the numbers periodically while assuring them the running track on the second floor would be theirs for however long they needed it because it would be left closed off to the gym members until they were done.

It was a utilitarian space at its best, but obviously set up for hard-core training. The track itself was probably about a quarter-mile around, because the long run took up most of the second floor. In the center of the oval was an odd collection of square boxes and wide A-framed triangles with a few hurdles scattered in between. Trey thought it looked like a giant toddler dumped their building blocks into the middle of the room, some of the build-outs nearly tall enough to block out the opposite side of the track. Everything was painted a doldrum gray, but the track was a speckled black ribbon, hard enough to run on, but gave slightly beneath their feet.

"The walls aren't very inspiring. They could have at least put up a mural to make it interesting. And why is the stuff we're running on black? Is it supposed to be a road?" The track surface was a bit spongy despite resembling asphalt, and Trey had lost count of how many times they'd gone past the fire extinguisher by the service entrance, the one bright spot in the whole room. "I feel like we're running in the world's ugliest hamster wheel."

"Did you forget the part where someone's trying to kill you? And be nice to me or I'll run you through the course. See how inspired you feel after climbing those frames." Kuro veered a little, nudging Trey's shoulder. It was enough of a hit to throw Trey off his stride, but he quickly recovered. "There's nothing wrong with running in a gym. And since the guy who owns this place owes me a favor, it was easy enough to get him to shut this down for a couple of hours so we could run."

"So you're willing to inconvenience everyone else who wants to use this track during peak after-work hours so I can get a run in?"

"I would shoot anyone who wanted to use the track in the knee just so you can get a run in," Kuro responded. "And you always run this slow? It must take you forever to get someplace."

"Fuck off." Trey laughed through a stitch in his side. "I'm pretty sure now they took you up to some sort of secret laboratory and replaced all of your bones with some kind of super metal. That's why—"

He'd gotten too relaxed, felt too safe being around Kuro, because when the service door blew in, Trey froze, shocked by the sudden explosive boom of the solid metal door hitting the cinder block wall. It took him a second to realize someone was rushing through the opening, and it wasn't until Kuro shoved him off the track and behind one of the obstacle boxes that he heard a burst of gunfire.

"Stay down and don't get killed," Kuro ordered, coming up with the gun he'd strapped to his ankle before their run. "We are going to end this right here and now."

KURO HAD little hope of Trey listening to him. It'd been stupid for him to trust Dan's staff, but it'd been a risk Kuro had been willing to take. Actually, he had no choice to take, because Trey was beginning to fall off the edge of his control and he needed to get out of the loft, peeling away the frustration and anxiety bubbling beneath his skin. The big guy who'd led them into the track had been nervous, glancing around even while they were in the elevator. Kuro assumed it was because Dan had given explicit directions to his manager about the track's use, but now he realized it was because the muscle-bound idiot sold them out.

He didn't question Dan's loyalty. Kuro pulled that guy's ass out of the fire more times than he could count, and everyone in the community knew Holly would have Kuro's back. While he cultivated a levelheaded reputation, she was known to exact revenge for even the smallest of slights. Something like a familiar bald man breaching a secured room wielding a gun was definitely the kind of incident Holly would bleed someone over.

"I just want the kid!" the guy shouted as he aimed around one of the obstacle frames, blowing a corner off of the cube with a single shot. "I'll leave the door—"

"I'm not a fucking kid!" Trey yelled back from somewhere among the structures. "I'm twenty-eight!"

Kuro cursed under his breath, knowing the man would be able to find Trey's position after he yelled. Ducking, he scrambled through the course, using the more solid shapes to give himself some cover, but when he got to the spot where he thought Trey was, he found himself instead staring at a man he'd shot at before.

His hair was a little longer, grown out to a dark stubble, but his face with its memorable canted nose had been embedded in Kuro's mind. Of the two men that night, he'd been the one who Kuro tagged as a professional. That opinion didn't change in the split second they stood across one another, staring each other down. At first glance, the man's dark clothing could have passed for workout gear, if one didn't notice the ammo belt slung across his hips. Wearing a black tank top, he'd probably hoped to blend in with the gym's clients, his bare arms nearly as thick as those of the weightlifter who'd brought them upstairs, but the similarity ended there. His body came from years of rough work, his large-knuckled hands blown out from punching flesh. There was an ugliness to the twisting of his mouth, an arrogant smirk plastered over his broad face, growing malevolent as he widened his stance and raised his gun to shoot a hole through Kuro's chest.

That was the moment Trey came out from behind one of the A-frames and plowed his foot up between the man's legs.

Kuro was on the move before the man's knees hit the ground.

The Glock was a forceful weight in his hand when he brought it around, punching the man across the chin. The angle was wrong to hit the nerves along his jaw to knock him out, but Kuro's next hit did the trick. Trey dropped away, dodging back down into the obstacle course, disappearing between two cubes. The guy was stubborn, refusing to let go of his gun even as his eyes rolled back. When his shoulder hit the thick mat in the center of the track, he tried to bring his weapon up one more time, wildly aiming its muzzle toward Kuro's direction.

Kicking the gun out of the man's hand, Kuro followed through with another punch, rocking his opponent's head back into the padded floor. He hit hard enough the man's skull bounced, and a firm thump of bone connecting with the hard surface beneath reverberated through the air. There was blood on the man's face, a trickle coming down from his nose, but the smirk was gone, probably wiped away by the first ball-bashing hit he'd taken.

Digging his knee into the man's stomach, Kuro twisted a hand into his tank top, pulling the fabric together tight enough across the man's throat to make him struggle to breathe. Pushing his left thumb against the criminal's eyeball, Kuro gouged down, putting enough pressure to threaten but not enough to pop the soft orb beneath his pad.

"Who hired you?" Kuro growled. "Give me a name."

He couldn't believe his ears when the subdued man whispered who'd sent him, but the muttered name made everything suddenly fall into place. Another tap across the man's chin took him down into the black, and Kuro caught up, shaking his hand as he went to retrieve the now-unconscious man's weapon.

"Who sent him?" Trey asked, sliding out from between a pair of inflatable balance balls. "You know who it is?"

"I know who it is," Kuro responded, a chill settling down in his blood. "And now I know who to go after."

Nineteen

"DO YOU know how long it's been since I've been on a strike?" Tatiana tied off her braid, wrapping a tight elastic around its end. It wasn't difficult to hear the excitement in her voice, even as she spoke around a mouthful of the knitted beanie she'd clenched between her front teeth. "I mean, I'm not ungrateful for the old man. He keeps me busy enough, and a lot of people hate his guts, so I have to stay on my toes, but I haven't seen real action since I left the agency."

"That is not a ringing endorsement for me to drag you along on the run," Kuro replied, checking the ammo in his clip. He'd done a full rundown of his equipment in the apartment, but it never hurt to double-check, even in the close confines of the Challenger's front seat. "Don't make me second-guess this."

Predictably, she rolled her eyes, muttering out the side of her mouth, "*Please*. Who else would you ask to go on this? Aoki? He is one teddy bear away from being the comic relief in a Korean War sitcom. And Bishop Three can barely wipe his nose without help."

"I'll give you Aoki," Kuro conceded, cocking his head. "But you're selling Trey short. He took down that guy in the gym. Or at least incapacitated him enough for me to punch his lights out."

"He shouldn't have come out at all," Tatiana tsked. "You're getting soft, Blackie. There was a time when you would've punched him in the face to knock him out so he would be out of the way."

"You forget we didn't work for the same agency. Not my style, Boom Boom." He caught her sidelong glance, returning it with a sheepish grin. "Okay, maybe I did that *once*."

"Markov's nose was never the same again." She clucked her tongue against the roof of her mouth. "And he'd been so pretty before. One might think you were jealous of the competition."

"Markov and I were never in competition with each other. He's straight."

"Wrong competition." Her grin was wide enough to make a Cheshire cat envious. "It was always a toss-up who was prettier until your fist took care of his face."

Kuro thought he was too old and jaded to blush, but it was a definite burn across his cheeks. Exhaling between his clenched teeth, he slid his Glock back into its holster. "You about ready to go?"

"How do you want to play this?" Tatiana tucked her braid under her beanie, craning her head down to peer out of the car's front windshield. "You said you can't guarantee the layout. How blind are we going in?"

"Pretty blind, but we've got one thing going for us. Our target is as paranoid as hell." Kuro offered up a pair of sleek black gloves to Tatiana. "Here. I brought some for you. They fit like skin, and you won't even feel them."

"You always had the very best toys," Tatiana murmured, taking the gloves from Kuro. "Can I keep them when we're done?"

"I don't know. Let's see if we can get what we came for. Then we can negotiate," he suggested. "But I'm leaning towards yes. Just don't get killed. I don't want to bury you in them."

What he was planning had been tried before, but Kuro had something others didn't—a banked rage and a fairly good knowledge of the grounds.

The curved streets and the infrequent streetlamps provided enough cover to hide them from curious eyes, the soft pools of light pouring down onto the road much dimmer than the rest of the city to avoid bleeding up and ruining the night sky for the nearby observatory. It was quiet up in the hills, a different world from where Kuro grew up. He'd cut his teeth—and feet—on the glittering streets to the east, barking his knuckles on hard heads and ruthless assholes. What he was going to do in a few minutes would violate every scrap of respect he'd earned along the way, damaging relationships he'd made over the years.

Was Trey worth it? That was a question he'd only pondered once… right before he opened up his gun safe and grabbed a pair of Glocks to take with him, shooing the cat out of the way before he shut the door on her tail.

"You ready?" Tatiana grunted, checking the fit of her beanie in the car's rearview mirror. "Because I left my girlfriend back at your house and I'd like to get home before midnight."

"She turn into a pumpkin or a mouse?" Kuro shot back, chuckling at Tatiana's lifted middle finger. "They're over at Trey's place, remember? He wanted to get some clothes."

"Is he tired of wearing your old rock-and-roll shit, Blackie?" She stuck her tongue out at him when he returned her gesture. "Are you sure it's healthy, him staying with you? You've known each other for what? Three days?"

"Months," he corrected. "And I like having him with me. Better than him being with the two of you. Kimber would shoot him before breakfast."

"Twice," Tatiana confessed. "She has… issues."

"Yeah, you could say that," he agreed. "Okay, let's go. Just remember, no killing unless you have to. There's only so much cleanup we're going to get on this."

"And here you said I could have fun," she snarked. "Fine, but you're buying me a milkshake on the way home. Chocolate."

They went in hard and quick, slipping in through a break in the wall near the garage. Kuro exploited every weakness he knew, holding Tatiana back in the shadows while he crept up on the large dark shape of a bodyguard hovering near the house's back entrance. There were flaws in the security detail's coverage, notably the abundance of thick man-wide columns spanning the rear of the ostentatious structure, but those design mistakes were exactly the sort of thing Kuro loved to exploit on a job.

Or at least he had loved. On this one, it was too personal, too close to his own skin, and as much as he was willing to dive back into his old life, he was only doing it because his new one was in danger of collapsing around him. It was too easy to slip back into old habits, like wishing he had something stronger than a horse tranquilizer to stab into the man whose neck he wrapped his arm around and wrestled to the ground.

"Come on, don't fight me," Kuro murmured, slowly holding the man down until the drug took hold. "Be glad I'm not using chloroform. That shit takes five minutes to work."

Gurgling, the man battled against the effects of the sedative, thrashing about in Kuro's arms. His shoulder began to throb, a not-so-subtle reminder it'd been spackled together with staples and bits of metal. Then a flailing elbow caught him right in the ribs, nearly unseating his tight grip.

"Could you hurry this up?" Tatiana hissed from her position against the outer wall. "What's taking you so long? Do you need me to do it?"

The man took one final heaving breath, then collapsed, nearly throwing Kuro off balance. Bracing against the dead weight pushing on his chest, Kuro slowly lowered the man down to the ground, then rolled him over to tuck him into a niche against an enormous planter bristling with ferns. Brushing his hands clean, Kuro stepped over the guard's legs, listening for movement in the house.

"Get the door. I'll cover you," Kuro whispered at Tatiana after she slunk up next to him.

He'd have preferred to run a silent mission, but they didn't have time to work out hand signals, and since they'd worked for opposing agencies, he had little faith they shared a common gesture reference. Drawing his Glock out, Kuro kept close to Tatiana's heels, sweeping his attention back and forth to watch for any other guards walking around the area.

Tall hedges separated the properties, but Kuro spotted lights through the thick copses. The U-shaped mansion cradled fountains and gardens in its gentle curve, with a colonnade following the line of the building, providing some cover from Los Angeles's nonexistent rain. Tall picture windows and french doors made up most of the lower floor's exterior wall, giving the illusion of easy access, but Kuro knew better. The panes were bulletproof and wired up to an alarm system that would bring archangels and hellfire down on them should it go off.

He couldn't see any movement through any of the windows around them, but most of the lights were dim or the drapery was too thick to let any illumination escape. They'd avoided a bank of floodlights coming in, and the security guard was on a half-hour route, only intersecting another guard on the opposite side of the house, far away from their entrance point.

The short recon they'd done was sloppy, a good enough job for a quick hit, but Kuro's stomach knotted tighter with each step he took. Standing behind Tatiana with his gun up, he listened to her work the lock, then swear a streak of icy Russian under her breath.

"What's wrong?" There was movement in the bushes as the wind picked up, sweeping through the canyons around them. Parroting her words right back at her, he asked, "What's taking you so long? Do you need me to do it?"

"Fuck you," she replied with very little emotion, turning the latch on the french door. "Only one lock was engaged. This is probably the door security uses to go in and out. And I almost put my foot in a pile of cigarette butts. But we're on."

"You don't have to go in if you don't want to," Kuro offered again. "I can take this."

"I haven't had any action since—not counting you in the bungalow—since I had to shoot that bus driver in the knee because he was giving me shit," Tatiana grumbled back. "If I don't bust some heads soon, I'm going to go crazy."

"Just remember, when you go berserker? We're on the same side now," he reminded her. "I don't want you to forget that and brain me across the back of the head with a unicorn lamp."

"I only did that once," she sniped back under her breath. "And it was a tissue box. Not a lamp. There wasn't enough room in that bathroom to swing a lamp."

"Not sure that matters to the back of my head," Kuro muttered back. "Let's go."

The inside of the house looked like a yard sale held in the parking lot of a store named Gilded and Tasteless. Everywhere they turned, something large dominated the space. Gold-trimmed armoires competed for space with oversized chairs held up by massive lion's-foot legs, with tall tables crammed into every niche and covered by overflowing flower arrangements or a knickknack heavy enough to do damage to a sturdy cranium. Kuro threw a smug smirk back at Tatiana when they passed a rampant horse statue placed on a round side table, a recessed overhead angled to spotlight its crystal horn.

She silently flipped him off, keeping her footsteps light while they worked through the lower floor, pausing only to let an older Hispanic woman in a gray dress scurry past them, her arms filled with a stack of folded towels. They waited, shrouded in a bit of shadow thrown out by an eight-foot-tall stuffed bear standing stiff and tall on a marble pedestal, keeping still behind its massive flanks while the woman muttered under her breath about pigheaded men and needing a new job.

Twenty minutes were left on their clock, barely enough to get in, find the right room, and get out before their shit would hit the fan. The second the woman was out of sight, Kuro was on the move, heading into the depths of the house to the one room he was gambling would have who he was looking for.

He was not disappointed.

The heavy drapes were closed, blocking off the outside with thick tapestry panels. There were very few lights on, but the room was bright enough, illuminated by a fast-moving game being played out on a television nearly the size of a twin bed. The volume was loud enough to make Kuro's ears bleed, and the rapid-fire Spanish blasting out of a row of speakers sitting on the credenza was almost too quick to follow. His target had a handful of Cheetos near his lips, his eyes pinned to the chaotic movement on the screen.

Of all of his jobs, this moment was the most surreal. His assignments were never personal. Not in the beginning. Some—like the one that got him retired out—became personal within minutes of him breaching the door while others remained simply a job, a dangerous situation he needed to go through in order for the good guys to get a point in a game no one would ever win.

Kuro wasn't used to dealing with emotions, and he was hard-pressed to push back on the conflicting swell bubbling up from his heart. It was easy enough for him to say Trey had to be his focus now. There was a future there. Or least he hoped there was one. It was something he'd never thought he'd have. There'd been too much death and carnage in his past for him to even imagine waking up next to someone he cared about the rest of his life. Now that was a real possibility—or at least he hoped so—but the only way he was going to get it was to walk over the raging embers of his past life, and there was no way to do that without burning himself.

Walking into the room, Kuro trained his gun on the man reclining across the corner of the red leather sectional and said, "Hello, Pops."

The older man immediately sucked in a mouthful of air, his face turning a grayish white, then proceeded to choke on the virulent orange puffed snack he'd just tossed back, his fingers filthy with a thick coating of cheesy dust. Alarmed, Kuro skirted the edge of the couch, his weapon still aimed at Pops's temple but his right hand clenched into a fist, ready to pound at the man's back.

"Jesus!" Tatiana hissed in a low whisper, shutting the door behind her. Crossing the room, she did a quick visual check, securing the other half of the space. "Aren't you going to ask him questions before you kill him?"

"I'm not trying to kill him!" Kuro kept his weapon out of arm's reach as best he could while striking Pops once between the shoulder blades. "At least not yet."

The soccer game blaring from the gigantic flat-screen television mounted to the wall a few feet away covered their entrance, as well as Pops's choking episode. Rubbing at his throat, he leaned forward, blindly scrambling to reach a remote a few feet away. Pops's elbow caught the bowl of chips, scattering its contents over the seat and onto the floor. Tatiana sidestepped quickly, then fell into a shooting stance when Pops made a grab for her.

"Oh no, old man," Tatiana scolded. "Blackie might have some sentimental attachment to your sorry ass, but I am more than willing to give you a third nostril."

"I'd believe her if I were you. Especially since you're the reason her girlfriend has been coming home late for the past couple of weeks," Kuro warned, circling the couch from the other side until he and Tatiana bracketed his former mentor. "And while we're at it, I'm going to go on record and say I'm not too happy with you either."

"Can't trust anyone to do the job," Pops spat. "You should be dead by now. You and that twink—"

"Do people still use that word?" Tatiana interrupted. "I'm not up on things."

"Yes. It's still a word, but I don't know if I would use it to describe Trey," he replied, stepping through the scattered puffs. They crunched beneath his boots, grinding down into the area rug in front of the sectional. Nudging the remote closer to him, Kuro lowered the volume a few levels. "Let's drop that down so you understand everything I'm saying to you. You'd already accepted the contract to kill me when I walked in that day, didn't you?"

"You were a bonus," Pops said, wiping his dirty fingers on his purple velvet tracksuit, smearing trails of orange dust across his thigh. "The hit was for Bishop. I told the boys to make it a two-for-one deal. Had to up the payment after you took out Bald Paulie."

"Is there a Not-Bald Paulie?" Tatiana gestured with her gun, sweeping her aim down the length of Pops's torso. "The nicknames you people come up with."

"You're called Boom Boom," Kuro reminded her. "And can we concentrate on what we came here for?"

"Sorry," she said unconvincingly. "I was just curious. Get your answers. We don't have much time."

"Who hired you?" Kuro growled. "Tell me who paid you to kill Trey Bishop."

"I'm not telling you jack shit." Pops returned fire, disdain creeping across his face. "I start giving out names to every asshole who threatens me with a gun and I'll be out of business or dead before I blink the next time. And don't act like you'd shoot me, boy. I fucking *made* you. Everything you are is because of me."

Pops wasn't wrong. Kuro's finger was on the Glock's trigger, but he wavered, probing at the edges of his torn loyalties. They'd been through a lot together, and Pops was the first person who'd made sure he had food and shelter. Kuro never expected to stand in front of the man who'd given him a gun and showed him how to use it. He'd learned more than just how to negotiate, standing behind Pops while people came to him to beg or pay for favors. Kuro picked up knowledge lurking in the corner of Pops's tight confines, from learning about weapons to how to plan a break-in. Graduating to organizing his own jobs after picking pockets and pulling street scams, he'd steadfastly worked his way into Pops's good graces, hoping to one day take over the man's underground empire.

He hadn't been ostracized for being gay. Everything he'd done for the man had been judged at face value, his devotion to Pops strengthening their bond right up until the day Kuro walked away, driven off by Pops's greed and flagrant disregard.

Also, Holly gave him an offer he really couldn't refuse… not if he was going to be true to the man Pops made him.

"Yeah," Tatiana snorted. "But you didn't make *me*."

The gun's sharp report was lost beneath a wave of cheers erupting from speakers as a red-shirted player scored a point and the sports announcer began a warbling celebration of the goal.

Pops's scream filled the air, drowned out by the jubilance of a soccer team's fans as their boys brought home a victory.

"Tatiana! Jesus Christ!" Kuro yelled across the room, grabbing a runner from a side table to staunch the wound. An arrangement of porcelain figures set on the fabric hit the floor in a smatter of tinkling crashes, and Kuro winced, knowing how much the ugly twisted forms cost. "You weren't supposed to shoot him!"

"Well, you weren't going to do it!" she shot back. "Someone had to, and he wasn't going to shoot himself!"

"Pops, stop wiggling around," Kuro ordered, crouching to press the runner against his mentor's injured leg. Pops's blood was hot, practically scalding Kuro's fingers, and he swore under his breath as it began to soak into the porous fabric. "It went right through the meat. You'll be fine. Just let me tie this off."

"None of this would've happened if he told you the name," Tatiana said calmly, unaffected by Pops's mewling. "Why is he making so much noise? It's not even serious. It wasn't like I aimed for his dick."

"She's fucking crazy," Pops gasped. "You brought a crazy person into my house!"

"You're not wrong," Kuro admitted with a slight grimace, wrapping the runner around Pops's thick thigh and tying it off. "I just need a name, Pops. Then I'll get someone to help you."

Pops glared at Kuro for so long, he was afraid the man would never give up the information or, worse yet, Tatiana would shoot both of them in frustration. Kuro never broke eye contact with the older man, staring into his timeworn face with its beaten-down expression. The gilded cage they sat in was proof to the old man that he'd made it off of the streets they'd come from, but he still shuffled down to the barbershop every day, probably unwilling to let go of the life he'd made for himself.

They weren't so different, Kuro realized. And crouching there, Kuro saw who he would have become if he'd stayed at Pops's side. If he hadn't taken a different path, it would be him behind that desk on Skid Row, a marionette in Pops's puppet show until the day he moved up after Pops's death and took his place on that very couch.

"Tell me who set up the contract, Pops, and we'll call it even," Kuro promised. "I'll walk away. No retaliation. No revenge. I'll even keep her off, but if you do me wrong, I'll be back, and you won't like what I bring with me."

He knew the moment Pops crumpled, his face giving way to a resigned resentment, but Kuro didn't care. The only thing that mattered was that Pops leaned forward, whispering a name into Kuro's ear.

"You sure?" Kuro pressed. "Because I don't want to be back here, Pops. I don't *ever* want to be back here."

"I'm sure," he replied, grimacing. "And if you don't take them out, you better come back here and kill me, because if I'm going to die, I'd rather you be the one to do it."

Twenty

TREY COULDN'T breathe.

He tried. God knew he was struggling to find some way to get air into his lungs, but it was impossible. There was too much in the way. He couldn't get his chest to move or even his mouth open. Sucking air in through his nose was useless, but Trey needed to breathe.

He just *couldn't*.

"It'll be okay," Kimber promised. "I'll help you through this."

That was a lie.

Trey longed to be childish. To scream at Kimber that she'd never been there before, why should he believe her now? But that also was a lie. She *had* been there. Standing against the storm of shit he'd thrown at her, a tempest of bad behavior and drugged-out disasters, Kimber was there. As hard as it was to embrace his culpability and what he'd done to her in the family, Trey was done lying to himself.

It was just hard to remember that sometimes.

Especially when he was standing in the remains of his bedroom, the long wall torn apart by large-caliber bullets and his best friend's blood still smeared across the hardwood floor.

"You don't have to do this," Kimber said. "You can wait in the car while I get your stuff together."

It would have been so easy to walk away. His bruises were fading from that day, or at least those on his skin were. Trey wasn't sure if he would ever stop bleeding inside, but he was working on it. Having Kuro in his life helped—so damned much—and the touch of Kimber's fingers along his back went a long way in soothing the scabs formed over their relationship.

"Thanks, but no. I've got to face this," he murmured, stepping over a fallen stack of books. "I can't just keep hiding at Kuro's."

He didn't know Kimber well enough to read all of the expressions she could make, but he recognized the one she had on her face when he turned around. There was definitely conflict there, an unnatural holding of her tongue, something she rarely did. If he'd learned anything over the past few weeks, Trey realized he liked his sister's brash honesty. She never really lied to him, not when it counted, and despite a few missteps, she really did try to help him, even when she didn't believe a word coming out of his mouth.

His sister hit something on the dresser, knocking it over with a loud clatter, but Trey didn't see what it was. He was too busy staring at the mottled stain on the floor. His brain was trying to make shapes out of the splotches, fitting Sera's body into its curves and negative spaces. He hated that he couldn't remember exactly how she lay, as if by forgetting that moment when she'd taken her last breath, he was somehow denying Sera her whole life.

"Did you hear me?" Kimber said, coming up to Trey's side.

"No, sorry," he apologized. "I just—"

"Let's get your stuff together and we can grab something to eat," Kimber suggested, gently leading him away from the side of the bed. "Just not ramen."

"I don't know," Trey said, working hard to keep his tone light. "The Tako Shop makes really good ramen."

"Yeah, I'm sure they do, but I can't talk to you about Kuro there." Grabbing a suitcase out of the closet, Kimber wrestled to get it past a pile of Trey's sneakers. "The offer is still open. You can stay with me."

It was an apology of sorts. The kind of gesture their father made. He never said he was sorry for something he did or thought, muddying the waters with gifts or praise. It took Trey a long time to realize that was how his family operated, masking their sentiments with verbal asides most people would take as shoving away any responsibility for their actions. Those people weren't wrong. Trey could sidestep with the best of them, and standing in the middle of his shot-up bedroom, he honestly didn't know how to respond to his sister.

"You don't like Kuro," he finally said.

"I don't *dislike* him." Kimber finally got the suitcase free, swinging it up onto the dresser. "I just don't know if it's healthy for you to be there. And I don't like you being with someone who I can't get a background check on. That kind of thing makes me nervous."

"Really? Because that kind of thing reassures me," Trey teased, grinning when she shot him a sour look. "You're just mad because you can't bully him."

"I'm a cop. I don't need to bully people." She held up a T-shirt with more holes than fabric. "Are you going to help me pack, or do I have to dig through this thrift store pile you've got in these drawers? Why do you even have this?"

"That was something given to me as a promo package and is worth around five hundred dollars," he informed her. "It's a designer shirt."

"I could wash lettuce in this," she grumbled. "I just don't see any longevity in a relationship with Kuro Jenkins."

"Did you think that with Tatiana?" He knew he scored a point when her shoulders stiffened. "Because something tells me if you ran a background check on her, you'd come up with a lot less than you would on Kuro."

"Talking about you, not me. I can take care of myself."

"I can take care of myself too," Trey replied softly, lightly squeezing his sister's shoulder. "I don't know where this thing with Kuro is going, but he makes me feel good about myself, and he's the first person I've been with who doesn't want anything from me. There's no agenda. There's no trying to score anything or have me introduce him to anyone. I just want all of this to end so we can maybe do some normal things, like go to the movies or pay for really overpriced hot dogs while we walk across Santa Monica pier."

"I just don't want him to break your heart," Kimber said.

"I think he's the one who's helping me put it back together." Trey leaned against the dresser, staring out of the bedroom through the holes in the wall. The angle was too low to see the sky, but there wasn't much to look at there anyway. At some point dusk slipped away, pulling the night down over them, and the bungalow was growing chilly, exposed to the cooling air. "I know to you it seems very quick. I get that. But he's kind of been a part of my life for months now, and I've always wondered what if he thought of me as someone he could be with."

"Does he?" Kimber opened up his underwear drawer, looking down at the balled briefs he'd crammed in there a week ago. "And tell me you haven't been going commando since this happened."

"No, Kuro grabbed me some from the store. It's just mostly I've been wearing his shirts and sweats." He began to tuck clothes into the suitcase, focusing on what he wanted to take with him instead of what had happened on the floor a few feet away. "Kuro knows I have baggage.

He's got some too, but he respects me, listens to me when I tell him how I feel. And he has a really cool cat."

"You just like him because with him around you don't have to cook." Kimber smirked.

"No, although that is awesome," he conceded. "To tell the truth, he makes me feel safe—not physically, but that too, but like inside—and I haven't felt that way in a long time. Maybe never. My biggest worry is I feel more for him than he feels for me, but I'm not ready to poke at that."

"From where I'm standing, he likes you a lot," Kimber replied. "He keeps saving your life, so I guess that's got to count for something."

Packing didn't take long. Mostly, he'd needed to go back to the bungalow, wanting to put the events into some perspective and, in a way, say goodbye to Sera. The brief phone call he had with her mother was long enough for Trey to know he wasn't welcome at her funeral, and he'd shouldered the blame for Sera's death willingly. His father made some noise about monetary compensation, a material salve for his conscience, but her family hadn't wanted a dime. Nothing the Bishop family said or did would bring back the vivacious, beautiful woman who'd been a good friend to him, and now Trey truly understood what he'd lost. It hurt not to have her there to tease him or to admonish him when he went running at two o'clock in the morning.

The only thing he could hope for now was to help bring the person who'd killed her to justice and not get himself killed in the process.

A car driving up through the gravel caught Trey's attention, pulling him from the excavation of his refrigerator. Kimber put down the garbage bag she'd been holding open for him, folding over the end so they didn't have to smell the rotting head of cabbage he discovered in his vegetable drawer. He was about to get up from his crouch when Kimber put a steadying hand on his back, murmuring for him to stay there, safely hidden behind the broad island.

"Were you expecting anyone?" She reached under her jacket, probably for the gun in her holster.

"No," Trey responded, trying to straighten up, but Kimber pressed harder. "It's probably the old lady next door. She's really nosy and—"

"Stay down," she insisted, drawing her weapon. "Right now, I'm not trusting anyone. And that includes nosy little old ladies."

"Hello?" The front door creaked open, and tentative footsteps on the front stoop crunched through a bit of gravel the gardeners couldn't sweep away because the house had been a crime scene. A tanned older man with a flowing mane of gray hair stepped through the doorway, his eyes lighting up when he spotted Kimber. "Ah, Detective Bishop! I don't know if you remember me, I am—"

"Stuart Gilder," Kimber finished. She kept her weapon to the side but took her hand off of Trey's back. "We've met a few times. You're the Mathers's lawyer. David, or so it appears. We still haven't worked out all of the details on that. You've been a hard man to get ahold of. Funny, you turning up here."

"I actually spoke to your sister Scooter just a little while ago, and she told me you were here. Since it was on my way home, I thought I would stop in and check up on your brother." From Trey's vantage point, he saw Gilder take a step forward. Then the man turned, his hand on the interior knob. Kimber shifted, blocking Trey's view, and he pushed at his sister's thigh, his legs cramping. "I thought Trey was with you. Did you come alone?"

"I'm not sure that's any of your business," Kimber replied, keeping her right side canted back, hiding her weapon. "I left quite a few messages at your office, and every time I tried to find you at home, I was told you were out. The last I heard from you was your voicemail telling me all of us inherited from the Mathers's estate. I would've thought you'd be eager to get ahold of me."

"About that," Gilder said pleasantly, but there was something in his voice Trey didn't like. "There seems to have been a mistake. From what I can see, you won't be inheriting anything. I've worked far too hard to let any of you take what's mine."

"*Fuck*!" Trey's chin hit the floor when Kimber shoved him down. "What the hell?"

His lip ground against the slick surface, a bit of grit working its way over his tongue, reminding him he hadn't swept properly in weeks. He was about to get back up when Gilder began firing the gun he'd been hiding behind the partially open door.

Before Trey could fully comprehend what was going on, he was back on that fateful day he lost Sera.

Except this time, he was going to lose Kimber too.

The gunfire was less erratic, but in the close confines of the front room, every shot shook the walls. Scrambling to stay behind the island, Trey caught a bit of tile shards across his cheek when a bullet aimed at his head struck the floor next to him. Sliding alongside Kimber, he pulled his legs up, unsure about what to do.

Kimber returned Gilder's fire, popping up over the counter to get off a shot, when her body jerked and she tumbled back down. Trey reached for her, but she shook him off, reassuring him she was okay.

Trey didn't believe her.

His sister glanced at him, her eyes tight with pain. Her shoulder was wet, her dark gray jacket turning maroon along her arm, and she switched her gun to her left hand, peeking around the island to fire. She shook as she took aim, resting all of her weight on one knee, but the blackened hole in her arm seemed to be swallowed up by the amount of blood pouring out of it.

"You've got nowhere to go," Gilder yelled across the room. "I've got two guns here and a man outside going around the back. You're not going to get out of here."

"There's no way you're going to get away with this," Kimber shouted, nudging Trey back with her foot when he crept forward. "Someone's probably calling the cops right now."

"It won't take me that long to kill you," Gilder said. "Kiss your brother goodbye, Detective. Because when I'm done with you, everyone is going to think you killed him when those men who shot at him the first time showed back up. It'll be very sad. Trey killed by friendly fire and you eating your gun in remorse."

"Like anyone's going to believe that," Trey muttered under his breath. Checking his pockets, he cursed, remembering he'd left his phone on the coffee table by the couch. "Let me see if I can get to the landline."

"You move one inch and I'll clock you over the head." His sister struggled to reload, her hands shaking. "Stay down and wait right here."

"Shit," Trey said with a grin. "Kuro! I've got something that can help."

"Kuro is not going to come rescue us," Kimber growled, slamming the clip in finally. "Crap, he's moving around. Stay on the opposite side of the island. Do not approach him."

There were sounds coming from the bedroom, of something crashing through probably what was left of the outer wall. Kimber stiffened, tilting her head up toward the noise, but Trey was already on the move. Digging through the cabinet on the side of the island, he found what he was looking for, the flat paddle cast-iron skillet Sera brought and Kuro used to cook the duck on. He'd cleaned it as best he could, hoping to return the pan in pristine condition when he saw Sera again, but they'd both forgotten about it, wrapped up in the investigation.

It'd been too long since he picked up the skillet, and Trey nearly dropped it on the floor, needing to grab it with both hands to get it out of the cabinet. There were now shouts coming from the other room, and he froze, conflicted between continuing around the island and staying at Kimber's side.

Gilder made that decision for him. The man rushed the kitchen, both of his hands gripping deadly-looking guns, his fingers pressing against the triggers repeatedly, shooting up everything in front of him. As Trey squatted at the edge of the island, he saw Gilder's eyes go wide when he spotted Trey, then the lawyer's closest gun swept to the left, aiming straight for Trey's head.

He'd learned some of the stupidest things on a television set. Trey knew how to jumpstart a motorcycle, do card tricks, pratfall on a banana skin, but most of all he'd mastered the perfect fight roll. It was something silly the stunt people showed him, how to tuck his body in until he resembled an armadillo, then come back up as if he were shooting a phaser at a hostile alien. It was a cliché he'd enjoyed learning, making a game of spotting the maneuver in every action film he'd ever seen.

It was exactly the skill needed now, and instead of coming up to shoot a phaser, he instead flung the six-pound flat cast-iron skillet straight at Gilder's head.

Much like he'd also learned how to throw a knife in the general direction of someone's body.

The skillet wobbled as it flew, but he had enough upper body strength to make it go exactly as far as it needed to.

The shoulder still ached from the graze he'd taken on the day of the shooting, and something popped when he finally let go of the cast iron, but elation struck him before the pain did. The skillet hit Gilder in the throat and the man's head snapped back, his flowing silver hair ruffling around his face like tinsel caught in the wind. Kimber took advantage of the distraction and stood up and punched three holes through Gilder's chest.

Gilder gasped, staggering back with his arms flung out on either side, a mockery of a crucifix hanging in midair for a split second before he tumbled to the ground. It seemed to take forever before he hit the floor, and the back of the bungalow sounded as if there was an army of men rushing toward them.

Trey scurried over toward Gilder, grabbing one of the guns from the dying man's hand as soon as it was in reach. Everything he knew about weapons was more for show, but he didn't have time to debate with Kimber about anything other than keeping them alive.

"Kick the other one over towards me," Kimber mumbled, her normally strong voice hoarse and weak. "He's not dead yet."

Trey kicked at the gun, seeing it go wide, but Kimber stopped it with her foot. After edging around the island, Trey waited, hearing his sister struggling to breathe a few feet away from him. Fear turned spit in his mouth to a cloying viscosity he couldn't seem to swallow, and his lungs were full of the scent of blood and gunpowder, but he didn't dare take his eyes off of the front door.

"No matter what happens," Kimber choked out. "I'm proud of you, baby brother. You did good today."

He didn't have time to answer her. To be fair, he couldn't find any words to respond, but life wasn't giving him the chance either. The archway separating the bedroom from the front space suddenly filled with a large, mean-looking man, his hand wrapped around one of the biggest guns Trey had ever seen, its black muzzle pointed straight at them.

If he lived past that moment, Trey knew he would be able to describe every inch of skin on the man's face. A bristled mane of coarse auburn hair seemed to sprout straight from his skull, the ends growing heavier a few inches away from his high forehead. His eyebrows were darker, a pair of deep brown bushes growing over his narrowed dark eyes, and a thick beard obscured most of his lower face, but there was enough to see of his ruddy features to embed him into Trey's memory.

The man was massive, larger than the staff member at the gym who'd betrayed them, and when he saw Kimber rise up from behind the island, her left hand quaking from the weight of Gilder's gun, he grinned malevolently, his yellowed teeth peeking out from behind his cracked lips.

"Oh, I'm going to have fun with you before I kill you," he said, his words thick with an accent Trey couldn't recognize. "Right after I kill your baby brother."

"I don't think so," Kuro said, kicking the front door open the rest of the way.

As gunfights went—and Trey had enough experience over the last few weeks to have an opinion on gunfights—this one seemed to be much shorter than any he'd had the misfortune of being a part of before. It wasn't something he mourned. All in all, a short few seconds of gunfire seemed to be exactly the right length, especially when it was Kuro doing the shooting.

Trey didn't know until right at that moment that brains didn't fly as far as blood did when bullets went through a skull.

If anything, it took the bearded man a long time to fall, much longer than Gilder, and oddly enough, the world seemed to be getting fuzzier, its sounds drifting away. He heard Kuro calling his name, then felt the shock of Kuro's warm hands on his arms, feeling almost as if Kuro set his skin on fire.

Then he was pulled into Kuro's embrace and the world snapped back into normal, screeching and caterwauling with the sounds of police sirens and the murmur of Russian spilling from Tatiana's mouth as she stroked Kimber's hair.

"Glad you could make it." Trey laughed, deeply inhaling Kuro's masculine scent. "I ran out of skillets to throw. I was going to have to toss the toaster next, but how was I going to get him into a bathtub full of water?"

"I don't understand a thing coming out of your mouth," Kuro said. "But I'm just glad you're okay."

"Thanks for saving me," he murmured, tightening his arms around Kuro's waist. They were on the floor, curled up around each other, and Trey had no intention of moving. "I thought I was going to die. I thought *we* were going to die."

"Never," Kuro whispered, tilting Trey's chin up with his fingertips. Brushing his mouth over Trey's lips, he deepened their touch into a soulful kiss, soothing the jitters in Trey's belly. "I made you a promise to keep you safe. And when I make promises, they're good for a lifetime."

Epilogue

"IT'S KIND of funny, me moving into a place two blocks away and I'm still over at your house having dinner," Trey pointed out, giving Yuki a stroke along her spine as she walked across their laps to get to the other side of the couch. "Of course, not that I'm complaining. I'll take you making me pad thai over a microwave pizza any day."

"You also don't have any food at your place," Kuro reminded, scratching at his cat's head. "I'm not sure that loft even has a kitchen. I didn't see it behind all of the boxes we carried up the stairs. Next time, make sure you find a place with a working elevator."

"The building was cheap, and the elevator guy was trying his best. Besides, I only have one flight of stairs. You live three stories up." He groaned, stretching out his legs. If there was one thing that made the meal perfect, it was being able to lean against Kuro after he was done eating. "If ever I can't go on a run again, I'm just going to go up and down your stairs a few times."

"So long as you stop by periodically to give me a kiss, then that's okay," Kuro murmured, pressing his lips gently on Trey's temple. "Is your dad going to rebuild the bungalow?"

"He offered, but I think it's best if it's torn down," he replied. "And honestly? I think it's time for me to move on. I've been walking in circles for the past couple of years, and I think it's time I made a few decisions about what I'm going to do with my life."

"What did you decide?" Kuro's fingers trailed up and down Trey's side and he worked his shoulders back, nestling into the crook of Kuro's arm. "Other than not buying food ever again so I have to cook you dinner every night."

"It's actually not a bad plan," Trey said, tilting his head back to look up at the man who'd been with him through the worst times in his life. "I was actually thinking about going back to work. Maybe seeing if someone will take a chance on me. Other people have made comebacks.

I kinda miss acting. I also kind of miss being in gunfights that aren't real, but mostly I just miss acting."

"I caught the first episode of the show you were on when you were a kid while Kimber was in surgery." Kuro laughed when Trey grimaced at him. "Don't make that face, you're good. And that show was pretty brutal. In a way, it sort of prepared you for the Mathers thing."

"Everything I did was make-believe. *Gilder*… nothing in the world could have prepared me for him." He swallowed the bit of sour coming up from his stomach, refusing to allow the dead lawyer any space in his life. "He kills one guy and convinces another to get surgery to look like his twin only so he can help build up a company just to drain it? He played hot potato with Robert's body for years because he did need his fingerprints, then has David killed because he was cracking under the pressure of being Robert. That's crazy."

"David apparently believed you really were Robert's son." Kuro shrugged. "You start to get older and regrets begin to creep into your head. Maybe he thought he needed to make amends. He went off the rails with starting to change Robert's will and holdings and there wasn't anything Gilder could do but *kill* him. Guy was probably just hoping you were still too far into the hole to care who managed the company."

"But why not go out and start your own company? Gilder, I mean. He should have taken what money was there and gone. Why all of this elaborate planning just to kill me?"

"Because everything was in a trust from Mathers's father." Kuro gave in to Yuki's nudging, using his other hand to scratch at her nose. "He was trying to find a way to crack into the bulk of the estate, thinking David would go along with anything he said, but eventually, every man has his breaking point, and David couldn't handle being a part of his brother's death. You've got to remember, every time they needed identity verification, they had to thaw out Robert. It's one thing to kill a man, but it's another having to face the fact you killed your own family, especially when the man who helped you murder your brother insists on you being there every time his body is needed for something."

"Best way to make sure he's implicated, right?" Trey shook his head. "I don't think I could ever kill someone. I mean, I guess I tried to kill Gilder with the skillet, but I was protecting Kimber. I don't know if I could just shoot someone."

"For some people it's harder than others," Kuro replied, grunting slightly as Yuki trod back over them. "Sit down, cat. You've got very sharp little feet."

"Have you ever killed anyone you regretted killing?" They hadn't ever talked about Kuro's past, but Trey had questions, and in the soft glow of the living room's dimmed lights with their bellies full of a good meal, it seemed like the perfect time to ask. "Because, Tatiana? I can totally see her shooting somebody in cold blood, but not you."

"I've regretted everyone I've ever killed," Kuro whispered, his hand coming to a rest on Trey's hip. "I'm not an angel. I'm not even a saint. I can't say that I've never killed an innocent person, because I've been in situations where people died and the higher-ups excused it as collateral damage. I don't ever forget those moments, and when I got burned out of the life, they stayed with me.

"So, while I have regrets about some of the things that happened, I don't have any remorse for any of the deaths I've caused over the last couple weeks. Everything I've done has been to protect you, and for the first time in my life, I've done the job for someone I care about." His smile warmed Trey's heart, and the kiss that followed stoked a fire in his belly Trey wasn't sure he was ready for. "I'm sorry you got tangled in this. If Robert Mathers wasn't already dead, I'd be happy to punch him in the face for him saying you're his son."

"It's what drove Gilder to everything. Or that's what the cops think happened. Gilder killed David because he was going to go to the police about Robert. Then when everyone started digging through the will, Robert saying I was his kid wiped out everything Gilder worked for." He pursed his mouth, accepting a blown kiss from the still-roaming cat. Yuki made another pass, then finally decided to meat loaf on Kuro's arm where it rested along Trey's side. "Kimber thinks the guys Gilder hired to move Robert's body stashed him someplace, so he couldn't produce Robert's DNA to deny the claim."

"It all just came apart around him. He also couldn't risk doing the DNA test. If it proved to be true, he was out millions. And when they dumped Mathers's body in the trash, he knew he was in deep trouble he couldn't fix. Not without killing you." Kuro wiggled his fingers, obviously trying to dislodge the cat, but Yuki wasn't having any of it. "He'd already murdered at least two people, what was a few more? His shitty luck you were the one person who'd seen Robert Mathers that night, but the universe hates lies."

"Little did he know, the intrepid yet battered Trey Bishop had a secret weapon at his side," Trey drawled. "His own personal protector, a mild-mannered ramen chef by day and a deadly assassin by night."

"Okay, all assassins should be deadly or else they wouldn't be assassins," he corrected smugly. "And I'm not an assassin."

"Really? Because I die a little bit inside every time I look at you when we're someplace I can't kiss you," Trey said, shifting his weight forward. The cat grumbled, dislodged from her perch, and she stalked away, stiff-legged and tail up, but Trey knew she'd eventually be back. "So, you and I. What do we do here? Where do we go?"

"We go wherever life takes us," Kuro replied, gathering Trey up in his arms and pulling him over until Trey straddled Kuro's hips. "I like having you here with me. It feels good, especially now since people aren't trying to kill us. I'd like to do some normal things. Go on a date. See a movie. Walk through a farmers' market with you, or maybe even cruise the Book Festival in the spring. All of the normal things a couple of guys who have probably fallen in love with each other do."

"Is that what this is?" The spark of something bright growing inside of Trey flared, and he could no longer ignore it. Working his fingers through Kuro's black hair, he lowered his mouth to Kuro's lips, kissing him until he was pretty sure they both saw stars. "You make me crazy, but with you around, everything seems sane. Even your naked cat seems normal."

"Hey, Yuki is totally normal. She just needs sweaters." Kuro returned the kiss, leaving Trey breathless and wanting more. "So, we're going to do this? Us?"

"Yeah, we should," Trey replied, then wrinkled his nose. "Maybe with a lot less trouble and murder."

"Honey, I've got a really bad feeling," Kuro muttered as he rolled Trey over onto his back, stretching them both out over the couch. "You're always going to be trouble."

RHYS FORD is an award-winning author with several long-running LGBT+ mystery, thriller, paranormal, and urban fantasy series and is a two-time LAMBDA finalist with her *Murder and Mayhem* novels. She is also a 2017 Gold and Silver Medal winner in the Florida Authors and Publishers President's Book Awards for her novels *Ink and Shadows* and *Hanging the Stars*. She is published by Dreamspinner Press and DSP Publications.

She shares the house with Harley, a gray tuxedo with a flower on her face, Badger, a disgruntled alley cat who isn't sure living inside is a step up the social ladder, as well as a ginger cairn terrorist named Gus. Rhys is also enslaved to the upkeep of a 1979 Pontiac Firebird and enjoys murdering make-believe people.

Rhys can be found at the following locations:

Blog: www.rhysford.com
Facebook: www.facebook.com/rhys.ford.author
Twitter: @Rhys_Ford

DIM SUM ASYLUM

RHYS FORD

Welcome to Dim Sum Asylum: a San Francisco where it's a ho-hum kind of case when a cop has to chase down an enchanted two-foot-tall shrine god statue with an impressive Fu Manchu mustache that's running around Chinatown, trolling sex magic and chaos in its wake.

Senior Inspector Roku MacCormick of the Chinatown Arcane Crimes Division faces a pile of challenges far beyond his human-faerie heritage, snarling dragons guarding C-Town's multiple gates, and exploding noodle factories. After a case goes sideways, Roku is saddled with Trent Leonard, a new partner he can't trust, to add to the crime syndicate family he doesn't want and a spell-casting serial killer he desperately needs to find.

While Roku would rather stay home with Bob the Cat and whiskey himself to sleep, he puts on his badge and gun every day, determined to serve and protect the city he loves. When Chinatown's dark mystical underworld makes his life hell and the case turns deadly, Trent guards Roku's back and, if Trent can be believed, his heart… even if from what Roku can see, Trent is as dangerous as the monsters and criminals they're sworn to bring down.

www.dreamspinnerpress.com

Murder and Mayhem: Book One

Dead women tell no tales.

Former cat burglar Rook Stevens stole many a priceless thing in the past, but he's never been accused of taking a life—until now. It was one thing to find a former associate inside Potter's Field, his pop culture memorabilia shop, but quite another to stumble across her dead body.

Detective Dante Montoya thought he'd never see Rook Stevens again—not after his former partner falsified evidence to entrap the jewelry thief and Stevens walked off scot-free. So when he tackled a fleeing murder suspect, Dante was shocked to discover the blood-covered man was none other than the thief he'd fought to put in prison and who still makes his blood sing.

Rook is determined to shake loose the murder charge against him, even if it means putting distance between him and the rugged Cuban-Mexican detective who brought him down. If one dead con artist wasn't bad enough, others soon follow, and as the bodies pile up around Rook's feet, he's forced to reach out to the last man he'd expect to believe in his innocence—and the only man who's ever gotten under Rook's skin.

www.dreamspinnerpress.com

415 ☆ INK • BOOK ONE

Rebel

RHYS FORD

415 Ink: Book One

The hardest thing a rebel can do isn't standing up for something—it's standing up for himself.

Life takes delight in stabbing Gus Scott in the back when he least expects it. After Gus spends years running from his past, present, and the dismal future every social worker predicted for him, karma delivers the one thing Gus could never—would never—turn his back on: a son from a one-night stand he'd had after a devastating breakup a few years ago.

Returning to San Francisco and to 415 Ink, his family's tattoo shop, gave him the perfect shelter to battle his personal demons and get himself together... until the firefighter who'd broken him walked back into Gus's life.

For Rey Montenegro, tattoo artist Gus Scott was an elusive brass ring, a glittering prize he hadn't the strength or flexibility to hold on to. Severing his relationship with the mercurial tattoo artist hurt, but Gus hadn't wanted the kind of domestic life Rey craved, leaving Rey with an aching chasm in his soul.

When Gus's life and world starts to unravel, Rey helps him pick up the pieces, and Gus wonders if that forever Rey wants is more than just a dream.

www.dreamspinnerpress.com

415 ★ INK • BOOK TWO

Savior

RHYS FORD

415 Ink: Book Two

A savior lies in the heart of every good man, but sometimes only love can awaken the man inside the savior.

The world's had it out for San Francisco firefighter Mace Crawford from the moment he was born. Rescued from a horrific home life and dragged through an uncaring foster system, he's dedicated his life to saving people, including the men he calls his brothers. As second-in-command of their knitted-together clan, Mace guides his younger siblings, helps out at 415 Ink, the family tattoo shop, and most of all, makes sure the brothers don't discover his darkest secrets.

It's a lonely life with one big problem—he's sworn off love, and Rob Claussen, one of 415 Ink's tattoo artists, has gotten under his skin in the worst way possible.

Mace's world is too tight, too controlled to let Rob into his life, much less his heart, but the brash Filipino inker is there every time Mace turns around. He can't let Rob in without shaking the foundations of the life he's built, but when an evil from his past resurfaces, Mace is forced to choose between protecting his lies and saving the man he's too scared to love.

www.dreamspinnerpress.com